I Hope You Find Me

Trish Marie Dawson

For Shane, Rory and Foxx. This is for you.

I Hope You Find Me

CHAPTER 1

I can't remember now how long their bodies burned but I do remember the sun setting before it was over, not far off in the distance, just beyond the still and dismal outline of downtown San Diego. Its flame-colored glare hit the Pacific Ocean and slowly, steadily, melted beyond the horizon as smoke drifted up in dark gray coils into the sky. The fleeing sun took the heat away with it, and as the first stars of the night made their appearance, the crisp chill of January returned.

Ash settled all around me, resting on my eyelashes and the tip of my nose…threatening to choke the oxygen from my lungs. I kept vigil over my dead family while I sat at the edge of the garden, slumped forward with my legs crossed and my hands resting loosely in my lap. A steady breeze from the approaching night collided with the draft from the fire, sending hot gusts of air in my direction. My face and arms stung from the warmth but the smell was worse than the heat. The strong odor of burning flesh kept my nostrils flared and stomach turning.

I knew that day it was true what they say; one can never forget the smell of a dead body. I know, I'll never forget.

***

After spending several days in bed crying, my broken heart didn't actually kill me like I had hoped it would. The weather felt cold and gloomy when I finally climbed out from under the covers and stumbled into the bathroom. I turned the water faucet on, but the tap was dry and for the first time that week, a stab of panic spread through my chest at the irony that I could die after-all…from thirst or hunger.

I blinked in confusion at the harried reflection in the oval mirror staring blankly back at me. The porcelain counter-top felt cool beneath my weak fingers as I leaned forward and stared at the hollow expression of the girl that resembled me. Her blue eyes seemed trapped in a stormy darkness, and the circles below them made her cheeks appear sunken in…completely defeated. Long, blonde hair hung from her scalp in greasy and knotted strands, having lost its luster.

I blinked again and pushed off the sink, wanting nothing more but to run away from that girl in the mirror, and my elbow grazed a small drinking glass, knocking it over the edge of the countertop. I gasped when it shattered on the white tile floor and watched, mesmerized, as a shard spun wildly away from my feet until it hit the edge of the fluffy blue bathmat, and bounced to a stop. I stared at the broken remnants of the glass with fascination, before I slowly reached down to pick up the large sliver that had nestled against the side of the mat, and pinched it between my fingers until a small bead of blood formed on the pad of my thumb. After letting the glass fall back to the floor, I rubbed the blood between my fingers until the warm fluid began to stick to my skin. Outside, the clouds parted briefly and sunshine teased behind the curtains, willing someone to open them, to let the light back in. When I looked back up at the mirror, it was me I saw.

***

I ran my fingertips across the grain of the distressed oak dresser, leaving thin trails in the dust as I stared at the picture frames, the generous pile of my son's miss-matched folded socks, and my wooden jewelry box. Inside the small glass door I could see the delicate necklace my daughter gave to me three years before on Mother's Day. I reached inside and tapped the golden locket until it swayed slightly on its chain like a pendulum, before carefully shutting the glass door, locking it inside the jewelry box forever. I stood in the doorway and looked at my neat bedroom and sighed. Everything was in its place, but I felt as if I no longer fit there.

It was the same feeling in every room I walked through, even my office, with the massive piles of school work I never got around to grading over the winter break that had snowballed out of control and spread along the desk top like weeds. A bright white piece of paper with a messy fingerprint on the right upper corner caught my eye, and I picked it up to read the name and title: Mariposa, The Happy Butterfly, by Cecy Aguirre. I read through the first paragraph about Cecy's fictitious garden butterfly before I remembered the class assignment. My third graders had turned in a fantasy paper about their favorite insect just before the school closed for the holiday break but I hadn't read any of them. An overwhelming sadness flooded through me, and I sat down at my desk, red pen in hand, and worked my way through the mound of papers, writing an "O" for outstanding at the top of each. When I was finished, I put the papers neatly in a stack, with Cecy's paper right on top and moved on to a pile of math papers, and went through those too. Even the ones with wrong answers got an "O" at the top, scribbled neatly in my red grading ink.

Afterwards, I sat at the desk with my face stretched out in a manic-like grin as I stared at the graded papers. I felt accomplished for the first time in weeks. Even though the papers would never make it back to their eight year old owners, at least they hadn't been completely forgotten. Earlier in the morning I had showered in the tub with cold, bottled water and put on a clean change of clothes before wandering through the house, feeling detached with a million fragmented thoughts running through my mind like wild horses. But with the papers done, a brief spell of peace calmed me, and all that was left to do was sit and think.

I pushed away the thought of starving myself by going back to bed for the next month, and because I had spent the last few years turning my house 'green' there wasn't anything harsher than vinegar to poison myself with. The strongest medicine in the cabinets was a half-full bottle of syrup for colds that was acetaminophen-free. I know because I checked the label. Twice.

And there was the dog to think about. The virus that had swept across the nation like an unchecked wildfire killing most in its path didn't do a damn thing to me, or our four year old black mini-lab/cocker spaniel mix. I leaned back in my ergonomic office chair and looked at the small furry body at my feet. Zoey was resting on her front paws, which often served as a pillow for her whiskered chin. Even though she appeared to be sleeping, there was a ring of moisture around her closed lids. I had no tears left, but the poor dog hadn't stopped crying.

3

So I really only had one option, as difficult as it was to comprehend. I had to leave. To get as far away as possible from the life I had lost; the life that threatened to kill me slowly by driving me insane. I couldn't walk down the long and narrow hallway between the bedrooms without hearing whispers, or feeling eyes on me. The edges of my psyche were beginning to crack, like the seams that held me together were unraveling, so I decided to go to my Mother's apartment in the city and figure things out from there because the longer I stayed in my own house, the more alien it felt. I was afraid the walls, or something sinister living inside them, would close in around me and swallow me whole.

Roaming through the house to pack my belongings didn't take long. What I really wanted to take with me was in a smoldering heap in the backyard. There wasn't much I needed other than food and water, some clothes and my little pocket first-aid pack. I sat down at my computer with a handful of flash-drives to copy pictures and videos of the kids since that was all I could really keep of them.

Out of habit I tried to go online but I wasn't connected; there was no internet service. I wondered briefly if the internet still existed at all inside the satellites flying around Earth or if it died from its own silent virus along with the rest of humanity. I guess I would never know, not that it mattered. Knowing the details wouldn't change what had happened.

I carefully tucked the flash-drives inside a sandwich bag before double wrapping it and sealing it shut. I rolled it all up delicately and set it inside a fabric pouch labeled *Tooth Fairy* in silvery-pink thread and put the pouch in a zippered side pocket of my back pack, next to Cecy's paper. For some reason, it felt good to take it with me.

I had enough food for about three days, and water for about one. Even though I could see the skyscrapers from our living room it was at least five miles to downtown and considering we might end up walking, I packed only what I could carry.

On our way out the door, I hesitated at the entryway where several framed pictures of our last snow trip to the mountains hung up neatly on the wall. I took down the one of the kids sitting on their sled and peered into the faces of the smiling girl and goofy grinned boy before slamming it up against the door frame. Zoey scurried away and looked at me reproachfully underneath her long dark lashes.

4

"Sorry girl." I apologized, as she carefully sat down in the driveway, anxiously waiting for me to exit the house.

I picked the broken glass out of the frame and removed the picture, holding it in both hands. She was 8 and he was 4. They were beautiful. I folded the paper in half and slid it into the front of my backpack, next to the tooth fairy pouch and Cecy's paper. When I shut the door behind me, I only turned around to make sure the note I wrote earlier was still firmly pinned into the red wooden door. I read the words silently, one more time.

1/9

Family and Friends: The dog and I have left to find my Mom. Most of you know where her place is, the corner of 9th and F. I'll leave a note there before I move on. Everyone here is…gone. I can't stay. I'm not sure when or if I will come back here but leave a message anyway.

I hope you find me. – Riley

I sighed heavily and turned around to face my dead neighbor's brand new cherry-red Jeep Wrangler, which looked out of place parked atop the weed-filled cracks of my driveway. Before I climbed into it, I ran my hand over the white *RUBICON* lettering that was printed along the side of the hood. It looked straight off the dealership floor, and even though my neighbor had brought it home six months before, he had taken exceptional care of it. Even the tires still looked untouched by the road. I had broken into someone's home, stolen their car, and honestly didn't care. As I drove the Jeep out of the driveway, I looked at the place that held so many of my memories. It felt like a cemetery, but I didn't see myself returning to visit any time soon.

***

There weren't many cars blocking the streets around my neighborhood but within a mile of the freeway the frozen traffic was bumper to bumper and I realized with horror and sadness that people had flocked out of their homes only to die in their cars. I couldn't think of anything more depressing. Even with most of the windows

5

rolled up tight, the smell of the decaying bodies wafted out of their tin coffins and surrounded the Jeep like an invisible fog, and I questioned, not for the first time, my need to go into the city.

During the last conversation I had with my mother, she had tried to hide it, but I heard the ragged breathing and could almost feel the fever through the phone and I knew she was sick too. Before the land lines went out I called everyone I could think of. My family, friends, coworkers and even my students, but most didn't answer their phones and the few that did were all sick. This wasn't a cold anyone recovered from; the virus was fast and efficient, killing the infected within forty-eight hours. The National T.V. called it the Cardinal Plague but the local radio stations mostly referred to the outbreak as the Red Death. I didn't care about the name, but it was efficient - more so than anyone could have possibly imagined.

Almost a week had passed since the power grid went off and only the tops of a handful of buildings had emergency lights still flickering on and off. At night the whole city seemed to disappear into the darkness, and I wanted to be out of the city by nightfall. I knew my Mom would be dead by the time we made it to her apartment, but I had to know for certain - I couldn't move on without knowing.

Once we made it within eyesight of the freeway on-ramp it was clear I wouldn't be able to drive into downtown from there, so I drove on side streets as parallel to the main roads as I could, slowly weaving between parked cars and driving on the sidewalks and embankments when necessary. Every street going in and out of the city was too congested to pass through freely.

The air was cool despite the morning sun as we inched along the streets leading into downtown. Eventually vehicles blocked the way forward, and with no room to turn the Jeep around, I had to leave it wedged between a chain-link fence and an old Buick, and decided to walk the rest of the way. All we needed for the day was shoved into my large back pack but I left the extra dog food since I planned on returning to the Jeep on my way out of the city.

Zoey looked at me as we wiggled between the cars full of rotting people. Her big, dark chocolate-brown eyes pleaded with me for answers and all I could think of to say was, "Don't worry girl, it's going to be okay." But I didn't believe my own words. When would it ever be okay again?

6

The silence of the city was overwhelming; a place that was once in a constant state of activity was completely devoid of sound and movement. Even the dog felt the heavy weight from the dead buildings. Loft windows seemed to watch us with sad, glassy eyes as we hurried down the empty sidewalks toward the epicenter of San Diego and I kept our pace quick.

We stopped at a corner and watched police tape flap about in the breeze that had been wrapped completely around a small parking lot that was full of medical vans and police vehicles. I carefully approached each car, peering inside. Every window of a plain black sedan with exempt plates had been shattered, its contents riffled through. Someone had already picked each vehicle clean. Piled up behind one of the vans was a heap of body bags, at least ten feet high, and equally as wide. I backed out of the lot before my mind had the chance to tell my stomach to purge breakfast.

One block further and parked at an angle in the middle of the street was a military tank. Part of the store front nearest the tank was blown inward, scattering huge chunks of concrete, glass and wood dozens of feet into the street. Pieces of trash and debris had settled on the front of the massive machine and the littered look of the scene gave the impression it had been there for years, not the weeks it had taken for the city to die. We kept walking, our eyes facing forward, feet pounding the pavement as a rancid, smoky smell drifted along the wind, similar to what my own backyard smelled like…burnt corpses. I did not want to find the source.

***

My Mother's apartment was on the fourth floor of a small corner complex. I stood in the street for a full minute, debating on whether I truly wanted to go inside. I had watched my son, my ex-husband and finally my daughter, take their last breaths in my arms. I wasn't sure if I was ready to find my Mother dead too in her small one bedroom apartment. So I stood there, staring at the entry door as if she would walk out of it at any second. With my eyes closed, I could almost hear the traffic and shouts and laughs of a once thriving public. But with my eyes open, all I could hear was my steady and slightly rushed heartbeat and the ragged panting of a nervous canine at my feet.

A raven flew out of a nearby tree, sending a piercing caw in our direction so loud that Zoey and I both jumped. It was enough to snap me out of my semi-trance and I squared my shoulders and closed the gap between the street and the front door in ten long strides. When I tugged on the metal handle nothing happened. It didn't budge. I slammed all my weight up against the frame and it rattled, but wouldn't give. The only option was to break in. The closest thing nearby that was heavy enough to go through the tempered glass was a metal trashcan. I had to roll it on its side to move it and it took several impacts against the door to crack the glass. After kicking the broken shards out enough to pass through, the smell of decay drifted from inside the building out into the fresh air. Zoey sneezed violently and refused to enter with me.

"Come on, girl. You can do it." I urged her.

She sat on the edge of the curb with a sad look, her droopy eyes moist.

"Let's go." I willed her toward me, my hands patting my legs. She mocked a sneeze and glanced away from me.

I stood with my hands on my hips, chewing nervously at my lower lip, wondering which would be less traumatic: leaving her outside, alone on the street, or carrying her unwillingly into the building and forcing her up the stairs with me. I glared at her, and just as I was about to turn and leave her sulking on the curb, a shrill scream erupted from down the street. Its echo bounced off the brick buildings with an eerie rhythm. The hairs rose on the back of my neck as I pondered briefly whether the scream was human, or animal, and Zoey's nervous glances up and down the sidewalk gave me the answer I needed. She wasn't staying outside without me.

***

All thirty pounds of her squirmed and wiggled under my arm as I stomped up the dark stairwell, cursing under my breath as she fought against me. On the second level I let her go and she followed at my heels until we reached the fourth floor landing. We stood there, the two of us simply looking at each other. At that moment if felt as if the narrow stairwell was the portal to some unknown universe, like leaving those steps would take us to a place we couldn't return from.

8

After pushing through the door, the smell of the hallway hit me like a brick and I swooned, fearing I might pass out from the overwhelming stench. Zoey whimpered at my knees as I ran to the end of the walkway and paused briefly in front of the last door. It was unlocked, but I still knocked gently and entered with a sleeved hand cupped tightly around my nose and mouth.

I was in the apartment no more than fifteen seconds. Mom had died in her bed, clothed in a nightgown, with a note folded in one of her bloated and discolored hands. A ray of sunshine penetrated through a gap in the blinds, sending a soft stream of light across her pillow, lighting her strawberry blonde hair and making the strands of grey shimmer. A dark fluid had begun to run down the side of the mattress forming a goopy puddle on the floor. I gagged as my stomach threatened to expel what little had collected there since morning, staying only long enough to take the scrap of paper, cover her and leave. I took the stairs down two at a time, choking back sobs, my eyes stinging with tears. My family, they were all gone. Everyone was gone.

***

After vomiting up everything that was in my stomach, and dry heaving for nearly five minutes, I collapsed up against the building and rested my head back against the cool red and brown brick until the sunlight felt hot on my face. Zoey lay next to me, her head resting on my thigh, comforting me the only way a dog knows how. I slowly rubbed the top of her head as I read my Mom's note out loud to her.

Sweetie,

Part of me hopes that you never read this letter. I know I'm dying and I don't want you to find me here like this. But if you came here, you must be safe and that is what comforts me now. I love you, so much. And I hope I said it enough. Humanity may have destroyed itself, but if you are here, if you are ok, then there is still hope. Never lose your hope. Love you, like you and care about you. Always.

Mom

***

I had to change. I so badly wanted out of my soiled clothes I was almost tempted to walk the streets naked. Even though I had only been in the tight quarters of my Mother's apartment for less than a minute, everything I wore, even my skin and hair, smelled like death. Zoey didn't smell any better and she knew it. God, we needed a shower.

Before we left the apartment I pulled a piece of paper out of my pack and wrote on it carefully before taping it to the inside of the complex lobby window.

1/9 12:30pm
Family and Friends: No one is alive here. It seems the City is dead. I'm moving on to the bus station then the airport. I'll leave a message for you at Terminal One.
I hope you find me. - Riley

I went back inside the building to the public restroom and tried the faucets but only a hollow echo vibrated through the pipes. It was quickly becoming an all-around sucky day.

Once outside again, I stood on the empty sidewalk looking up and down the street, squinting into the sun. It was maybe a thirty minute walk straight to the bay. The water would be cold, but it would be better than walking around with that stench clinging to my body, checking building after building, hoping for a working faucet.

We turned west toward the mall. It took a while to find replacements for what I was wearing, as well as what I'd need to scrub my skin and hair. When we made it back to Broadway, over an hour had passed; the sun was directly above us but there was a chill in the air. The bus depot was before the bay so we continued west, and as we walked through an empty intersection I saw movement out of the corner of my eye.

"Help me." A man's voice whispered from behind my right ear.

I jumped and uttered a startled yelp but when I whirled around, the street was empty. If Zoey hadn't bristled and growled I would have thought I'd imagined the whole thing. I stood very still as I looked up and down the buildings and store fronts for any sign of movement.

"Hello?" I couldn't keep my voice from shaking.

Taking a few more steps into the intersection I cleared my throat and tried to hide the tremor in my voice as I yelled once more, "Hello... anyone there?"

From one of the corner buildings, a metal door slammed shut with a heavy bang, causing me to flinch. Zoey began turning in circles and barking loudly in the direction we had come from. Then, she bolted. Not knowing what else to do I ran after her, calling her name, struggling to hold onto my bags while the pack thumped heavily against my back. Twice I looked over my shoulder and the second time I thought I saw someone watching us from a street corner, but I didn't stop running until the stitch in my side became unbearable. I could see Zoey off in the distance, a small dark speck on the horizon.

Well that's just great. I muttered to myself.

As I collapsed to my knees, my eyes strained to take in everything around me. Every sense I had was heightened. I could smell the salt in the air from the nearby ocean mingling with the rot of the city. While my knees pressed into the concrete of the sidewalk, I listened to the creak of the tree branches and the scraping sound of a small paper cup as it rolled along the gutter, and an empty humorless laugh escaped my mouth at the fact that I was losing my mind.

I inhaled deeply and started moving again, but Zoey was nowhere to be seen. For a little dog she sure could run. I was more than irritated that she bailed on me, which wasn't her usual protective style but I knew something (*or someone*) must have really scared her. Every few feet I whistled for her, and called out her name. Two blocks past the bus depot and there she was, standing on the sidewalk, cowering behind a large metal trashcan, looking at me sheepishly. I stopped about ten feet from her and put my hands on my hips. A gesture she knew well.

"Yeah, you know you blew it, don't you?" I asked her with a mocking edge of firmness to my voice.

I waited for her to creep her way to me and when she got to my feet I folded my arms across my chest and raised an eyebrow at her and glared. She flopped down and rolled submissively onto her back waiting for a tummy rub. Several minutes later, after the petting and soothing on my part and face licking on her part, we started walking again, back to the depot.

I told myself we were both seeing and hearing things that weren't there, but that didn't keep me from looking over my shoulder every few seconds and staring nervously into the shadows around us. Zoey kept her tail tucked between her legs and her head low, as if something would attack us at any moment. The longer she continued on like that, the more I felt we weren't alone.

I couldn't shake the feeling that we were being watched very closely.

***

There was no reason to go inside the Greyhound station. People had flocked to the small transit station hoping to get on a bus that would take them out of the city, but the buses couldn't get them far, and there were more people trying to leave than there were buses.

Hundreds of suitcases and bags littered the entryway, haphazardly strewn about the sidewalk. Someone had written on the wall in bright red spray paint: *NO MORE BUSES. PLEASE GO HOME.*

One peek through the glass doors told me no one was alive inside. Bodies were slumped shoulder to shoulder up against each other. Some people sat and others lay slumped on the floor under blue blankets. My heart sank as I noticed all the parents that had died with their arms cradled around small children. A dark grey stroller lay empty, turned onto its side with the contents of a pink and yellow polka-dotted diaper bag dumped out onto the ground. I kept my hand clasped tightly around my nose, trying to ignore the smell from the building until I saw a police officer who sat awkwardly on the linoleum leaning against a wooden desk, a gun in his hand, and dried blood caked along the side of his lowered head, and my stomach lurched.

I turned around so quickly that I tumbled over a red and black suitcase, and just before I landed on all fours, watery vomit flew from my mouth ungraciously, splattering against the pale sidewalk. I shook and lurched until I was sure I would heave my stomach lining out onto the dirty concrete. Zoey whined at my side, unsure of what to do

12

and dodged away from me as I stumbled to my feet, swaying a bit before turning my back on the depot.

I didn't look back as we continued on to the Bay. I walked slowly, taking each step deliberately, wanting to run, but knowing that if I did my knees would buckle underneath me and send me face first onto the concrete. Even though I willed my nerves to calm down, and told myself I was going to be fine, my body betrayed me. I was shaking with fear from the inside out.

CHAPTER 2

I sat on the edge of the narrow wooden dock with my naked feet dangling slowly over the water. I left my bra and underwear on, as if the small amount of clothing would protect me from the cold. For a bit I listened to the creak of the nearby boats as they gently bobbed in the murky water, every so often leaning into their dock slips with a groan or a sigh.

When my shoulders felt warm from the sun I knew it was time to jump in. The challenge would be getting the dog to go with me. We could have just climbed across the rocks and walked right into the water, but the dog hated baths…even if I carried her in and kept her leashed, she would drag me out, or die trying. Anyhow, the bay water near the shore looked disgusting.

But at the end of one of the small boat piers there was nothing but water, she would have to swim a bit before escaping to dry land – which is exactly what I wanted. The only way I'd be able to rinse her off properly would be to haul her into the deep water and be able to keep her there long enough to scrub the bubbles out of her thick coat. At the time, it seemed like a good plan. She stood peevishly at my feet, her thick dark coat lathered thickly with shampoo. I was prepared for her to hate me forever.

She put as much distance between us as she could, fully aware that I had leashed her for a reason she wouldn't like. When I pushed off the pier with the strap wrapped around my hand I tried to sound happy as I said, "Jump, girl!" but my words lost their breath when the cold water cut into my core like ice.

It started at my feet, and quickly spread up my legs into my torso…a painful stinging sensation, like I was being jabbed everywhere with thousands of angry needles. For one very terrifying second, I was sure I was being stung by jellyfish, and I thrashed at the

15

water around me until I realized the pain was simply from the cold water.

I managed to close my mouth after gasping for air just before my head slipped under. The last thing I heard was Zoey's nails scraping along the edge of the pier as she tried to pull against the taut strap. She crashed, indecorously, directly on top of my head, feet pummeling, struggling to find something to stand on. I let her kick circles around me while I struggled to open the shampoo bottle I dove in with, and pour it all over my hair. I washed what I could, and did my best to rinse the dog's head before swimming back to the ladder to heave myself out. I made the mistake of taking the leash off my wrist and suddenly, Zoey was gone.

I spun around in the water and saw her swimming away from the dock, deeper into the bay. I pushed off the ladder with enough force that I felt it rattle underneath my hand. I struggled to catch up to the dog.

"Zoey!" I tried calling for her, but soft waves of water lapped over my face as I swam, and I mostly choked out her name.

She doggy-paddled further out to sea, clearly terrified, not aware that she was swimming away from the shore, rather than closer to it, and with each stroke of my arms, the water became colder beneath me as if a giant hole had opened up somewhere in the depths below. I fought back the urge to panic at the thought of what could be swimming freely just a few feet beneath me.

"Stop!" I yelled, "Zoey, come here!"

Eventually she turned and saw me, and made an awkward and slow turn back in my direction. The gentle waves splashed against my face and into my ears as I tread the water, waiting for her. As soon as she was within touching distance, I reached for her leash and secured it to my hand again.

"Damn dog." I said, as my body trembled violently. "I don't want to drown out here, let's go." I tugged on the leash and she began swimming next to me, her dark eyes rimmed red from the ocean water and an almost comical expression of fear in her gaze.

By the time we got back to the dock, I was certain I swallowed an unsafe amount of saltwater during my struggle with the dog, and the impromptu swim had taken most of my strength. The cold was debilitating; I was shivering so hard my teeth were banging together, and my legs felt like solid lead.

Climbing back up the ladder seemed almost impossible with my semi-frozen limbs but I reached up anyway and gripped the rough metal for support. My hands were numb as I slumped my forehead up against the first metal rung in frustration. Zoey barked beside me, treading the water in tight circles. As my fingers tightly gripped the frame, I willed myself to pull up and get the hell out of the water. With my eyes closed, I raised one hand up at a time. By the third rung I couldn't feel my fingers anymore so I hung there unable to move up as my legs floated in the water below me, my knees pressed into the ladder frame for support. I refused to let go and fall back into the water.

After counting to ten, and funneling what was left of my adrenaline-packed swim into my arms, I pulled myself upward, and the lower rungs of the ladder broke off beneath my feet. I gasped as the whole frame tipped forward and came apart in my hands.

"Damn it." I hissed, in disbelief, as my body slammed back into the water.

What was left of the old ladder slipped under the water line and disappeared into the dark blue of the bay beneath the pier like a metal skeleton. I swore again at my luck and glanced nervously up at the pier, knowing it would be difficult to heave myself the few feet out of the water over the edge without a ladder. I could barely climb the rungs as it was.

Pushing away from the pier in frustration, I floated onto my back, looking up at the warm sun which was a total contrast to the freezing bay water. Zoey barked loudly and swam past me, tugging on my arm, bringing me back to where the ladder had been hanging just moments before. Exhausted, and unable to swim anymore, I reached my hands up as high as they could go, and gripped the edge of the wooden dock with my fingertips.

I stayed like that for several minutes, letting the flow of the water push my body and feeling the warmth of the sunlight penetrate into my hands and arms, until something dry and warm closed around my wrists and yanked me upward. I felt strong arms go around my waist as I was tugged over the edge of the dock, but I didn't have the strength to lift my head and look at my savior.

17

I flopped, water-logged, back onto the pier like a fish and tried to stutter out the words *"My dog"* but it came out sounding like, *"Ny og."* instead.

A few seconds later Zoey was scrambling onto the pier, shaking her body every two steps. The water droplets flying from her wet coat went so high up into the sky that they fell back down all around me like rain drops.

I stayed on my side, curled in a ball, breaths shuddering in and out of my mouth, ignoring the sharp pin-pricks of the roughly sun-warped wooden planks digging into my cheek. The marina swayed in and out of my vision and I was startled by a deep male voice above my face.

"You must be out of your mind!"

With no energy to answer, I nodded in agreement as a dark haired man loosely wrapped one of the fluffy white department store towels around my shoulders, rubbing my arms for a few seconds. Then he went to work on Zoey with the other towel, vigorously rubbing her up and down until her tongue hung from her mouth in satisfaction.

In the background I noticed an older couple standing on the shoreline. They were holding hands, watching us with sad expressions on their faces. The pier heaved softly with the water; distorting my vision and making the couple appear to shimmer in the sunlight, almost like they were bobbing up and down on the rocks. I gave up trying to focus on them and closed my eyes, listening to the steady creak of the wood underneath my cold body until his hands were on me again, so gentle and reassuring. When I opened my eyes the couple was gone.

"Hi." He peered at me curiously from clear blue eyes, his dark brows furrowed with concern.

He was close enough to my face for me to see how long his eye lashes were. And they were long, insanely so. His full lips were flushed the same color pink as his cheeks. Long, dark brown strands of hair framed his face and for a moment I thought I knew him. *There's no way I've met him. I could never forget a face like his. But I know him, from somewhere.*

When I realized I was staring at him and he was staring back, I cleared my throat and tried to speak. My teeth clattered together violently as I answered him, "Um…Hi."

He smiled. Wow. It was a beautiful thing really; the roundness of his mouth parted, showing off a perfect set of bright white teeth, and as his smile deepened and his lips curled upward. I thought it should be illegal...having a smile like that. The little voice inside my head said softly, but firmly, *a smile that amazing can only mean one thing...danger.*

I slowly shifted up onto my elbow and Zoey casually walked up to me, licked the side of my face and sat down by my hand. Her brown eyes were open wide as she peered at me, then the stranger, then back at me, waiting for one of us to speak again. It wasn't me. I didn't trust my voice at the moment. Even though this man had pulled me out of the frigid bay, I was sitting before him half naked, half conscious and realizing my dog now saw him as the post-bath rub down person; which meant at this moment he was more in her favor than the woman that dragged her into the frigid water.

"Are you alright?" The man asked me quietly, a trace of smile still playing on his lips.

When I didn't immediately answer, he gestured to my dirty clothes heaped at the end of the pier and said with a wisp of a European accent, "It's kind of cold to go swimming, don't you think?"

He shifted back on his heels and I took in his whole frame for the first time. He wasn't a huge guy, he had a slight but strong looking build and again I got the overwhelming feeling I knew him.

"I'm fine. I..." I trailed off with a wave of my hand, not feeling comfortable trying to explain to a perfect stranger why I jumped into the Bay in the middle of January.

Feeling self-conscious, I straightened my shoulders and said, "Thanks, for the help. I should probably get dressed now." I was painfully aware that I was sitting in front of him, wrapped only in a towel.

He smiled again, stood and took the few strides to the end of the dock and scooped up my pack and shopping bag. After he casually walked back to me and dropped them in my lap, he bent down and picked up the second wet towel and held it out in front of him.

"I won't look, I promise." His voice had a hint of playfulness to it and he turned his face away from me as he talked, "What's your name?"

I slipped into a clean bra and underwear as quickly as I could. My voice was muffled as I pulled a blue cotton Henley shirt over my head, "Riley. What's yours?"

I sensed the slightest hesitation before he said carefully, "Connor. Nice to meet you Riley." He laughed softly and I heard his accent thicken somewhat when he asked, "So, do you make a habit of jumping off docks in winter?"

"Not really," I let myself smile a little. "There's a shortage of hot, running water, in case you haven't noticed."

I pulled my new jeans up my legs, jumping up and down as the fabric stuck to my wet skin like spandex. Standing barefoot, I rummaged through the last bag and brought out a pair of converse shoes, socks and a large hoodie. When he heard me zipper up the sweatshirt he turned to face me again and lowered the towel.

"It's nice to see another living person." He said quietly. "For a while I thought it was just me."

We stood there for a moment, looking at each other, until I remembered the man and woman on the shoreline earlier. "Wait, what about the older couple?"

"Older couple?" Connor raised an eyebrow and looked at me quizzically. "Where?"

"They were standing over there, watching us." I pointed at where they had been, holding hands. "When you pulled me out, I saw them but I don't know where they went."

Connor looked up and down the handful of docks, scanning the shore and turned back at me, shrugging his shoulders. "Why would they leave?"

"I don't know." I sat down hard on the pier to put my socks and shoes on. Zoey seemed anxious to get away from the water but didn't appear to be suffering from the cold anymore. Despite the dry clothes, I was *still* shivering. My muscles were trembling in painful waves, making my entire body ache. It felt like I would never feel warm again. I pulled my brush out from my pack and tried to work through the knotted ends of my wet hair before giving up and pulling it all back into a messy bun.

"Well, we could look for them…if you want." He said it almost like a question.

"We?"

I looked at him curiously as he shifted uncomfortably and ran a hand through his wavy hair, obviously trying to pick his next words carefully. His face showed a wide range of emotions, his gestures almost familiar.

He shifted around a bit and then turned his body away from me. He stood with his hands shoved into his back pockets, and asked, "Are you leaving the City?" He nodded at my pack and added, "It seems like you're carrying a lot in there for just a day trip."

I blinked, unable to answer him at first, "I came here to look for someone." I paused long enough to wrap my arms around my waist, "And now I'm heading to the airport. I don't know what I expect to find there though."

"The airport is full of the dead." He said it with no emotion.

"Oh." I couldn't think of anything better to say.

I knew I still had to go there to at least leave a note, to keep my trail fresh for anyone looking for me, but I hadn't thought of where I'd be going next. I knew in the back of my mind I had hoped to find other survivors. Now that I had, I didn't know what to do. *Now what?*

The week before the power went out; I had called one of my closest friends, who lived in Las Vegas. She was bed-ridden when I talked to her. She was lucid one minute and confused and vomiting the next. She hung up after saying she was going to call her father. He died seven years ago from cancer. When I called her back an hour later she didn't answer. There was no one else left for me to look for, but the urge to keep looking was there. The desire to be found was stronger than ever.

I blurted out, "Will you come with me? To the airport, I mean. There's something I need to do there." I didn't want to be alone again, with all these dead people and nowhere to go, no one to find.

His pale blue eyes seemed to pierce through me and I was certain he would say no. That small voice inside my head warned me not to trot off into the distance with a strange man, no matter how attractive and nice he seemed to be, but I refused to listen. It somehow seemed worse to be alone when I knew others were around, than if I was the only person left standing. Besides, the dog was comfortable around him, which at the time, was enough for me to trust him.

"Okay." I felt the muscles in my shoulders relax after he agreed.

21

He turned, and started up the pier toward the land and for the first time I noticed a large backpack leaning up against a crate near the entrance of the dock. He slipped his arms through it as Zoey and I jogged to catch up with him. A sigh of relief escaped from my mouth.

Walking side by side, we left the marina and crossed an empty parking lot to reach North Harbor Drive. We passed the USS Midway and the Maritime Museum, following the street as it curved to the west until the tarmac was in sight.

An explosion that sounded like a sonic boom erupted from somewhere nearby, blowing the glass out of a nearby building and shaking the ground beneath our feet. I landed on my knees, holding tight to the dog's collar. I pulled out Zoey's leash and clicked it into place, not ready to chase after her again. Confused, the three of us huddled there for a moment, kneeling on the pavement. When Zoey barked it was muffled, I felt deaf but I could hear the tinker of glass falling to the ground. It reminded me of wind-chimes and for a second it sounded almost beautiful.

Connor and I looked at each other wide-eyed, and then back at the sky above as it started filling with clouds of smoke. *Did a plane explode?* Neither of us spoke right away, there wasn't much to say, especially if for the moment neither of us could hear well.

After making it to our feet, Connor told me he had heard a similar explosion earlier in the day, and saw smoke in the sky. He was downtown to see if he could find the source of the fire. We stood together, staring into the distance where the airport stretched out before us. If the runway was on fire, we might have a chance of making it to a terminal, but only for a few moments. What I thought we might find there, I didn't know. But I couldn't turn back. I had nowhere left to go.

***

The road leading up to the airport was a complicated web of chaos. A blood-orange glow pulsated from some distant and unseen part of the runway where a fire was burning fiercely. Dark rolls of smoke twisted and bellowed upward, obscuring the view of any structures behind it. Vehicles were everywhere; on more than one occasion we had to slide over roofs and trunks to make it through the entwined metallic mess. The military had attempted to block access to the airport terminals but it was obvious the public had forced their way in. As we carefully climbed around the collapsed military temporary fencing blocking the entrance, we saw more and more vehicles riddled with bullet holes. In the end, the military had turned on the civilians.

A fine layer of ash had settled on mostly everything, leaving a trace of our footprints behind us and messy skid marks on whatever we climbed over. It smelled of fire and fuel and something organic. *People.* Connor gestured for me to cover my mouth with my shirt sleeve. I nodded that I understood and we clamored our way through the disaster until we reached the terminal's first set of double doors but they were completely barricaded with suitcases and trolleys. We followed the glass wall as it angled on towards set after set of doors that we couldn't squeeze through. My eyes were stinging, and my head hurt from the burnt and toxic air I was breathing. I was just about to give up when my hands reached a bent piece of window frame where the glass had been completely blown out. Connor pulled me inside behind him.

There wasn't much to see. The halls were dark where smoke had filled the upper half of the lobby and the air was rotten. I understood it would be pointless to wander around. It wouldn't be hard at all to get lost in the hazy air.

Connor stood before me, and gripped my shoulders. Dark rings were starting to form around his nostrils, his eyes were watery and bloodshot and his hair was dotted gray with ash. He held me firmly as he asked loudly, "Do you see? Do you see? There is nothing – *no one*, left here?"

I nodded but still he did not let go of my shoulders so I uttered a weak, "Yes."

His hands finally dropped, and he pushed past me, back outside the broken window into what little fresh air was left. The smoke billowed greedily out after him, escaping the confines of the building. Zoey had stayed outside and was watching anxiously, sneezing every so often. The smoke was too much, we couldn't stay anywhere nearby. Even if there were answers, we didn't know what we were looking for or where to find it. Another massive explosion could level the whole place.

This was a mistake. Why did he come with me, when he knew we would find nothing? I thought to myself.

I turned to follow Connor when something brushed gently against my back. I stopped abruptly, my feet sliding along the bits and chunks of fallen glass but after looking over my shoulder, I saw no one. Staying absolutely still, all I could hear with my partially damaged eardrums was the sound of fire hungrily eating its way through the building toward me. My eyes were watering, and even though I had my arm across my mouth, every breath I took was heavy with soot.

"Hello?" I called out between my fingers, but only the whistle of the oxygen being sucked out of the room answered.

I ran outside, unsure if it was the fire or the lingering feel of a hand on my back that spooked me. I rushed past both the dog and Connor and stopped at a red pick-up truck to catch my breath.

Connor came up beside me, heaving, and for a moment all we did was lean against the truck and watch as flames licked at the back of the building. A series of small explosions shook the ground, rattling the frame of the truck. Without discussing it, the three of us retreated to the barricade. Our tracks in the dust and ash were the only signs we had been there.

***

We headed back the way we had come in silence, half walking, and half jogging. Other than our labored breathing and the fire raging on the runway, there wasn't anything else to hear. My ears popped a few times and though my head hurt, it seemed my hearing wasn't permanently damaged. I could hear the cracking of glass behind us, the collapsing of walls and the rushing of fire. It sounded like a distant waterfall.

We went back toward the bay, leaving the airport behind us, but before we left the intersection I panicked. In our rush to leave the airport I hadn't considered a place to put my next message. Exhausted, I sat down on a bus bench and scanned the street. By morning there wouldn't be much of the airport left. With no one to put out the fire, it could burn down half of downtown, or worse.

Another series of booms erupted somewhere out of sight and the fire cloud above the airport doubled instantly. The ground beneath us trembled and Zoey cowered behind my legs. The rational thing to do would be to go back to the bus depot and leave a note there. I had no idea what I would write but at least it would be proof that I was still alive, if anyone was looking for me. *If anyone is left.* I thought to myself.

I closed my eyes and leaned into the bench, with Zoey slumped between my feet, panting heavily. Connor sat to my right, riffling through his bag. I heard him open a zippered compartment and the unexpected crunch of plastic made me jump. When I opened my eyes he was holding out a bottle of water and gestured to Zoey.

"Wash her face off, and make her drink. Hopefully we didn't inhale too much of that smoke." He said. His voice was hoarse, thickening his accent.

"Thanks." I replied, my own voice just as strained.

I watched him settled up against the bench, his hands gripped together behind his head. Without thinking I blurted out, "I know it might seem weird but I feel as if I've seen you before."

He leaned forward slowly, putting his arms onto his legs and lowered his head, running one hand aimlessly through his dark hair.

"Guess I have one of those faces." He mumbled, with a flick of his hand in the air, as if to dismiss the topic.

So change the topic I did.

"What do you think happened? At the airport, I mean?" I asked him, after Zoey had lapped up half the bottle of water from my cupped hand.

I downed what was left in a few gulps, not realizing how hot and dry my throat really was till the cold water passed between my chapped lips. Connor finished his own water, before he rested his elbows onto his knees and put his hands to his head. From that position he looked almost juvenile, small and fragile. I immediately felt embarrassed by this thought. Based on the little amount of time I had spent with him, there didn't seem to be anything weak about him. Despite his young looking frame, his face showed his maturity; not in an aged way, but in a wise way. I guessed he was in his early thirties, somewhere around my age.

I flinched when he sighed loudly and sat up, rubbing the back of his neck and looking at me as he said, "I don't know what happened. The fire wasn't burning yesterday. Someone could have set it." He said the last few words carefully, deliberately, as if he wanted me to consider them.

I sat up straighter. "Why? Why would someone try and blow up an airport?" I asked him, a hint of incredulity in my voice.

"Who the hell knows? But obviously we aren't the only people out here."

"No, I guess not." I went silent, and it dawned on me that being alone might not be as bad as finding more people alive. The idea that someone would deliberately set the airport ablaze made me nervous. Was someone trying to keep those of us left from leaving...or keeping someone else away? I remembered the voice on the street earlier that seemed to whisper in my ear, the old couple on the shore that disappeared before offering to help, the touch on my back that seemed to belong to an invisible hand. None of it made sense to me but it was obvious we were *not* alone, not completely.

"Well, look," I said, as I stood up and began brushing ash off my new clothes and out of my still damp hair, "We can't stay here, not in the City anyway. It's obviously not safe to be anywhere near the airport. It'll get worse before it dies out. Maybe it will even catch these buildings on fire as well."

"I agree." He said with a feigned grin on his face, "So, what's your plan?" He shook the ash out of his hair and quickly dusted his arms and legs off. "You're not thinking of taking another dip in the ocean, are you?" He grinned at me.

My knees weakened slightly and I frowned, I didn't like the fact that my body seemed unable to control itself around him. I planted my hands on my hips and glared into the distance. Less than an hour before I was clean. Sure, I was wet and freezing, but clean. And now here I was, covered in soot and ash and smelling of fire. Stinky again. I was more than a little irritated at the irony.

"My plan?" I shrugged, "I don't really have one, but we can start with the bus depot. I want to leave something there."

"Leave what?" He asked with a hint of suspicion.

"A note." I replied simply.

"For who?" He turned in a semi-circle, his arms outstretched.

When he faced me again, I wasn't sure what to say. I was afraid to admit to myself that everyone I knew was gone, that no one would come looking for me. But I couldn't just walk away from my life like

I no longer existed. Leaving the notes felt like I was tethering myself to my past, and I wasn't ready to let go, not yet. Several times I found myself wanting to pull out the folded photo of the kids and trace the contours of their faces but I knew if I did that, I wouldn't want to go on without them. I couldn't let them down by quitting, not yet.

At the intersection I decided to leave a note anyway. I wasn't sure if the area would be safe if the fire moved off the runway and started down the streets, but it felt right to at least try and leave a message.

"Hold on a minute." I mumbled.

Connor watched me open my pack and pull out the small notepad and large permanent marker. I used the hood of a car to write on before tearing the paper from the pad. I walked up to the largest military truck in the intersection and taped the note to the side. The white paper noticeably stood out against the camouflaged green paint. *Good.*

1/9 4:00pm

I found someone today, he found us actually. His name is Connor. The airport is on fire – no help there – so we are heading back to the depot. Tonight I'll find a place to sleep before we make a plan to leave the City. I'll leave a message again soon. I hope you find me. – Riley

When I turned around to rejoin Connor I was startled to find him standing directly behind me. My forehead bumped into his chin and even though I blushed and stepped back, he didn't move, but instead peered over my shoulder with interest and read my message aloud. After shoving his hands into his pockets he looked at me curiously.

"You leave a note everywhere you go?"

"No, not everywhere," I replied, defensive. "If someone is out there, looking for me, it makes sense to tell them where I'm going. To let them know I'm okay."

He didn't say anything, just continued to gaze at me with curiosity. I realized then how close we were standing and began to edge my way past him, lightly brushing against his arm as I passed.

27

Connor rocked back onto his heels before turning to follow me. "It's not a bad idea you know. Smart actually." He said when we were walking side by side again.

Not sure if he was being sarcastic or not, I felt the need to once again be defensive. "Sure." I quipped.

I walked faster, hoping it gave me the lead and he would fall back behind me but he kept my pace. I could feel him glancing at me every few steps.

"Did I upset you?" He asked after a few minutes of awkward silence.

We had rounded a street corner and were heading back into the heart of downtown. I sighed, not certain if I was really upset with him or the seemingly impossible reality we now faced.

"No," I started, "I'm not upset with you. It's this shitty world we now have to survive. I don't know what the hell to do. *Why are we here?"*

I felt my cheeks flush with anger and turned away from him, arms crossed, glaring at the empty street, fuming. A picture flashed through my mind of my daughter, when she was upset, standing the same way, her lips pulled tightly together in a pout so comical it took most my control not to laugh. My eyes instantly welled with tears and I couldn't bring my hands up fast enough to hide them. The warm trickles spilled down my cheeks and I rubbed them away with disgust. I didn't want to cry, I wanted to hit something.

"Shit." It was all my voice could manage before cracking.

Connor had squatted down near Zoey and was scratching behind her ears when I finally turned around to face them. She walked up to me quickly, rubbed against my legs and sat directly on my left foot, her head tilted up with her tongue protruding from her mouth slightly with each pant, eyes gazing innocently into mine. I wondered if her eyes would forever look sad. I reached down and rubbed the top of her head and she licked my hand.

"Okay then?" Connor asked. For a moment I had almost forgotten about him.

I nodded and we were off again, walking back the way I had come just a few hours before with Zoey. I could no longer see the sun directly, it had moved over and beyond the buildings. Long, craggy shadows reached out at us from every stationary object. The dog seemed jittery, and remembering how she bolted earlier I kept a firm grasp on her leash. She seemed almost grateful for the bond, as if she thought I might up and disappear when she wasn't looking.

"The hotel I'm staying at isn't that far from here. There's plenty of room for you both," he gestured at the dog, "I have water and food. I've been stocking up." He said with a soft laugh, "Sorry, there's no room service, but it's clean and safe enough."

"You're staying at a hotel?" I asked. *Why didn't I think of this – before I jumped into the bay?*

"Well, yeah. I'm not a local." He shifted his pack on his shoulders, and continued, "I was supposed to be here on business. Actually tried to leave the City last week but the traffic was impossible. So we holed up in the hotel. The emergency generators kicked on when the power went out and well, it's just me now." He turned to look at me and for the first time, the smile on his face was completely forced.

We walked the rest of the way in silence with only the scuff of our shoes on concrete and the occasional boom of something exploding far away at the airport echoing softly around us. The shadow of a tree loomed toward me, and for some reason I felt compelled to step around it. It looked too much like a person with an outstretched arm.

When we came upon the bus depot, Connor made no move to follow me; instead he stood at the corner of the building, nervously glancing up and down the streets. I noticed he stayed in the sunshine. Maybe he was seeing things in the shadows too. I told him I would hurry and did just that, but instead of pulling out my notepad I wrote directly on the glass door.

1/9 5:00pm

On my way to the Grand High Hotel. Plan on leaving the City soon with Connor and Zoey – will leave another message before we go. I hope you find me. – Riley

CHAPTER 3

The air was heavy and stagnant, and rushed by us on the breeze with urgency. On the more narrow streets, the wind whistled between the buildings, and rustled the trees with an unspoken vow that it would return to displace more leaves as the cloud cover thickened above us with the promise of an oncoming storm. The change in the air felt electric and made the walk to Connor's hotel rushed, taking less than half an hour. Twice we stopped, thinking we heard people in the distance, but never saw anyone. We were all on edge with our senses maxed out and we were exhausted and thirsty but we hurried through the empty streets as darkness settled around the city, because none of us wanted to be outside in the dark.

The hotel stood out before us like a mountain made of concrete and glass and in the fading light it seemed ominous and sinister. Following behind Connor, I stumbled through the large and dimly lit lobby and groaned with each flight of stairs we took up. A small emergency light was on at the top of each landing, and the dusty yellow hue gave off just enough light to guide the way up each flight of steps. When I felt for certain I couldn't climb any further, Connor pried open one of the stairway doors and we stepped into the dark walkway of the twentieth floor. A moment later and his flashlight lit the way to the end of the hall. I felt my stomach clench with nerves at the thought that I had followed a man up to his hotel room, with only a 30lb dog for protection.

What an idiot, I thought to myself, as I watched him smoothly stride away from us. Panic began to rustle inside me, and for an instant, I almost bolted back down the stairs. But then Connor spoke, and turned to smile at us and even in the dim lighting, the piercing calm of his clear eyes showed nothing but kindness. So I walked to meet him.

"I think the bulb burnt out in the hallway. The others still seem to have the emergency power on." He said casually as he stopped in front of a large door. "The locks are battery operated, see?" He slid an electronic key out of his back pocket and inserted it quickly into the lock. A dim green light blinked once and the door clicked ajar.

He held it open and gestured for me to go in, but I stopped just inside the room. It wasn't just one room, there were at least three that you could see from the door, the place was massive. The style was the same as the lobby, expensive and modern with clean lines and a handful of solid neutral colors. Two large windows took up the corner of the main sitting room with glass reaching from the floor to the ceiling, flanked by massive plum-colored velour curtains. A door stood open that led to what looked like a large bedroom, and the complete kitchen was overflowing with canned goods. Lined up neatly inside the entry way were large water coolers, all full.

"Wow." It was all I could manage to say.

Connor raised an eyebrow and gestured for me to follow him. I heard the click of the door as it closed behind us. "Well, it's nothing special, but there's still electricity, so we can use the kitchen. And I hauled up every water cooler I could find on the main floor. The canned stuff came from downstairs too." He paused and shifted uncomfortably from one foot to the other before adding, "I don't like to spend too much time down there. I never feel alone."

He cleared his throat, and asked, "So, who gets that shower first...you or the dog?"

***

Two long hours later and I was blowing my hair dry with the small handheld dryer attached to the hotel bathroom wall. It had taken both of us to wrestle Zoey into the master bathtub, and I ended up climbing in with her to keep her from jumping out. I was wet and soapy from the waist down by the time we were through. Connor toweled her off after showing me to the second bedroom, with its own equally impressive bathroom. One very long, lukewarm shower, and a dangerous amount of floral-scented soap suds later, I was able to dry my hair after brushing the tangles out. I actually felt somewhat normal again.

Before I came out of the bedroom the smell of cooking food enveloped me and for the first time that day, my stomach lurched with something other than nerves...hunger. I stood in the sitting area and almost laughed at the sight of Connor bustling about the kitchen, wrapped in a large bath sheet, with Zoey perched atop the closest sofa like a cat, watching his every move.

"I feel amazing. Thanks for the shower and for dinner too?" I aimed my voice in the direction of the kitchen but walked toward the windows to take in the view, except there wasn't much to see, since most of San Diego was dark. A few of the nearby buildings still had their red emergency beacons flashing on the roofs, but from where I could see no one else seemed to have lights on inside.

Connor smiled over his shoulder and said, "I showered too. Kinda had to since I was covered in dog hair." Zoey mock-sneezed then stretched out along the top of the sofa back. In so many ways she resembled a cat more than a dog.

"I noticed my clothes are gone." I said as I walked over to Zoey.

"Oh yeah, I put our clothes into the wash. There's a washer and dryer in the bedroom closet. Hope that's okay?" He asked.

"Of course!" I wasn't going to complain. I didn't have many changes of clothes, and after the airport, our clothes definitely needed to be cleaned.

He turned to look at me and seemed startled by what he saw. "You look different." He said after a moment and made no effort to hide his gaze as he looked me up and down, twice.

"Different? If you mean dry and not covered in ash, well then yes, I guess I do look different." I laughed a bit nervously as I tucked a wavy strand of blonde hair behind my ear.

"Your hair is blonde." He said, sounding a bit surprised.

"And you're cooking in a half-lit kitchen for a stranger and her dog, wearing only a towel." I rebuffed.

He laughed, but before he turned away I thought I saw the color in his cheeks darken a bit. Good, I thought to myself, *let him be the embarrassed one for a bit.*

"There's wine on the counter, help yourself." He gestured at the open wine bottle.

"Wine? Well, now I'll never leave." I paused, "Just kidding of course."

"You're welcome to stay as long as you want. But I don't know how long the generators will last." And the reality of the situation came rushing back to both of us.

I sat down with a less than gracious thud onto a kitchen stool and poured myself a generous amount of wine into one of the large glasses. It was a white wine, and tasted deliciously cold and sweet. I didn't bother to use the stem of the glass, and instead, cupped my hands around it to drink.

"What are you making?" I asked him in between long sips.

"Veggies mostly, and some rice." He turned with two plates of heaping food in his hands and placed them down on the counter. He slid onto the stool next to me, close enough that our legs touched and I shifted nervously at the heat that threatened to burn my cheeks crimson.

"Oh, almost forgot." He got up and returned to the kitchen, and gestured at a bowl near the stove. "Can she have this?" He asked me.

"Sure." I watched as Zoey flew off the sofa and trotted into the kitchen and began licking at the food. Before Connor sat back down the bowl was half empty. The heat of his partially naked leg radiated through my jeans again, but I didn't want to move away. His warmth felt comforting.

The first bite was delicious. "It's very good. Thank you." I said to him, after my second swallow. I pushed my bangs out of my eyes as I leaned in for another spoonful. I was unusually comfortable around Connor already, but the meal still felt awkward in a way.

We ate in silence for a while, sipping our wine in between bites. Half way through the meal Zoey stretched out along the top of the sofa again, lying on her stomach with all four legs dangling over the edge of the cushions and within seconds she was snoring. I offered to clean the dishes but Connor joined me near the sink and towel dried as I washed. Twenty minutes later and the kitchen was clean and the small talk was over.

Connor disappeared into his room for a bit and returned to announce the clothes were in the dryer. "Should be ready in an hour or so." He was wearing a loose fitting white cotton shirt and sweats.

"Thanks." I smiled in his direction and topped my glass off with wine before crossing the room to sit down on the couch opposite from

Zoey. I didn't want to disturb her, since she seemed to be getting the best nap she'd had in weeks.

Connor did the same with his glass and surprised me by sitting down next to me. He sat at an angle, with one of his legs on the coffee table, and the other bent at the knee, resting on the cushion not far from my feet. I wasn't sure if I should move away from him, or stay still. *Don't you dare move!* A small voice inside me screamed.

"So," he began after clearing his throat, "You want to leave the City and go where exactly?" He was staring at me, sipping his wine. His hair was dry now, his waves tousled and a bit wild looking. The darkness of his hair contrasted with his fair skin and clear blue eyes. He blinked and I jerked my gaze away.

"Yes. Well, that's the million dollar question isn't it?" I thought to myself for a moment and then added, "I called my friends and family, and some of them live out of State. I think this, whatever it is, spread out all across North America." I risked looking in his direction.

He was nodding, and said quietly, "It's not just North America. It's overseas too." He shifted a bit, settling further into the cushions and took a long drink from his glass before continuing.

"The last time I spoke to my family was almost two weeks ago. My parents, who are in Dublin, were on their way to the Hospital. Everyone I spoke to in London was sick." He paused there, as if considering what he said. "There were others I couldn't get a hold of. I don't know what happened to them." His words came out heavy and soon he seemed lost in his thoughts.

We sat there, unconsciously listening to the dog snoring. After a bit I broke the silence, "So are you from Ireland, or London? I can't quite place your accent." I took a sip of wine.

"Me, I'm from Dublin," he said.

"I thought so, but your accent's very faint." I waited for him to explain further, and when he didn't I continued on. "I'm Irish too. Not directly, but a lot of my ancestors were Irish." I smiled at him. I didn't know what else to say.

"Is that so?" He asked, and smiled back at me, looking first at my blue eyes, and then to my blonde hair – as if sizing me up.

"Have you ever been?"

"To Ireland?" I snickered softly, "No, I haven't been out of the Country. I planned to go there, but I think deep down I knew if I did, I would never come back *here.*"

Connor laughed long and hard, and tossed back the rest of his wine. "Maybe one day." The words hung in the air as he stood up, and with his hands on his hips he stretched his back. We said good night to each other and retreated to our separate bedrooms, with the exception of Zoey, who was still asleep on the sofa.

***

I left my door cracked open for the dog. I knew eventually she would wake and go looking for me. So in the early hours of morning when I felt the gentle pressure of the bedspread move next to me and a body snuggle up against mine I wasn't alarmed...not until an arm slid over my side and a hand rested on my stomach. Startled, I yelped and pushed myself up in bed and banged into the wooden headboard loud enough to make Zoey bark at the echo from the other room. She came running into the bedroom growling, and Connor came rushing in behind her a moment later, looking a bit dazed.

"What...?" Connor mumbled, rubbing at his face with one hand, the other holding onto the wine bottle we had emptied earlier in the night.

"*Someone's in here.*" I whispered. I kept my eyes on the bed as I fumbled with the bedside lamp until I found the switch. Light flooded the room but it still felt dark.

Zoey stood at attention near the door, and only when the light came on did she stop growling. She jumped onto the bed and turned in circles sniffing the blankets and pillows. Eventually she sat down near me and rested her head on my legs. She whimpered at me and I absentmindedly began rubbing the top of her head. My hand found her ears and scratched behind them. I was trembling all over.

"No one's in here but us." Connor said, still sounding sleepy. He put the bottle down on a small dresser near the door.

"I swear someone was in this bed next to me." I looked around nervously. The only place someone could have gone was into the bathroom or under the bed. I drew my legs up to my knees, suddenly feeling like I was eight years old again. Zoey shifted and laid her head on her paws and watched as Connor flipped the bathroom light on.

"All clear in here." He said, as he leaned into the bathroom door frame, his arms crossed at his chest. He made no attempt to cover a yawn.

He was obviously not going to check under the bed. So I bent forward and rolled onto my stomach and leaned over the side, slowly pulling up the sheet and blanket to peer under the mattress. As my eyes adjusted all I could see was the carpet, shrouded in night, but then the other side of the bedspread flipped up and there were Connor's eyes, looking back at me. A strangled scream escaped my mouth before I registered it was his face and not some intruder's and I lost my balance and slid off the bed, crumpling into a heap on the floor. I lay there on my back a moment, breathing heavily while Connor sat on the edge of the bed, laughing at my expense.

"Oh, shut up." I said, half serious, as I stood and straightened my tank top. "You scared the crap out of me, what were you thinking?"

"Did you really think someone was under the bed?" Connor replied, holding one of his hands up to his mouth to cover his smile.

"Something *was* in here. I felt someone lay down right next to me!" I stood with my arms crossed and an indignant look on my face. I was half tempted to stick my lower lip out at him in a petulant pout.

"You were probably dreaming." He paused and glanced around the room seriously. "I've had some strange dreams myself lately."

"I wasn't dreaming." I glared at him, aware that my face was flushed with heat.

"Okay, you weren't dreaming, but nothing is here now. Except the three of us, of course." He gestured around the room. He stood and ran his hand through his hair, a move I found more enticing every time I saw it, which immediately annoyed me.

Connor moved toward the door, and turned to face me. "You going to be okay in here?"

I rolled my eyes at him, and patted the space next to me as I slipped back under the covers. "I'll be fine; I'll keep Zoey in here."

"Okay, good night then." He smiled, and closed the door behind him.

***

37

Connor lay still in his bed, resting on his back with his arms shoved beneath the pillow, staring up at the ceiling tiles. The room glowed slightly from the moon, making everything around him the same dusty, bluish-grey color. His room smelled faintly of detergent and wet dog as he replayed the day's events in his mind.

He had been startled awake earlier that morning by a loud explosion that vibrated through the hotel. He had seen the smoke in the distance and wasn't sure but it looked to be coming from near the airport and he wondered if a plane had tried to land, and crashed instead. So when the smoke got worse instead of better, he set out with a days' worth of supplies in the afternoon to see what happened. He had been to the airport just last week. There were so many bodies inside and the runway was littered with planes that even if someone was left to fly them, they wouldn't be able to taxi down the runway. He doubted a plane could land at all but perhaps someone had tried anyway? Either way, it was worth seeing what was going on.

He weaved through the streets, walking briskly, with his hands shoved into his pockets. As he rounded a street corner he stopped short as somewhere in the distance a dog barked loudly. He stood still, holding his breath, listening. The barking stopped as abruptly as it started, so he couldn't pin-point its location. The streets seemed hollow, and sounds bounced off the buildings, making it nearly impossible to find the source.

He stepped off the curb, still moving in the direction he thought was west when he heard a yell. It sounded just as far away as the dog, and again, he stopped to listen. He turned in circles, as the echoes vibrated down the streets and felt confident it wasn't coming from behind him. He broke into a run, still moving west, and after passing through one city block the yelling stopped. It sounded like a child or a woman, calling for someone. He wasn't sure, but he did know one thing, he wasn't alone after all.

He waited for more yells to come, even whistled a few times, hoping to hear the dog, but all was quiet once again, so he continued to jog down the streets, his pack slapping against his back with each stride, but he ignored it. He stopped only in the intersections to look down each street and listen. He ran nearly four blocks when he saw the first glints of the bay ahead of him. Though he was still almost a *mile away from the shore, far off in the distance he thought he saw a tiny figure blotting out the sun for a second, before it passed behind a building and was gone. He began to run again, this time at full speed. He wanted to find whoever it was before they disappeared.*

A handful of minutes later and the street he was running on merged into Harbor Drive. The bay lay before him, old ships docked to his left, and larger, private and commercial vessels intertwined with small floating piers to his right. He looked down the street to the south, where the figure had disappeared, and glanced up North Harbor Drive before noticing the smoke in the sky. The airport had to be on fire.

"Fuck." He said quietly.

Out of breath, he stood frozen in place, not sure where to go next, when to his left he heard a woman's voice in the distance. After crossing the street, he jogged half a block, peering into buildings and around the boats. And then he saw her. Down the street, and across a parking lot, at the end of one of the piers he saw a girl jump into the water, and what looked like a black dog jumping in after her. He crossed the road and ran along the sidewalk, looking for a way down to the docks. By the time he made it to the parking lot, he couldn't see her anymore, and wasn't sure which pier she was near, so he paced the shore line, hopping along the rocks that lined the bay, hoping to catch sight of her. He could hear barking, but couldn't see them, anywhere.

Frustrated, he retraced his steps through the parking lot and jogged to the end, where a large commercial pier stood jetted out behind a seafood restaurant. At the end, he saw them swimming back to the pier.

"Hey!" He shouted, and waved his arms...but the woman didn't respond.

He ran back down the pier and returned to the smaller docks, until he found the one she was closest to. He dropped his pack at the gate, and jogged by the boat slips, the breeze above the water was cold, easily biting through his clothing and chilling his skin. There were so many places in between the boats that she could be, that it took him a full minute to reach the end and in the middle was a bag next to a pile of clothing.

After looking down the side of the dock for any sign of life, he saw the dog first, paddling around in circles. He stepped to the edge and noticed pale white fingers holding onto the edge of the pier, he looked down, and there they were, treading water, several feet below him. An attractive long-haired woman with dark blue eyes was holding on for dear life, wearing not much of anything, and the dog splashed around her feet, clearly not sure of what to do. After fishing them both out of the water he knew then there was hope. Hope that others were out there.

He didn't regret the rest of the day; following them to the airport, even though he knew only the dead were there, and that the place was most likely on fire. And he didn't regret inviting them back to the hotel for food and water, and safe shelter, even though the invitation slipped out of his mouth before his brain caught on. But he did regret lying to her, to Riley. When she asked for his name, he froze. Everything was different now, who he was two months ago didn't matter, and she obviously didn't recognize him.

For years he wanted his privacy back, to feel normal again, to be seen as normal, to be treated normally, he just didn't think it would happen because the world died, leaving him completely alone. He didn't think it would happen like this. So he lied, and gave her his last name. He could be whoever he wanted to be now and Connor was just as good a name as any other.

He actually felt happy with Riley around. Like there was a purpose in even trying to make it through the day. He could even get used to the dog slobber. It felt safer with them...comfortable and like it was okay to laugh again. He could be himself, his real self with Riley because she didn't know him as the rest of the world had.

Plus, she was gorgeous, though a bit careless, and she had a plan, even though he didn't know what it was exactly, it was better than sitting in a luxury hotel waiting for the power to finally die out and having nowhere left to go.

The real colors of the room were starting to come back to life as the sun struggled to pierce through the darkness of night and warm the land with its rays when he finally let his eyes close. Sleep took him quickly, eagerly, and gave him no dreams to struggle through.

CHAPTER 4

It hadn't taken long for Zoey to fall asleep curled up against my legs but I kept my eyes open until dawn. When the sunlight started streaming into the room it forced away the shadows, and I didn't want to move until the darkness was gone. The room was awash in pale yellows and oranges when I rolled onto my side and buried myself under the covers. I woke two hours later with Zoey nudging my face with her wet nose. I stumbled out of bed, dressed quickly in my jeans, leaving my tank top on and let her out of the room. She seemed disappointed to find the bowl on the kitchen floor empty.

I noticed Connor had closed his door as well during the night, so I approached it quietly and carefully leaned near the frame and listened for any sounds coming from the room. Satisfied he was still asleep, I ventured into the kitchen and hunted around the cupboards for coffee and mugs. I decided to make a full pot and the smell alone as the coffee brewed helped me relax and wake up a bit. I took my hot mug to the windows and looked at the city around us. There was a partial view of the ocean that I couldn't see during the night and this early in the morning the sunshine made the water look like colored glass. The glint was almost blinding so I shifted my gaze up and down a few of the streets. In the direction of the airport the sky was hazy, the wind must have been blowing the smoke away from us, but it seemed there was still some sort of fire burning in that area. Zoey allowed me to enjoy my coffee for exactly two minutes before she sat at the front door, whimpering to be let out. This meant walking down twenty flights of stairs. *Great.*

"Alright, alright. Give me a minute girl."

I went into my room and pulled on my converse and took Zoey's leash from my pack, sliding it around the back of my neck like a thin pink scarf. I grabbed the key card from the counter where Connor had left it the night before and quietly slipped out the door. The dog and I jogged down each flight of stairs till we reached the main floor landing.

The lobby was bigger than I had remembered from the night before. There were chairs and tables scattered around one side of the main room for socializing, and a small bar took up the furthest corner. The main desk itself was the most impressive thing in the room to me, with a large rugged marble top and a back-splash of colorful blue tiles.

Once outside I could smell the smoke in the air and it seemed the wind was shifting, blowing the airport fire in our direction. I silently chided myself for not wearing something warm on my arms since at 6:00 a.m. it was nippy outside.

Fortunately we didn't have to walk far from the hotel entrance before finding a patch of grass for Zoey to do her business. While she scouted for the perfect spot I walked to the corner of the building and glanced down the street. The sun hadn't yet reached the cars and most were still covered in frost. I squinted my eyes at each of the building windows looking for signs of life, but nothing moved, nothing breathed. Zoey sniffed behind me and together we passed back through the lobby and headed up the stairs.

On the fourth floor landing, when I was talking to the dog about breakfast and being polite to our host, one of the hall doors below us opened with a loud squeak and promptly slammed shut. The noise startled the dog enough to send her dodging up half a flight of stairs. I froze in place. I wasn't sure if I should call out, or stay hidden. Eventually I leaned over the railing enough to see down the spiral but it didn't appear like anyone was climbing the dark stairs below us. Suddenly Zoey barked loudly, causing me to jump so badly I bit my lower lip. The air went heavy and the already cold stairwell dropped in temperature causing my arms to break out in goose bumps.

"Damn dog!" I hissed at her, "*Ssshhh.*"

She stopped barking but stood nervously at the railing above me, looking down below…her hackles up, her tail tucked stiffly between her legs. I no longer felt the need to know who had opened the door and I burst out into a full on run up the stairs, taking two at a time. We made it to the fifteenth floor before I had to stop and catch my breath. I had a stitch in my side that hurt like hell and Zoey was panting heavily but whined at me to catch up as she ascended to the next landing and sat down, waiting.

"Hold on." I was practically panting myself.

We took the next few flights a bit slower, but still made it to the twentieth floor in good time. I was sweating when I leaned my back against the hall door. Zoey stood, nosing the crack of the door, waiting for me to open it but I wanted to make sure we hadn't been followed before starting down the hall. Again, I leaned over the railing and saw nothing below, and heard nothing either. If someone was down there, they weren't paying attention to where we were on the stairs, so they shouldn't know which floor we got off at. I decided to risk it. We left the stairwell quietly and jogged down the hall. Once inside the room, both the dog and I relaxed.

Connor was up and drinking his coffee. He nodded at us, and whistled at Zoey, leading her into the kitchen where he had a bowl of food out for her.

"I figured the dog needed a potty break," he said. His hair was disheveled, like he literally just rolled out of bed. "Morning." His voice was still husky from sleep. Daytime Connor was sexy, but Early Morning Connor...there were no words to do the man justice.

"Hi." I was out of breath still. He handed me a bottle of water and when my chest stopped heaving I told him, "I think there's someone else in the hotel." I chugged at the water bottle till half of it was gone.

Connor didn't respond but he was looking at me curiously. I traded my water for my still warm mug of coffee, and relayed the happenings in the stairwell. He raised his steamy mug to his mouth again and listened without commenting. What he said when I was done surprised me.

"I think you might be right," he said quietly.

"Really?" I thought he didn't believe me, like he didn't believe me the night before when I felt someone try and cuddle with me in bed.

"After what happened last night it got me thinking." He paused to chew on his lower lip. "Well, sometimes I hear things too, but I've never seen anyone, at least not completely." He sat down on the arm of the sofa, blowing the steam off the top layer of his coffee.

"What does that mean? Not *completely*...?" I didn't understand what he was trying to say. I moved in front of him, waiting for him to make eye contact.

When he looked up at me, his face was tired and serious looking, the laugh lines around his eyes seemed to have deepened since the day before. He asked one simple and yet complicated question.

"Do you believe in ghosts, Riley?"

***

It was as if all the air was sucked from the room by some giant vacuum. Part of me wanted to laugh in Connor's face at the incredulity of what he was suggesting but the other part of me, a much *bigger* part of me accepted it, completely. I had been seeing and hearing things and even feeling things that couldn't or at least shouldn't be real. I sat down heavily on the sofa, and Connor pivoted on the arm rest to face me.

"So it's not just me?" I asked.

He blinked at me. "No, I don't think so."

"Good." I paused to close my eyes just long enough for my mind to transport me to my house...and I opened my eyes warily, not wanting to suffer through those memories again.

"Good?" Connor seemed surprised.

"Well, yes. This means I'm not going crazy. Thank God."

Connor nodded, then shuffled over to the counter, and sat down beside me, his shoulder slumped as if holding the weight of the world on them. He smelled lovely in the morning...his faint musky sweat mingled with a light fresh linen smell. For a moment, the scent of him overwhelmed me, and I found myself leaning toward him slightly as he began talking.

"I flew into town from L.A. for business three weeks ago with two others." He paused to clear his throat before continuing. "It's funny because looking back now, I remember seeing a handful of sick people in the airport. This guy and his kid on the flight were sick actually. Anyway, we were here for three days before the quarantine notices went up, and the transportation systems were shut down."

I interrupted, "Shut down?"

"Yeah, closed off. We left the hotel and tried for two days to get a flight out. People just mobbed the airport. They ran through the security systems, toppled over gates. And half of them were sick. My friends were showing symptoms that second day so we decided to come back here. The military had started separating people, just grabbing them and taking them away. They announced the airport was shut down – nothing in or out." He took a sip of coffee and then leaned forward and sat the mug on the coffee table. I sat, riveted, unable to look away from his face while he shared his story with me.

"So, we headed back to the hotel but took a different route, and there was this mobile clinic, and a big truck parked in this lot and people were lined around it, trying to get in. It was total chaos. But there were military nurses and doctors inside, we could see them. I left my friends there." Connor looked down at his hands. I reached out and slowly touched the side of his hand, just slightly, to let him know I was there.

"They were sick; I didn't know what else to do. My friend Grant, he was so ill he couldn't walk anymore. He kept shaking, and started bleeding from his nose, his mouth and I just panicked." He brought his hands up and dragged them down his face. His eyes were red and watery when he looked over at me. "Jesus, I just left them there to die. With all the other sick people. I just left them."

He balled up his hands into tight fists and pushed them up against his eyes and stayed like that for a long time. When he finally lowered his arms and looked at me, I said quietly, "There was nothing you could have done to save them."

"Right." He said, with a touch of sarcasm.

"What happened next?" I asked him.

"Well," he sighed heavily, "I came back here. By then, this place was pretty much cleared out. Only a handful of people had stayed. The staff had mostly left too. I holed up here, in my room. The streets were full of wandering people, and the sick. I called my parents and they told me half of Dublin had it. My friends in London were either sick or unreachable. Everyone around here died within a week. I've knocked on each and every door. No one has answered. I moved the bodies I found into the conference room. I didn't know what else to do with them." He paused again, leaned forward and pinched the bridge of his nose. He sat down on the sofa, leaned his head back and

45

stared up at the ceiling. With my hand, I reached out and gently squeezed his shoulder. He smiled down at me faintly.

"The next day I was down in the kitchen and it felt like someone was in there with me, following me around, you know? Every time I've been in there since, it feels like I'm being watched. I hear things too, like whispers or talking. And one morning I woke up after something brushed across my cheek. Before, I dismissed it, you know, as stress or something. But after last night with you, well, I can't stop thinking about it." He brought his gaze down and fixed it on my face.

"So, you think that what we've heard and felt...that there are ghosts, or apparitions here?" I asked him.

"It makes sense if you think about it. I mean, all these people died, probably billions if it's still spreading across the world, and it happened so fast. There was no closure. For anyone." He turned around so that his whole body was facing me. "If you believe in stuff like this I guess."

"Well, I'm a Stephen King fan, I believe in almost anything." I couldn't think of anything else to say and I grinned shyly. Connor laughed.

It did make sense, with so many people dying, of the same thing, the same illness, and dying so quickly. There would be millions of people who didn't get a chance to say goodbye to their loved ones. If a spirit was ever to have a reason for unfinished business, this would surely qualify.

"What do we do now?" I sat there, with the question hanging in the air, knowing neither of us knew how to answer it.

"I have no idea. Keep living, I guess," he replied.

***

I sat on the floor with my legs crossed, as I gazed out the window. Being twenty stories up in the air was dizzying at first, but the longer I stared down at the streets and the smaller buildings around us, the less my vertigo threatened to take control of my body. The view would have been magnificent on a clear day if the layer of smoke drifting on top of the air like smog didn't filter out a good portion of the sunlight. We could smell it inside too. The faint wisp of smoky air was everywhere.

Connor came up behind me and tapped something gently on the back of my arm. I looked over my shoulder to see him leaning forward, holding out a green apple. I took it from him and nodded a thank you. I had packed the fresh fruit I picked off the neighborhood trees before heading into the city. A small bag of apples was one of the things I dumped out of my pack the night before to share. It seemed fair, considering Connor was sharing everything of his, with not only me but my dog as well.

He perplexed me most of the time. He had been through a disaster, lost his friends and probably everyone he knew overseas, dealt with a handful of dead people from the hotel and seen the swarm of sick overrun the airport. Yet, he smiled, all the time. He laughed just as much as he blinked. His attitude was contagious but I was beginning to think it was a show. No one could possibly be as balanced as he portrayed himself and still be human.

Be careful, that nagging inner voice said to me, and rather than push it aside, I listened to it. It wasn't that I didn't trust him, I felt the opposite actually. I trusted him as if I'd known him half my life, but for some reason it seemed too early to share my story. I felt, even though he had shared a great deal of his, that my story should stay private. I wasn't ready to talk about my children...or their father. We had been divorced for two years but were still close. We tried hard to make life normal for our children and I was sad to have lost him, but devastated with my daughter and son. It seemed the right thing to do, to move on and find others and survive, but I knew in my heart, that part of me would never recover. I would never be able to smile or laugh without their faces flooding my memory. I didn't think I'd ever understand why I didn't die with them, like I should have.

As I sat at the window, eating my crunchy green apple, I wondered again about where to go. It would be unsafe, in more ways than one to stay in the city. I considered traveling north, to L.A. but the stilled traffic up there had to be bad. The illness took people quickly, but it didn't stop them from jumping in their cars and driving off only to die behind the wheel a few hours later. Going north would be a bad idea.

47

That left two choices, go east into the mountains and the rest of the country, or travel the short distance south to the Mexican border.

"Connor, do you speak Spanish by any chance?" It was random and caught him off guard.

"Uh," he choked down a mouthful of apple. "Not really." He shook his head, "Why? You planning a trip down south?"

"It was a thought. But I don't speak Spanish either." I sighed heavily.

He bit his apple, and I watched as his jaw muscles flexed effortlessly and when he ran his tongue innocently over his lower lip, I blushed and looked away from him. *What* was *it about this guy?*

"East it is then," I said aloud to no one in particular.

"East? Is that where you want to go?" He looked at me, still chewing. I tried not to watch his jaw.

"Why not? I think it would take a really long time to get to L.A. especially if we'd have to walk some of it." I continued, "And going south across the border would be a mess too. Even if we did find people there, we might not be able to communicate and that could be dangerous." I considered for a moment.

"There's a resort-type lodge up in the Laguna Mountains, called the Big Laguna Hideaway. Have you heard of it?" I asked, forgetting for a moment that Connor wasn't from California.

He shook his head no, so I went on to explain. "Ok, so it's a lodge more than a resort. I've never actually been there but when it was built the owners made a point of advertising its eco-friendly design all over the County."

"Still not following you." He said. He licked his lower lip again and I looked away. *Jesus, Riley...knock it off!*

A pleasant sort of anxiousness came over me as I remembered pictures I had seen of the place tucked away in the mountains. "It's an eco-friendly mountain resort. It runs completely on solar power." I looked at him, and watched as what I said registered.

"Completely solar operated?" He asked with a hint of excitement in his voice.

"Yes, and it would have its own water supply too, probably welled." I shifted around so I was facing him. "There's one problem, well, not a problem but it could potentially be."

48

"What's that?" He got up and walked to my side of the room, fruit still in hand. Zoey stretched from her napping place on top of the sofa when he sat down.

"Well, it gets cold enough up there for snow. Every year portions of the highway are closed down due to ice and snow conditions." I watched him ponder over what I had said.

"The cold doesn't bother me. I guess our biggest problem would be having enough food." He settled deeply into the cushions and continued eating. He was chewing the apple down to the core, and for some reason I found it extremely sexy. "We have plenty here to take with us, but how would we get it there?"

"I left my Jeep on the outskirts of the City. If we could find something here to drive we could try and leave downtown by the streets and back-track parallel with the freeway. The roads are congested mostly around downtown and the major interchanges. We could probably drive more freely once we hit East County." I was excited now, just a little, at the prospect of having a plan. Now we just had to put it in motion.

We sat quiet for a while, chewing our apples and as I nibbled around the core, I bit a seed off and tried to discreetly spit it out of my mouth into my hand. Instead, it stuck to my lip. I definitely could not eat an apple as sexy as Connor.

"Let's do it," he said, oblivious to my apple seed incident.

"Let's do it," I repeated. "I'm tired of the warm weather anyway." We smiled at each other. A plan. We had a plan. Now we had to get out of the city with our supplies and drive the hour and a half up into the mountains. It felt good to know where we were headed, but it wasn't the most forgiving of places to venture into alone.

As if to further support our decision to move on, something across town exploded. Looking into the distance we could see more smoke rising up from where the airport was. It was still burning, which meant the fire had probably spread past the tarmac.

***

As I pulled the covers up around my ears, I listened to the quiet of the hotel suite and wondered if Connor was asleep yet. I let my mind drift a bit, thinking about Connor, the trip out to the mountains and without warning, a memory I had with my kids at the Zoo from the summer before blazed through my mind. I fell asleep as I had every night since the day my children died, with my eyes swollen and my pillow damp.

CHAPTER 5

The lace curtains moved away from the window, then settled back against the frame, and this happened over and over as if the window itself was breathing and the curtains were being expelled to freedom with each breath, only to be sucked back in a second later. My gaze followed the curtains for what seemed like hours until they just stopped, suddenly. The air had stilled in the room, and I was aware of the warmth of the new day working its way through the coldness. I watched as the sun rays hit the window glass, making bright prisms sparkle like giant diamonds. The light filtered through the lacey fabric, casting an intricate pattern on the floor, full of swirls and different sized circles. My daughter was an early morning person and now that I awoke in her room, I understood why. Her view of dawn was glorious. The carpet fibers lit up inch by inch as the rays of sunlight crept over them and devoured the shadows.

I watched, wide eyed and alert, as the sunshine slithered up the side of her bed, and I could see the pinks and yellows of her quilted blanket. I didn't dare blink as the light moved up and over our toes, showing our matching red nail polish. Her bare feet touched at the ankles, and were tucked up neatly against the side of my right foot and I focused on her chipped and uneven polish for a moment. I finally blinked. The blonde hairs on her skin glittered as the sun swallowed us up, legs first. I couldn't see above her shins, because I had covered her with a fleece Winnie the Pooh blanket. The overwhelming urge to see her knees came over me, so I shifted until the blanket moved, exposing her right knobby knee with the bruise from her last tree climbing adventure. I couldn't smile, but it somehow made me happy to see that bruise.

I felt the warmth of daylight as it hit my right arm, and rushed over my shoulder, exploding into my face, causing my eyes to water. I closed them for only a moment and in that instant I saw her big and round, bright blue eyes, her small, perfectly puckered red lips that rested below her little button nose, the curve of her jaw line that led to her slightly big ears, and all her blonde hair that curled at the ends. I could see her freckles and could count each one...she had four on her face and one on the top of her right ear. I saw all of this and held onto it before I opened my eyes. That girl was gone. I wanted to remember her face, the face she had before death took her from me.

When I opened my eyes the sun had filled the room and it was all there for me to see. I was looking at her stomach, where her arm rested and her little hand lay still inside mine. She had a freckle on that hand too. I didn't want to look at her face just yet so I kept staring at her arm, willing it to move on its own, but it didn't of course. At some point I realized I couldn't feel my own left arm, which was tucked under her head, or most of my left side for that matter. And I didn't care. I had cuddled up next to her during the night when the hallucinations started, and held her in my arms while I sang Into the West by Annie Lennox, over and over, like I used to do when she was a baby. I sang to her, even when her fevered body stopped seizing. When her shallow and uneven breathing quit, I was still singing to her, gently and methodically rocking her back in forth in my arms.

Her very last minute was peaceful. Her chest rose slightly and then fell slowly and I felt the hot air of her last breath tickle my cheek as I whispered to her...The ships are here now, baby. They are taking you home. I held onto her, my first born child, my only daughter, until the new day reminded me that my family suffered these awful and horrible deaths and I was somehow kept alive to see it happen. It was my own personal Hell. So I stayed next to her, my beautiful daughter, and cried. I cried until my heart broke and I thought that for sure would kill me, but it didn't.

And now here I am, lying next to her, willing myself to look at her face. I force my gaze up her throat, over her chin and her slightly parted lips, which are no longer the color of my favorite rose but an unnatural bluish-grey shade. I ignore the blood that had flowed from her nose, spreading down her cheeks, pooling on the pillow beneath her head. The rusty brown color of it was dry and caked on her skin almost like paint. I couldn't stop now, so my gaze moved up even

52

further to her eyes, but instead of the deep ocean blue I was used to seeing, her eyes were red, blood red. The scream started low in my gut and came out of my mouth almost strangled. I screamed until I was hoarse. I screamed for my son, who was dead in the room next door, tucked neatly in bed. For the husband I once had, but lost to a broken heart two years before, and for my daughter, now dead and cold in my arms. I screamed and screamed until the wind made the curtains dance again. I screamed until the sunlight started fading from the room and the shadows took me over.

***

My eyes flew open and a mournful groan escaped past my lips as the image of my dead daughter silently faded away to that place in the brain where nightmares hide. I bolted out of bed, my chest heaving with anxiety. My lower lip was trembling and for several seconds I didn't know where I was. It was dark, still night, but something was wrong. Zoey was barking at the bedroom door, nervously looking from it to me and back at the door again. I blinked back a new wave of tears as I realized I was standing in Connor's suite. A hollow thumping sound was coming from the other room. It must have been what woke me. I wiped my hands across my eyes and moved past the dog to open the door an inch or so. Solid dark shadows shrouded the room but there was enough moonlight filtering through the windows for me to see Connor moving toward the suite's front door in long strides. I followed him, as Zoey rushed ahead of us, still barking. We stood, silently, inside the hotel room. I shushed the dog and commanded her to move back. When I squatted beside her, my legs were shaky and unreliable. Connor was looking through the peep-hole on the door when another bang made him jump.

He glanced at me before asking, "Who's there?"

We heard voices talking before a man answered, "Hey!" He said with some excitement in his voice, "We're looking for Riley, Connor and...Zoey?" There was more hushed talking behind the door.

Connor moved aside and let me look through the peep-hole. I didn't recognize the man, and it looked like a young woman was standing beside him. I heard a click behind me and the entryway light washed over us. I blinked at Connor and he looked just as confused as

I felt. Then I remembered the notes I'd left, I had led these people here. I didn't know if I should feel excited or panicked.

"*They've been to the depot,*" I whispered to him.

"Look, we don't mean any harm we're just excited to find you. We saw the message on the window at the bus station. We've been searching this place for a while. We heard your dog barking, started knocking on doors till we found you." He paused before asking, "Can we come in?"

Connor had stepped away from the door slightly and was nervously rubbing the back of his neck with one hand. I walked up to him and asked quietly, "What do you think? I put the messages out there to help people find me. I guess I wasn't thinking about strangers finding us, but they look harmless enough."

"You can tell that through the peep-hole, can you?" He seemed irritated.

"They know we have a dog," I reasoned, "They don't have to stay with us, but we could at least see who they are."

When he didn't answer, I told him, "It's up to you."

He nodded and went back to the door, "If you have any weapons leave them on the floor." I pulled Zoey back with me and squatted down so I could put my arm around her and hold onto her collar.

Connor unlatched the security bar and pulled the door open. The man had backed away from the door and peered into the dimly lit suite tentatively.

Connor stuck his hand out. "I'm Connor."

The man took his hand and a smile broke out on his face, he pumped Connor's hand up and down and called over his shoulder, "You coming?"

When Connor stepped aside to let the man in, he nodded at me and the growling dog and said, "My name's Matt." He gestured behind him, "This is Mariah."

Mariah slipped inside carefully, her eyes darting around the room. She was obviously on edge. Zoey issued a loud bark, making both of the newcomers jump.

"Zoey, shush," I told her. I didn't want to let go of her just yet.

"So if Zoey is the dog, then you must be Riley," Matt said to me.

"Yes, I'm glad you found us."

Connor broke the awkward silence that followed by flipping on the kitchen light and pointing to the bar stools that rested beneath the counter top. "Have a seat, are you thirsty?" He asked them.

"Do you have anything warm?" Matt asked. Mariah hesitated to sit down. She was still eyeing the dog wearily from the entryway.

I let go of Zoey and she rushed the newcomers, wagging her tail so vigorously her back legs threatened to lift off the ground. She sniffed at Mariah who seemed to relax when she realized the dog wasn't going to eat her, feet first. Next, she checked out Matt as Connor turned the coffee maker on. He popped an individual serving of coffee into the machine and watched it brew directly into the mug.

Mariah was about my height, maybe an inch shorter, with shoulder length, curly brown hair and big brown doe eyes. Matt was tall and stocky, also with brown hair and intense, dark eyes.

"This is a nice place." Matt said. "Is it running off a generator?" He aimed the question at Connor, who was placing the mug in front of him on the counter.

"Yeah." Connor began fixing another cup of coffee for Mariah. "I was staying here actually when everything…you know. Riley here is a local." Connor nodded at me. He seemed much more cautious with these two than he was meeting me on the pier. He barely cracked a smile at either of them. I realized that Middle of the Night Connor was not as sexy as Early Morning Connor, and the thought made me stifle a laugh.

"Really?" Matt asked. He glanced around the large suite, taking in the jugs of water and canned goods piled up around the kitchen. "Are you two planning on staying here then?"

Connor and I exchanged a look. "We were just talking about that actually." I paused, deciding to hear their story before sharing our plans. "What about you? Did you meet in the City?" I aimed the question in Mariah's direction but she was busy rubbing the dog's head and ears and wasn't looking at me.

"Oh, no…we didn't meet in the City. Mariah and I are twins." Matt leaned into the counter, clearly enjoying the hot drink. His oversized USCD sweatshirt hung off his muscled upper body but he filled his jeans perfectly, accentuating his lean hips and long legs. I stared at his backside, wishing for a moment he wasn't sitting.

"Wow." I said, "What are the odds of that?"

"Pretty well in our favor when you think about it." Mariah spoke for the first time. She looked up from the dog and glanced at Connor before resting her soft gaze on me. "You know…same genes and all." She smiled.

"Thanks for leaving that message. We were starting to freak out wondering where we would be sleeping tonight," Matt said, his mouth hovering over his mug.

"You're welcome, I guess." I laughed softly. "I left it for family or friends, in case anyone is left. I didn't really think about anyone else reading them." I suddenly felt foolish.

"Well if you hadn't we would still be wandering around downtown right now." Matt slid off his stool and handed the second cup of coffee to his sister. "Mind if we crash in one of the rooms down the hall, and maybe chat again in the morning?"

Connor replied, "Not at all, in fact I have the key to the suite next door, it's a single bedroom but it has a comfy couch." Connor smiled at Mariah. She smiled back at him as she raised her hand up to brush a curly section of hair away from her neck. I wasn't sure, but the stirring in my stomach felt almost like jealousy.

"Yeah, I think we can figure it out." Matt winked at me, and asked if they could return the mugs in the morning. After Connor assured them we had plenty, and not to worry about it, we walked them to the door. Mariah seemed truly sad to part with the dog, and made a point to lean in to Connor and touch his arm as she said goodnight.

Connor seemed genuinely happy to see Matt go. I was genuinely happy to see Mariah go. I went to my room that night with the overwhelming feeling that the next day was going to be a long and possibly unpleasant one.

CHAPTER 6

Connor was awake the rest of the night, listening to the sounds of the hotel. He didn't trust Matt; there was something about the way he looked at Riley that disturbed him. He understood how Riley must feel, having the dog with her. Zoey wasn't just her companion but she was a reliable, walking and barking, alarm system. He left his door open, wide open, and if he shifted to the left side of his king size bed, he could look across the sitting room and see unobstructed into Riley's room. They had agreed to leave the doors open so Zoey could freely move about the suite during the night, in case their visitors returned. Zoey seemed to sense the difference because she didn't sleep much either. She wandered between the two bedrooms, sniffing around Connor's bed and then returning to Riley's room.

He lounged, completely still, on top of the comforter and imagined meeting Riley under different circumstances. He let himself close his eyes for just a moment and pictured her happy somewhere, perhaps with family, or with friends, carefree and without the emptiness in her eyes he saw when he first met her. He envisioned a light burned there once and she had the kind of smile that could truly bewitch most men, the straight ones at least. The shape of her body was alluring but she didn't flaunt it. In fact, she seemed to go out of her way to hide it - covering her curves with jeans and loose fitting sweat-shirts or baggy tops, but Connor had still noticed. She had an inner strength that pulsated through her personality, marking her as a damaged woman, but a woman who would never give up, which also made her extremely attractive to him.

She hadn't told him anything of her life before the day they met, but he knew on the pier she was fascinating, and it wasn't because she was the first live thing he found amidst all the death festering around him. There was something about her that made him forget *what he had lost. When he sat near her, he almost felt like he would be okay. He wanted that, needed that feeling, but it came with a sharp pang of guilt. Because across the land of the country he was now marooned on, and over the vast expanse of ocean water, there was a little boy, his own little boy, and he was probably dead, as was his mother.*

He couldn't force the images of his innocent little Roan and his ex out of his mind. He rolled onto his stomach and punched his pillow until his face was efficiently buried in it and he wept silently for the son he would never see again.

***

The day started when Zoey jumped onto the bed, whining at my feet. I had curled up under the covers but was unable to fall back to sleep after Matt and Mariah left. The curtains were drawn tightly closed so the only clue that it was daytime was the faint line of light along the ground below the window. I rose from the bed slowly, and it took a considerable amount of force to make my feet move. The blur of the last few days had clouded up my mind. I was afraid to sleep; for fear that nightmares would haunt me. I felt secure with Connor but at the same time confused about how I felt about him, and now there were two new people down the hall.

I decided to shower before taking Zoey outside. She gave me a displeased look and forced a sneeze when I passed the bedroom door and went straight into the bathroom, shutting myself inside. Fat droplets of water burst from the silver showerhead, pelting the glass doors with a sort of rhythmic and excited frenzy as I draped my clean clothes across the long marble counter top. I brushed my teeth while the steam from the shower began to fill the large bathroom. The hot water was something of a gift, but I kept the shower short, and dried my hair again before dressing. When I opened the door, the steamy smell of my shampoo filled the bedroom and *almost* covered up the stench of fresh dog shit.

The offender was nowhere to be seen. But in the furthest corner of the room, just in front of the draped windows, there it sat, one little dog turd.

"Zoey!" I hollered loudly at her, forgetting that Connor had gone to sleep just hours before. When she didn't come, I stalked out of my room, ready to scold her.

"Zoey, *come here.*" I said sternly to the empty sitting room. I walked to Connor's room and looked inside. The bed was empty and the master bathroom was dark. I realized he must have taken her outside himself and guilt washed over me. I rushed back to my room and pulled my converse over my naked feet and shoved the extra keypad into my back pocket. I yanked the door open and stepped into the hall, turned to my right, and walked straight into Matt's chest.

"Shit!" I gasped, into his cotton t-shirt. He smelled freshly showered and his face was clean-shaven.

Matt had gripped my arms when I stumbled into him and slid his hands down to my elbows to steady me. When I looked up he had a big goofy grin on his face, but the darkness of his eyes unnerved me.

"Sorry," I mumbled, "I didn't see you." I leaned away from him but his grip stayed firm on my elbows.

"Where are you off to, so early in the morning?" He asked in a teasing voice. "You aren't doing the walk of shame are you?"

My mouth dropped open, and he smiled at me. I saw that his eyes were full of mischief and something else…desire, maybe? I snapped my mouth shut so hard that I bit the tip of my tongue.

"What? No, no…it's not like that." The words tumbled out of my mouth. I had to straighten my spine, and shake my head to regain my composure.

I yanked my arms from his grasp and took two full steps backwards. "Connor and I just met a few days ago, besides, even if we were…whatever, it's none of *your* business." I shifted on my feet and pointed behind him. "Do you mind, I was on my way downstairs." I said it even as I moved past him.

"Whatever. I mean, it is what it is, right?" He said from behind me. I didn't bother to look at him but I could tell he was following close behind me.

"What does that mean?" I challenged him.

"You and Connor," he said simply.

"What about me and Connor?" I asked, a little too innocently.

"Like I said - whatever."

We had reached the end of the hall and I pushed open the stairwell door. I turned to face him, and put my arm up to block his passage.

"What's downstairs?" He asked as he peered past my shoulder into the empty stairwell as if the answer would be hovering in the air behind me.

"My dog." I didn't like how close he was leaning towards me. I gave him a blank look. "Look, I'm not a morning person, and I just got up. How about we meet up with the others, in say, half an hour?" I hoped this would keep him from following me down the next twenty flights of stairs.

He didn't answer me right away, but he backed off and nodded. "Okay, whatever you say Boss Lady." He winked at me and I rolled my eyes in response as I moved away from the door and let it slam hard in his face. I jogged down the stairs, pausing every few landings to listen to the hotel around me. Twice I risked leaning over the rail to look above me and make sure Matt wasn't in silent pursuit.

When I opened the door to the lobby, I whistled for Zoey. I pushed the heavy glass doors open and walked over to the grassy spot that I had been taking Zoey to and it was empty. I frowned and turned around, whistling. I called out for Connor but got no response. The horizon was dark to the north, but thankfully the wind was still pushing the smoke away from us. The grey clouds above the distant skyscrapers gave me an ominous feeling and I tried to rub the chill from my arms. The sky seemed to be teasing the earth with the prospect of a storm, for days I thought it would rain, but the clouds always ended up parting and allowing the sunlight to filter through. This day was different though, the static in the air ran through my hair and along my skin, and the clouds looked heavy enough to dump a year's worth of rain onto me at any moment. I felt exposed, standing in the front of the hotel, alone, and though it made no sense at the time, I was certain I was being watched from the apartment complexes and businesses across the street.

I headed back the way I came and reached out to open the doors once again but a reflection in the glass moved just above my head, stopping me. I looked up, startled, and saw my face but also a man, standing behind me. The view I had of him was murky, almost cloudy in the glass, but it was easy to see that he was tall, shirtless and had blood dripping from his nose. He reached out to me with his hand and I spun around, flattening myself against the door. The air twirled around me furiously, lifting my hair from my shoulders and whipping across my face, nearly blinding me and I shrank back from the man in horror. Where his eyes should have been were only empty holes, and the sick color of old blood covered his face from the nose down. His mouth was moving but I heard nothing he said, because my own screams were so loud they vibrated through the glass behind me and echoed down the street. Just before his outstretched fingertips grazed the front of my shirt, I clamped my eyes shut and screamed for Connor. I waited for the man to touch me, but the air stilled instantly and my hair dropped back down to my shoulders in fluffs.

When I opened my eyes, there was no one there. I looked all around the front walkway; it was wide open so he couldn't have disappeared that quickly. I realized I was holding my breath so I let it out in one long exhale and watched as the vapor clouded before me as I felt a chill pass through my body and I frantically fumbled with the handles until I had pulled one of the doors open enough to squeeze through. Once inside the lobby I bolted for the stairwell door.

I ran up three flights of stairs before I heard the squeak of a door somewhere above me. I shrank away from the railing but I was certain that if I hadn't been seen yet, whoever was there would be able to hear the thumping of my heart rebounding off the walls. There was a soft shuffle of feet, and a clicking sound, and I slammed my hands against my mouth to keep from screaming. When Connor's voice reverberated down the staircase I nearly broke out in tears with relief.

"Riley?" He called.

"Oh, thank god." I said to myself.

I moved close to the railing and peered up. Connor was two flights above me, and Zoey was standing next to him, her tongue flopping out of her mouth. When she saw me, she rushed down the stairs to greet me with a series of her customary wet slobbers.

"I'm glad we found you." Connor said, as he descended. He smiled down at me and I struggled to keep myself from rushing up to him and throwing my arms around his shoulders in relief. Instead, I kneeled down and bear-hugged Zoey till she squirmed away. Before she got too far, I tugged on her collar and brought her face level to mine.

"You do not poop in the house." I said it sternly, emphasizing each word clearly, but even the dog knew it was a moot point.

"Yeah, she came out of your room after you got in the shower and circled around my feet till I agreed to take her out." He smiled at me, and reached down to stroke the top of Zoey's head. She glanced up at him and sneezed. Connor and I both laughed.

He looked at me before asking, "Are you alright? You seem pale."

I nodded a bit too quickly and swallowed hard before speaking. "Yeah, I'm fine."

"You sure?" He pried.

"Yeah, of course. So, how did you get upstairs without me seeing you?" I asked him. I was eager to change the subject to *anything* other than what happened downstairs.

"Oh, we took the elevator. Have you been taking the stairs every time?"

I blinked at him like he was speaking to me in Swahili. "The elevator works?"

When he was done laughing at me, he nodded and said yes, the service elevator worked.

"Then why the *Hell* did we climb up twenty flights of stairs when you brought me here?" I gaped at him, and smacked his arm playfully.

"I don't ride it often, in case it breaks down or something, plus I avoid it at night. I guess I forgot to tell you it was working." He laughed again, "I'm so sorry."

"Right. Of course you are." I smiled at him and pointed up at the nearest landing. "So we can take it upstairs from there?"

"Yep. When we got back to the suite and didn't find you, I figured you went downstairs looking for us." He led the way up the stairs and opened the door.

A solitary bloody handprint had dried on the wall just below the light switch. I hadn't noticed it before, so I raised my hand up to it as I passed by. The whole print fit into my palm. I snatched my hand away from the child-size print and followed Connor into the hall and around a corner to the elevator. I watched him push the call button but didn't get excited until a dim yellow light glowed...a signal of life.

"I thought you might have been Matt when you opened that door." I didn't look at him.

"You saw him this morning already?" Connor looked surprised but sounded almost irritated.

"Yeah, he's a bit of a jerk I think." I slightly regretted it after I said it, but the words felt true. I snuck a glimpse at Connor and he was eyeing me carefully.

"Why?" He asked in a low voice.

"It's probably nothing." I was interrupted by the ding of the elevator as the doors opened before us. Connor went in last and pushed the button for the twentieth floor. He turned to look at me, with his hands on his hips, and a frustrated look on his face.

"What'd he do?" He asked me carefully.

"He didn't *do* anything. Let's just say the guy has no gift with words." I shrugged and braced my hand against the railing. I never felt comfortable in elevators, not since I was fifteen and spent over thirty minutes trapped inside one in between the tenth and eleventh floors of my grandmother's senior complex.

"Well, I don't trust him," Connor said and turned so that all I could see was his profile. I looked at him and thought his was a face that an artist would draw or paint incessantly...unable to achieve true perfection on canvas.

"So," I chose my words carefully. "Should we hold off on heading out east? At least, until we know more about these two?"

"Definitely." The word came out rushed and he looked at me after he said it. I was sure he was going to say something else, but the elevator slowed, causing the pit of my stomach to lurch, and the doors slid open.

The only sound in the hall as we walked back to the suite was the sound of Zoey's padded feet thumping along in rhythm atop the worn Berber carpet.

***

We hadn't been in the suite for ten minutes before our new neighbors knocked on the door. I intentionally stayed sitting on the couch with my coffee, petting Zoey, as Connor let Matt and his sister

63

inside. Zoey flew off the couch and welcomed the visitors with wet sniffs and stretched out submissively at Mariah's feet.

"Awww, she's so sweet!" Mariah gushed. Zoey rolled around on her back, wiggling underneath Mariah's hands and allowed her to rub her belly. It wasn't something she did with strangers, but the pickings had been slim in the attention department.

Matt sat down at the bar, rapped his knuckles onto the counter and said, "So, Mariah and I want to head north, maybe make our way to Nevada. We have family in Vegas."

"Really?" Connor was the only one to respond. He set hot coffee in front of Matt.

"Yeah." Matt paused and then took a long look in my direction before continuing. "Of course, if you don't have any travel plans, you're welcome to tag along."

I avoided looking at him, and chewed on the inside of my lip to keep from saying something rude, but Connor beat me to it.

"Well, isn't that kind of you, inviting us to *tag along*. I think we're good here though, thanks."

My teeth clamped down hard and I uttered a strangled yelp. Everyone turned to look at me.

"Sorry, I bit my cheek." I blushed, and licked my lips nervously; avoiding Connor's knowing gaze and Matt's glare.

Mariah stood and for the first time I noticed she had a canvas shopping bag slung over her shoulder. She moved from the entryway to the kitchen and held the oddly shaped bag out to Connor, almost like a peace offering.

"Breakfast." She smiled at him. "We really appreciate you letting us stay, and we have plenty still. It'll go bad if we don't share." She sent a sideways glance at Matt, who looked away from her. I got the feeling he didn't want to share much of anything.

"Thanks, what is it?" Connor asked her as he opened the bag. "Oh wow, yum." His reaction made Mariah grin.

Curiosity got the best of me, and I left the sofa to join them in the kitchen. Connor reached into the bag and pulled out two mini watermelons.

"Did you find those in a store?" I was surprised, since it was off season but our whole food markets always had fruit. How they had stayed fresh this long after the power went out shocked me.

"Yeah, we found them yesterday at a little ethnic market on the other side of downtown. Almost everything was rotten. Matt wouldn't even go in the store it smelled so bad. But I wanted to check. There were a few things that I found, still edible." She beamed with pride.

"That's great, thank you." Connor said, smiling at Mariah. I cleared my throat and offered to cut the melon myself while the others gathered around the bar counter.

"So when are you planning on heading north?" Connor directed the question at Matt.

"I don't know. Was thinking soon but now that we found you guys and this place, I guess there's no rush." Matt shifted on his stool and leaned forward so his chest was resting on the counter. He was watching me slice up the melon and place the pieces into a large glass bowl. I could feel his eyes on my back. He lowered his voice to a mocking tone, "Unless we're intruding, of course."

Clunk. Clunk. Clunk. The knife hitting the cutting board was the only sound in the room. I kept slicing through the fruit, pretending not to hear the hidden implications in his statement.

"Uh...no, you aren't intruding." Connor was the one to break the awkward silence.

"Great!" Mariah jumped from the stool and came into the kitchen to take the bowl from me before I could fully turn around with it. She set it in front of the two men, and faced me again. "I can't tell you how glad I am to be around another woman." She nodded over her shoulder at her brother, "I mean, I'm so grateful to have Matt and I love him and all, but finding you two, this is just amazing! Don't you think?" She spoke so fast that she couldn't possibly have had time to breathe.

I smiled at her, "Yes, it's...great." I glanced at Matt, who was watching me, while sucking on the end of a melon wedge. Mariah leaned in to hug me and I froze. I hadn't actually touched so much of a person's body since before my own family got sick. It felt alien in a way. I instantly remembered my kids. I patted Mariah's back quickly and stepped past her, hoping that no one saw me fighting back tears. I excused myself to the bathroom and once behind the door, splashed my face with cold water from the tap. After a few deep breaths, I towel dried my face and opened the bathroom door to find Connor standing there.

"You okay?" He asked quietly.

"Yes, why?" I cleared my throat. I stood as tall as possible, but still managed to feel small in front of him. He took a step forward and slowly reached out and lightly stroked the side of my forearm. He lowered his hand but kept his gaze where he had touched me. A tingling sensation spread from my wrist up to my shoulder. When he spoke his voice was just above a whisper.

"Are you okay?" He repeated.

"*No.*" I could barely squeak the word out. I closed my eyes, not wanting to look at him, not wanting to look at anyone. In that moment I just wanted to cry.

"Want to get out of here for a bit?" He asked me, his quiet voice was tender, almost soothing and his accent was a bit stronger, masking the sound of the letter 't' a bit.

"Yes." I finally opened my eyes and we stared at each other. I saw something in his expression that mirrored my pain. For a brief moment we just stood there, exposed, raw, and broken. Connor reached out again and this time took my hand, leading me out of the bathroom and across the bedroom.

Connor's fingers slipped away from mine as Zoey met us at the door, and I bent over and rubbed her head. She knew I needed the love more than she did. When we joined the others back at the counter, Matt was talking to Mariah about something inaudible and they quieted as we approached. Not sure what to say, I took a piece of the cut fruit and nibbled on it. I didn't have the heart to tell Mariah I hated watermelon. She smiled and pushed the bowl closer to me, and I smiled back at her but avoided looking at Matt.

"So Riley and I were thinking of heading out to get a few supplies, we should be back in a few hours. Will you guys be okay in the hotel by yourselves?" Connor was standing behind me, with Zoey at his feet.

"Oh." Mariah said, sounding disappointed. "Oh, no, that's fine, we'll be fine." She tried to sound more upbeat but had a confused look on her face. "Is everything alright?"

"Yes." Connor and I spoke at the same time.

66

"Of course."

Matt slid off his stool and raised his arms in a stretch above his head. I felt the move was an act to show off his defined abdomen. He flexed his arms outward and locked his fingers together, cracking the knuckles. I looked away from him.

"Ah, its okay, Mariah. I think these two want some alone time." He winked at me, and I glared at him. I felt Connor place a hand on my lower back, and lean in closer and I stiffened, not sure if it was an act to piss off Matt, or an innocent gesture of affection.

Mariah seemed momentarily deflated. Then she brightened and asked if we could all eat dinner together. Connor, Zoey and I followed them out into the corridor and we agreed to meet again by sunset. We watched them open the door to their room and hurried down the hallway...I couldn't get out of the hotel fast enough.

We didn't speak a word on the elevator, or when we walked out of the lobby. We stood outside and let the spotty sunshine warm our faces before Connor directed me to a pathway lined with palm trees and neatly trimmed Birds Of Paradise bunched tightly with other tropical plants I didn't know the names of. The brown cobblestone walkway curved around the side of the building and opened up into a cabana style pool area. I gasped in surprise. From the street, none of what I saw was visible. I didn't even know there was a pool tucked away behind the building. I followed Connor to a covered lounge area and we sat down on rattan chairs covered with brightly colored canvas fabric. Deep reds, ocean blues, fresh greens, and lemony yellows danced on the pillows and seat cushions. A lightly floral and citronella waxy scent wafted through the air from the open candles that sat neatly on the table tops nearby.

Zoey dashed happily into the perfectly planted landscape that surrounded our little private cabana. After a series of patrols she found the perfect spot to dig and I watched as clods of soil flew into the air around her. I laughed as she came up for air, dirt piled neatly in a tiny pyramid on top of her snout.

"Thanks for bringing me down here." I sighed, breathing the air in deeply.

"It's nice, isn't it? Relaxing." His chair squeaked as he shifted around to get comfortable. He plopped his feet onto a matching rattan footstool the length of a small dining table.

I leaned into the cushions, sitting sideways with my feet underneath me. I stretched my sleeves up to my palms and then tucked my hands under my chin, making myself as small as possible in an attempt to ignore the coolness in the air. I felt Connor's eyes on me.

"Are you cold?" He asked.

"No, I'm good." I lied, as a chill worked its way up my legs and arms and tickled along my spine. I smiled at him, as if that would hide my shiver.

He rose from his seat and crossed the small distance between us. He tapped my knees with one hand and gestured for me to move my legs. "Scoot over." He said to me with a smile.

I turned my legs and pushed myself over to the side of the chair as he edged in beside me, and after he put one arm around my shoulders, he gently pulled me close to him. My face was just below his so I didn't dare look up at him.

"Better?" He murmured.

"Mm-hmm." I didn't trust myself to speak.

We sat together, watching Zoey dig up the garden until she found an ideal place to doze in the sun. I had started to think Connor was asleep too until his hand moved from my shoulder, down my arm and back up again, slowly rubbing along my sweatshirt. The friction was warming and I let my head rest on his chest, just at his collar bone where I could feel his heart beating. I wanted to freeze that moment and hold onto it, so I closed my eyes and listened to the steady thump of his heart as my cheek rose and fell with his chest as he breathed.

Connor raised his hand up to my face and tucked my hair behind my ear, and slowly trailed his long fingers down my neck, before returning his hand to my arm again. I fell asleep curled up next to him some time after, as he caressed my arm. It was a peaceful, dreamless sleep.

***

When he led her outside he wasn't sure where he was going to take her until he started moving. The pathway to the pool seemed to beckon him, so he moved them in that direction. He wanted to talk to her, but it seemed right to be quiet for now. He knew something upset her upstairs, and in her room it was as if they shared a certain understanding between them. Taking her hand was a bold move, but he wanted her to know he cared, and he didn't have the words to tell her that, at least not yet.

Down by the pool he wanted to hold her close to him. He wanted to tell her she was safe, he wanted to tell her not to leave. But instead he held her tighter, tried to warm her against him and watched as her dog made a mess of the landscaping.

When he thought she was asleep on his chest he dared to touch her hair where it had slid forward over her face. He let his fingertips graze her neck and he felt her adjust slightly, burrowing against him. He took his hand away and put it back on her arm, and leaned his head closer to her ear.

"Who did you lose?" He whispered.

Drowsy, she answered him without opening her eyes. "My world."

"Me too." He said, as he gently kissed the top of her head.

CHAPTER 7

We woke up when the sun was past its apex, and the wind from the impending storm was strong enough to slap the cabana curtains against our chair with fury. When I opened my eyes I was looking at a zipper. At first, I couldn't register what I was seeing. I mean, I had known what a zipper was for over thirty years, but this zipper was completely foreign to me and definitely didn't belong two inches away from my nose. I was laying on something soft and warm and blue, and as I blinked the sleep away, what was underneath me moved. I snapped my head up, and realized it was Connor's chest I had been resting on, the zipper belonging to his pullover sweatshirt.

He was yawning with his eyes shut, and I took the opportunity to sit up and put some distance between our faces. Zoey was lying at our feet. She had moved under the cabana after her siesta by the pool. She sat up and stretched as Connor and I came to terms independently that we had just slept next to each other.

I was the first to get up. I stood so quickly that my head spun, and my vision went blurry and I lost my balance, bumping into Connor's legs. He placed a hand on my hip to steady me and I laughed nervously and suggested we go upstairs and talk about Matt and Mariah, and driving out east.

Fifteen minutes later we were upstairs, rinsing the dog off in Connor's oversized bathtub for the second time that week. Even with the nap, I was exhausted and overwhelmed. We tossed all the towels we had used to rub the dog off and wipe down the bathroom into the washer along with our clothes. I scrubbed the smell of wet dog off my arms with one of the hotel scented soaps neatly displayed in a silver bowl on my bathroom sink. After pulling my hair back into a messy pony tail, I changed into my tank top and sleep shorts and pulled on

71

one of the hotels thick, cotton-weaved, white robes while I waited for our clothes to dry.

When we met in the sitting room, Connor was barefoot, wearing a pair of his faded blue jeans and a thin white V-neck shirt that showed off the sleek and smooth definition of his collarbone. I tried not to stare, but failed, epically. I was grateful he didn't talk about our nap outside, because if he had, I was sure I would have blushed the most unattractive shade of red possible. So, I lost myself in the kitchen for a while, taking a mental inventory of the canned goods, bottled water, perishables and cooking supplies we could use for our journey into the mountains. The fact was we had more supplies than we could ever take with us, at least in one trip, especially if we planned to retrieve the Jeep. It didn't have a huge amount of storage space, but at the time that I decided to use it...or more truthfully, at the time I stole it from my dead neighbors, I wanted something sturdy, not too large and with good tires. The Jeep would get us there, but not with all this stuff.

"We should make a list of things we absolutely need to take with us." I said out loud to myself. Connor made me jump a little when he spoke from just behind me.

"You said you have a Jeep?" He asked.

The space around me filled with the scent of his airy cologne. I breathed it in deeply before answering him.

"Yeah, I only brought my backpack with me into the City. There's a bag of dog food in the Jeep and I threw a few extra pairs of clothes and some boots in there. Oh, a gallon of water too." I didn't turn around when I spoke to him, I didn't trust myself so close to him.

"What about taking two vehicles up there?" He asked, after a pause. He was leaning on the counter now, still just two feet or so behind me. I could see the sleekness and nakedness of his arm in my peripheral vision.

"That's probably a good idea. I was just thinking of everything we have here." I finally turned and leaned against the counter opposite of him. "I mean, we have no idea if the lodge is stocked with anything. There might be people there already or it could be completely gutted."

"We don't know much, do we?" He smiled and gazed at me with his crystal blue eyes.

Don't look at his eyes, Riley, whatever you do, or you might lose yourself in the blue. I cleared my throat softly and glanced around the room, searching for something else worth commenting on. I couldn't seem to handle looking at him, and he couldn't seem to stop looking at me. I felt like a foolish teenager with a crush, but it also felt forbidden. I wasn't ready or altogether willing, for life to move me along so quickly. Officially, I had been single for most of the last year. I had dated one man for a handful of months after my divorce was finalized but I wasn't much of a browser. Dating was a challenge with two young children in tow, finding a man that accepted that had been hard to find. And unlike my ex-husband, who was working on girlfriend number three by the time our divorce hit its one year anniversary; it was hard for me to move on. Really hard. Anything that happened with Connor made me feel like not only was I cheating on the dead memory of my ex, but our children as well. I didn't like that feeling, it made me sad in places of my heart that I didn't know existed.

When I glanced back at Connor, he pushed off the counter and stepped forward with one of his hands outstretched, "Riley, look…" He was cut off by a loud knock and Zoey let off a flurry of barks as she flew off the sofa and darted to the door.

"I'll get it." I said a bit too hurried, and I felt the slightest touch of his fingers along my cheek as I slipped past him out of the kitchen and to the door as fast as I could.

It was Mariah, and she asked what our plans were for dinner. I told her it was going to be coming from a can or a bag and she laughed. I invited her and Matt over to eat with us without asking Connor and she promised to be back soon, with her brother, as I watched her walk the short distance to the next suite.

Connor was still in the kitchen and I risked a quick look in his direction. I couldn't see his face but his shoulders were slumped and his head was tilted downward. I knew he must have been at least a little upset with me, but I didn't have the energy for the conversation he seemed so eager to have.

"I hope that was okay."

"What?" He didn't look at me.

"Inviting them over, I hope it was okay?" I watched him carefully. He didn't make eye contact with me, but instead moved around the kitchen, opening and closing cabinets, apparently searching for something.

"Oh, sure. Why not?" He said the words lightly but I felt tension in the air between us.

"I'll cook, I make a great spaghetti." I hoped I hadn't hurt him.

"Sounds fine," He said something under his breath as he rummaged deeper into a cabinet and then loudly exclaimed, "Ah! There you are!" He set a large unopened bottle of Bushmills 21 onto the counter with a solid thud and I eyed the amber liquid with curiosity.

He said half joking, "There were several a few weeks ago. Now there's only this one left. The bar downstairs has a great selection of alcohol though, if you aren't interested in this." He gestured to the bottle.

"It looks expensive." I told him. Connor shrugged, and set two glass tumblers down beside the bottle.

"Depends on what you consider expensive." His tone was a bit saucy.

"If it's more than $20, it's expensive to me." I said.

Connor laughed loudly, and said, "Well, it's more than $20."

The most I had spent on alcohol was a $30 bottle of wine I bought as a gift a few years back for a friend. I couldn't even properly read the names on the label. I would never admit that to Connor though.

"Try it, you might like it." He filled nearly a quarter of one glass and put only a shot in the second and pushed it across the counter to me. I picked it up and was surprised at the weight of the tumbler. I brought the glass to my nose and inhaled. Connor smiled as he took a sip of his own drink.

"It smells sweet." I downed the tiny amount in my glass and thought I had survived it but the smooth citrusy fluid that first touched my tongue became a burn that rushed down my throat like lava. I very indecently choked out a gagged cough. *"Oh my god!"*

Connor rocked back on his heels and laughed. He took another sip and set his glass down. He popped open a can of soda and handed it to me, "This will help."

I took a few large gulps of soda before asking him, "Is there liquorice in that?!"

"Very good." He laughed.

I stuck my tongue out at him, "I hate liquorice…that was nasty."

"Guess that just leaves more for me." He winked and walked away with his glass.

"I think I'll go downstairs with Mariah later and look for some wine, because that…" I pointed with exaggeration at the bottle of Irish Whiskey sitting alone on the pretty marble counter top that probably had some fancy Italian name I couldn't pronounce, "…would kill me."

Connor began to laugh so hard his face turned red and for the first time, I saw him cry. I chucked an apple at him that had been sitting in a floral shaped metallic bowl by the sink but it missed him and grazed the coffee table instead. Zoey ran after it and chased it around the sitting room like a ball. Connor was still laughing through his tears when I retreated to my room to change into a pair of jeans.

I vowed to get him back later in the evening. I considered dangling him upside down from one of the windows but that required too much upper body strength.

While I yelled at him from my room, I hopped into my jeans, "Be careful, you have to sleep sometime!" I giggled despite myself, even though my pride was slightly bruised, it felt good to laugh. Maybe a bottle of Moscato was exactly what I needed.

***

"Well, you came baring gifts."

I hated to be even the slightest bit kind to Matt, but there he was standing before me with flowers in one hand and a shiny gold box wrapped with a wide brown ribbon in the other. The flowers looked like they were from one of the flower beds that surrounded the palm trees out front and I was a little leery of what was in the box. He handed both to me, and I stepped aside, giving him and Mariah space to enter the suite. Mariah smiled at me and gently put her hand on my arm as she passed by.

"It smells great in here!" Mariah followed her nose into the kitchen and asked permission to peek inside the simmering pot on the stove.

"Hope you don't mind pasta." I said to her with a smile. I set the mysteriously wrapped box on the counter, and put the flowers inside a large drinking glass. I set the arrangement in the middle of the small dining table that was in between the kitchen and sitting area. There were orange and red carnations and a yellow daisy. I wondered if Matt had picked them, or if Mariah had made the selection.

Matt noticed the bottle of expensive malt whiskey sitting on the counter and pointed at it, "That's not there for decoration, is it?"

Connor had already set out extra tumblers and poured a glass for Matt and offered Mariah some. Thankfully for me, she passed.

"Great! This means hopefully someone else will drink wine with me?" I said in a joking manner.

After Mariah agreed to raid the hotel bar with me in search for wine, we left the boys and took Zoey on the elevator ride downstairs. We made it to the nineteenth floor before Mariah blurted out, "Oh my god, Riley, Connor is just gorgeous!"

She looked juvenile in that moment, standing before me in a fashionably short black dress with a light pink sweater so tight around her tiny middle I was sure it was cutting off circulation to her legs. Her curly hair bounced off her shoulders as she danced on her toes, tightly squeezing her hands together. She had 'Sorority Girl' written all over her but she seemed a bit old for that phase of college. Her joyful personality also seemed out of place considering the circumstances, and I wondered if she was still going through the denial stage.

I smiled and said simply, "He's okay."

She stopped bouncing and grabbed both my arms. With a very serious look on her face she asked me, "Have you slept with him yet?"

I was dumbfounded. Of all the people that could have stumbled our way through the city, we wound up with two horny siblings.

"No...of course not. I've known him less than a week, Mariah." I shifted so she would loosen her grip on me.

"Are you serious? You've seen him, right?" She stared at me, wide-eyed. We were obviously not speaking the same language.

I sighed deeply and tried my best to not let my irritation show. "I've seen him, yes. I've also seen a couple hundred dead people since last week." I looked at her, and she reddened in the face.

"I'm sorry. I know. It's awful." She stepped back from me and the rest of the ride down to the lobby was silent. I felt slightly bad at hurting her feelings, but as the doors opened up into the dark main floor, the image of the shirtless man out front earlier took over my thoughts and I stared carefully into every shadow...afraid he might jump out at any second.

After I let the dog relieve herself outside, we found the wine stash. I grabbed two bottles of Moscato and Mariah grabbed two bottles of champagne. What we had to celebrate, I wasn't sure, but at that moment I realized that I was most likely going to drink those two bottles of wine myself anyway.

***

All of us were laughing, draped across the sofas with drinks in our hands as Mariah did an encore performance of her best drunk runway walk through the sitting room. She was actually quite good until she turned...she wobbled her hips like she was balancing an invisible hula-hoop as she stuck her arms out and flapped like a bird to keep her balance.

We laughed even harder when she insisted she wasn't drunk with her cheeks flushed pink and her slightly round nose scrunched up in defiance. She pointed her slender finger at Connor and plopped down next to him on the sofa and took a sip from his glass. Connor had pulled various bottles of alcohol out of the cupboard, so I had no idea what was in that glass but I was pretty sure it wasn't going to mix too well with the bottles of champagne Mariah had finished on her own. The wrapped box Matt gave me was sitting on the coffee table torn open with half its chocolate contents missing.

"So, what's *your* hidden talent?" Her words were slurred and she leaned into Connor as she drank from his glass.

I watched Connor shift his position so he was facing Mariah and smiled at her. She had one of her bare arms resting loosely around his shoulders. I didn't like what I saw, at all.

He laughed and said, "Not sure it's a hidden talent, but I can play 'Freebird' on the guitar."

"You lie." I said to him with a chuckle.

His face went serious and for a second I thought I insulted him. "We'll just have to find us a guitar."

"So you can butcher Lynyrd Skynyrd? Sorry, I can't allow that." I said to him with a laugh.

He tossed a pillow cushion at me and it bounced to the floor, its clear sequins spraying prisms of light along the ceiling tiles above us. We all laughed again until Mariah asked, "What's *Freebird*?"

"What?!" Connor and I both said it at the same time and looked at Matt who raised his hands in the air defensively.

"You've never heard 'Freebird'?" I couldn't believe it.

"No, who's Lenny Skinny?" She looked perplexed, and hiccupped.

I looked at Mariah like she had three heads.

"Matt! Please tell me you've heard of classic rock?" Connor was sitting upright, his hands in the air while Mariah picked up his tumbler once more and drank freely from it.

"What's *classic rock*?" Matt said innocently, and Mariah cursed at him and pillows were flying through the air again.

Matt insisted if we had a piano, he could play Twinkle, Twinkle, Little Star with his feet. We all agreed through fits of giggles we were happy with the fact that there was no piano nearby for him to prove that claim.

"That leaves you." Matt said to me.

"I'm sorry, what?" I played dumb.

"Oh come on now." He said as he rose from his seat and plopped down next to me. "Surely you have a hidden talent you can share with the group." He leaned in close to me and playfully tugged at the hair tucked behind my ear. I tilted my head away from him even though his smell was enticing and his body felt warm against me and the darkness that filled his eyes penetrated me.

I lifted my glass to my lips and smiled sweetly at him, hoping he didn't pick up on my unease. "I have many talents, most of which you will surely never see."

Connor whooped and Matt threw a glare in his direction, and reached for my glass.

"Refill?" He asked me.

"Just a little." I handed it to him. I watched him walk away in his too-tight jeans and even tighter shirt. I decided I liked the back view of him much more than the front. I conceded he was a bit more attractive when I was buzzed on wine. But he was still an asshole when he opened his mouth. He returned with my glass filled nearly to the top. "That's way too much!" I gushed.

He sat down next to me again, so close our thighs were touching. I looked from his leg up to Connor, who was eyeing Matt coolly. He had control of his drink again and with one swig finished the last of it. His tumbler made a hollow clunking sound when he set it on the table a bit too hard. He settled deep into the cushions and propped his feet on the table. Mariah had curled into the corner of the sofa and began to doze.

For a short while the three of us just sat quietly while I sipped my wine and Matt nursed his own drink. He broke the silence and the light-hearted conversation from before took on a more somber tone.

"What if Mariah and I didn't head up north right away?" He was looking at Connor when he asked the question but then turned to me and flashed a toothy smile. He put his arm up along the back of the sofa, making the space between us diminish and I didn't like it. Matt's smiles seemed forced to me, and his stares almost predatory. A warning shiver ran up my spine and I remembered how uncomfortable he made me before.

"Huh?" I was sure I hadn't heard him right.

"You know, I've yet to hear what *your* plans are." His voice was lower, softer, but it didn't hide the sharpness of his gaze.

I blinked at him and then blinked at Connor. My head was fuzzy from the wine; the room seemed smaller and warmer than it was minutes before. As I bent forward to set my glass on the coffee table, Matt lowered his arm from the sofa and rested his hand on my lower back, just above the waistband of my jeans. Connor made a move to get up but I bolted from Matt's hand before he noticed the red flush that had crept up Connor's face.

I stood, uneasy with the friction that had started weighing down the air and attempted to form a solid yet simple answer for Matt that wouldn't include the details of what little planning Connor and I had made.

"What's wrong with this place?" I gestured around me. "If we kept the generators going, I'm sure we could stay here a long time." I looked at Connor and he was watching only Matt.

Matt stood and faced me. "What about family, don't you have anyone that you want to find?"

My voice was flat when I answered, "My family is dead." I tried to move around Matt to take my glass to the kitchen but he stepped in front me of me, blocking my path.

"Excuse me." I tried to push past him but he gripped my arm. I staggered back a step in surprise.

"So what, you want to die here too - with him?" He tightened his hold on me and I gasped at the uncomfortable pressure in my upper arm.

Connor was instantly on his feet. "Let go of her." He kept his eyes on Matt as he maneuvered around the table behind me.

When I yanked away from Matt he put his arms up. "It's okay, I get it." He said with a forced smile on his face.

"No, you don't." Connor moved in front of me, putting himself between me and Matt. I slowly set my glass down on the table without taking my eyes off the two of them.

He snorted and looked over Connor's head at me. "What exactly is the deal here? We wouldn't be here at all if you hadn't left that note. Obviously you wanted someone *else* to find you, so why stay with this asshole?"

Connor moved at him and Matt squared his quarterback sized shoulders. His voice was low and threatening, "Man, I can snap you in half, don't even try it."

"It's time for you to go." I could see the muscles in the back of Connor's arms tighten as he spoke.

"Or what, you'll call the police?" Matt sneered.

Zoey had picked up on the change of vibe and was standing on all fours, watching us. I knew I had to do something before fists and possibly fur started flying.

"Matt, you should go to Nevada with Mariah, to find your family." I had backed up so that I could walk around the sofa and approach them from the side. "You can take whatever you need, there's plenty here to share."

He glanced at me quickly and then at his sister, who was fully asleep. He said to me, anger creeping into his voice, "We don't need more shit. And you know Nevada is as dead as this place."

"So what do you want?" I asked him, frustrated.

"I thought that was obvious?" He winked at me. And that's when Connor hit him.

The punch took him by surprise and he reeled backwards, stumbling over his own feet. He landed on the ground hard. He rolled onto his side, cursing and covering his face with both hands. Blood started to seep through his fingers and Connor stepped back, away from Matt's thrashing feet.

Zoey began barking madly, rushing back and forth between me and Connor, clearly confused. Matt had wobbled back up onto his feet, continuing to curse while I struggled to get a hold of Zoey's collar. She stood next to me, shaking and whining.

Mariah pushed herself up and looked around the room. "Matt?"

A guttural sound came from Matt as he lunged at Connor. Zoey rushed in between them barking wildly at Matt and nipping at his shoes. Mariah was on her feet, unsteady, and her eyes widened at the sight of Matt's bloody face. He got one good swing in at Connor, striking him in the jaw before Zoey bit his leg. He howled and backed away, kicking at the dog. She forced him backwards to the kitchen area before I called for her to come to me. Mariah was crying and Connor was yelling for Matt to get out.

I felt horrible for Mariah but I gently pushed her towards her brother and tried to tell her calmly to take him back to their room, that he was drunk. He was still cursing and yelling as they left, and the vibration of their door slamming shut down the hall shuddered through our suite.

My entire body was shaking so badly I didn't trust my legs to hold me so I went down to my knees and hugged Zoey to my chest to calm us both, telling her over and over, *good dog...good dog.*

Connor locked the bolt on the suite door and slowly crossed the room to me. Zoey approached him cautiously before rolling onto her side so Connor could rub her belly. He murmured to her in a soothing voice and when he looked up, he asked if I was okay.

"Me? What about you?" I stared at his face, where the bruise was already forming on his jaw. I reached up and touched the spot gingerly. "Are you okay?"

"Yeah, I'll be fine. He barely grazed me." He tried to smile. He lifted his hand and his knuckles were swollen and red.

"I'll get you some ice." I stood and went into the kitchen, and wrapped a few ice cubes in a clean dish towel. He had moved to the sofa and Zoey had followed him. She looked at me anxiously when I approached them with the makeshift ice-pack. I held the towel to his face first and he winced.

"Matt's a jerk." I said to him, as I examined his knuckles with my free hand.

"He's dangerous." He looked at me.

I moved the towel to his hand. "Maybe."

"There's nothing stopping anyone from doing or taking what they want now." He paused, waiting for me to make eye contact. "You understand what that means for you, right? As a woman?"

"I'm a big girl Connor; I can take care of myself."

"If it was just you and him in a locked room, would you really believe that?" He sounded angry.

I sat back on my heels and looked up at the ceiling, feeling the alcohol buzz through me like a live wire. "We should get some sleep." I let go of the towel and stood up. I walked to my room with Zoey at my feet and shut the door behind me quietly and I sat on the edge of the bed. A short time later I heard Connor's door close loudly. I pulled my shirt over my head and stepped out of my jeans and went into the bathroom to wash my face before retreating to the bed and crawling under the covers.

***

Connor sighed and rolled across the bed and peered into the darkness of the room, wondering if Riley was asleep or lying awake as he was. He could hear a low humming sound beyond the closed door, coming from the kitchen area...the fridge, he supposed. The rest of the suite was silent. The air still felt heavy from tension, and it was unusually cold.

He grimaced when he shoved his hand under the pillow, the swelling around his knuckles made it hard to close his hand. He felt like an idiot. Fighting over a girl he couldn't claim as his own. The night had been so cheerful for all of them, and he had to blow it by letting that ass get under his skin. Even now, the memory of Matt's hand on her back, the way he looked at her and watched her, it

82

threatened to unhinge his every nerve. He couldn't stand the sight of him touching her.

Twice, he threw the blankets off and got out of bed, intending on marching into her room to apologize for the way the night ended but both times he turned around and tumbled back onto the mattress, not sure he could apologize for hitting Matt, because for that, he definitely wasn't sorry.

He caught the fleeting looks Riley made his way during the night when Mariah got too close. Mariah was nice to him, and a bit touchy-feely, but he wasn't interested in her, so all he did was smile at her advances. All night he wanted to pull Riley aside and tell her that but she was never alone. Matt hovered around her the whole damn night, like a vulture, waiting to make his move, even though it was obvious he made her uncomfortable. Matt thrived on attention, and if Riley didn't give him any, he took it by putting her on the spot, or touching her every chance he got. The guy was a douche. He tried to push Matt out of his mind and for a moment that left room for only Riley.

He struggled with his sheets as they threatened to strangle him and he ended up face down under his pillows, cursing at the World for its apparent disdain for him. His life was stripped away from him, leaving only an empty shell version behind. And then Riley came and he didn't know what to do. It wasn't just about being lonely. He didn't want to ruin what very slim and unlikely chance he had with her but in such a short time she had begun to fill his thoughts completely, consuming the darkness that haunted him, pushing it away and replacing it with...light. She radiated. He didn't know how to tell her that, or if she was ready to hear it from him.

Part of him was thankful for Mariah, because after her arrival he knew for sure how he felt about Riley. He felt nothing for Mariah. She was young, she was pretty and she was interested in him, she all but said it, but it only made him want Riley more.

He tortured himself with these thoughts as he laid face down in bed on the side that wasn't bruised, and the last thing he remembered was the feeling of waking up outside by the pool with Riley asleep on his chest, how her arms were tucked up against his stomach, her knees resting on his leg. It felt amazing to hold her like that. He loved the feel of her perfectly shaped body next to his, and the faint lemony *smell of her wavy blonde hair that mixed perfectly with the subtle coconut fragrance of her skin.*

That was the image he had in his mind when she came into his room in the middle of the night. At first, when he saw her outline, sitting next to him on his own bed he thought he was still dreaming, but she was real when he touched her. She was real when her lips brushed softly against his and he wanted nothing but to hold her again.

***

The room was dark and cold and smelled faintly of smoke. No matter how far down under the blankets I went, I couldn't get warm. I wondered if Connor was asleep yet, and thought about what he said. It was absolutely true. Things were different. Any people we met, we couldn't trust based on appearance alone. It was every man for himself. I wondered what it would have been like if I had run into Matt in the city. I was lucky to have found Connor first.

Eventually I kicked the covers off and wrapped myself loosely in the bathrobe. I opened my door to see darkness all around the suite. I quietly crossed the room and stood at Connor's door, listening for any movement or sounds within. When I opened it slowly and peeked inside, his room was just as dark as mine was, but I could see his form in the bed.

"*Connor?*" I whispered.

When he didn't answer I moved deeper into the room and carefully climbed on top of the bed. His back was to me, and his head was buried underneath his pillow. I crawled to the middle of his bed and touched his shoulder with my hand. His body jerked and he sprang upright, startling me.

"I'm sorry." I said in a hushed voice. "I didn't mean to wake you."

"Are you okay?" He asked, groggy with sleep, dragging his hand through his hair. It was a gesture I could watch him do over and over again and never get tired of.

"Yes, I'm fine. It's stupid." I paused, suddenly embarrassed. "I couldn't sleep." I hesitated before saying, "I just wanted to say thanks - for earlier."

When he didn't say anything I began to move away from him, certain that I shouldn't be there, sitting on his bed in the middle of the night, but then he reached out and clutched a handful of my sleeve. His hand moved up my arm and down the front fold of my robe as he tugged me closer to him.

Our faces were inches apart. I spoke just above a whisper when I repeated, "*I didn't mean to wake you.*"

"*You already said that,*" he whispered back.

"Sorry," I laughed softly.

"You already said that too," he teased.

I smiled, even though it was dark and he probably couldn't see much of my face. I felt his palm move across my collarbone, just inside the opening of my robe and a soft gasp escaped my lips. His hand slid across my bra strap and grazed up my neck and he ran his fingers along my jaw, slowly tracing the outline of my mouth. I leaned into him and touched my lips to his. Connor's hands wrapped tightly around me, pulling me in to his chest and I nuzzled my face into his neck.

We sat in the center of his bed until the heat from our touching bodies wasn't enough to warm us anymore. Connor pulled his shirt over his head and handed it to me and I slipped the robe off my bare shoulders and wiggled into his cotton shirt. We slid under the covers together and I pressed my body against his and let him hold me close. We stretched out onto our sides facing each other, with one of his arms tucked under the pillow, the other draped naturally around my waist. My head rested just below his chin and our legs became enmeshed together. The feeling of his thighs pressed against mine was thrilling, and oddly comforting.

I closed my eyes and listened to Connor's steady breathing and felt the thudding of his heart in his chest. I drew in his aroma, his clean, fresh masculine scent. I wanted to stamp his smell into my memory; it was refreshing but also calming.

"*Can I stay with you all night?*" I murmured into his bare chest.

He whispered into my hair, "*I'm not letting go.*"

***

When they had settled under the covers, Connor felt the contours of her body relax and mold into his, and he felt whole beside her. She had one arm around him, and it rested in between his shoulder blades so that when he breathed, he felt the pressure of her hand rise and fall slightly on his back. She curled her bare legs around his and buried her feet into his flannel pajama pants.

Her soft skin felt perfect as he ran his hand gently from her neck, down her spine and over her hips. When she sighed, the fullness of her breasts pressed into his ribcage and he draped his arm around her waist, holding her to him. Finally, he could hold her the way he imagined so many times since he met her. He tightened his embrace when she asked if she could stay with him. And when dawn finally rose, they were still nestled in each other's arms, sound asleep.

CHAPTER 8

When morning came, it wasn't the sunshine filtering through the gaps in the curtains that woke me; it was the continuous drumming of rain drops pelting the window panes. I opened my eyes and a shiny sea of sateen white sheets started at my nose and flowed down the length of the bed. I knew I wasn't in my room and after blinking at the foreign set of sheets with their matching duvet cover, I tilted my head upwards and the silky fabric slid off my mouth, cascading delicately down my neck. I was lying on Connor's bare chest, and he was asleep, on his back, with his face tilted towards mine. I gazed up at him, and took in every detail of his neck, his full mouth, his nose and his long dark eyelashes. They fluttered delicately and a gentle sigh escaped from between his lips. I was afraid to breathe for fear that I'd wake him, he looked completely peaceful.

I continued to visually inspect the curves of his upper body, starting from his neck, where I could see his pulse beating steadily under the skin just below his ear to the hollowed space between his collar bones. My eyes traveled along his pectoral muscles, pausing to take in the perfect roundness of one of his nipples. Below my left hand I could feel the edge of his ribcage and I lightly slid my palm down to his navel and rested it there. His chest lifted slightly below my cheek and I glanced up at him. His pale blue eyes blinked sleepily at me.

I leaned my hips into his and shifted so that I could prop both my arms on his chest. We smiled at each other as his hand slipped up the back of my shirt.

"Morning," he said with a grin.

"Hi," I replied with a giggle as his fingers tickled their way teasingly up my spine. When his hand reached the back of my neck he gently squeezed and then buried his fingertips into my hair. I felt the muscles in his abs flex and tighten as he leaned his head down to me and kissed the end of my nose.

Zoey ruined the moment when she jumped onto the bed at our sides and began licking every exposed limb she could find. We groaned and shivered as the blankets slid off our bodies and scolded the dog good-naturedly as she climbed across our heads and attempted to bury herself underneath the pillows. Her wagging tail hit the padded headboard with a rhythmic whacking sound and I rolled off Connor onto my knees after I told her I got the hint.

Connor sat up and grabbed my hips and said playfully, "You're not getting up yet."

"No?" I teased.

"Not without this." He murmured as his fingers stroked my face and his hand darted up my shirt again. He leaned into me and crushed his lips to mine, kissing me deeply and leaving me breathless.

***

By the time we emerged from the room, the persistent rain had turned into a full blown thunderstorm, and each time the sky boomed the dog yelped and circled the suite nervously. We opened the windows, pushing the heavy fabric aside to reveal an angry sky, full of pregnant clouds that were continuously punctured by the sharp bursts of crooked lightening, releasing a torrential downpour on the city below. I loved thunderstorms, we had them rarely, but witnessing one twenty floors above the ground was overwhelming. I watched from behind the thick glass as nature lashed out all around us. The wind howled and buffeted the building and the temperature inside felt as if it had dropped to just above freezing. I shivered in my robe, even with Connor's shirt and a spare pair of his pajama pants on, I was cold.

He came up behind me and kissed the back of my neck lightly and I let myself smile and enjoy the moment. We had crossed a line the night before and although I was prepared for things to be awkward the next day, it was the opposite. I felt comfortable and happy with him and I could tell he felt the same way too. We shared an unspoken need for each other, a craving of sorts, and for the time being, I welcomed it.

He handed me a steaming mug. I deeply inhaled the subtle honey and green tea aroma and wrapped my hands around the ceramic to warm my fingers.

"I love this weather." He said, embracing me from behind.

I sighed. "Me too."

I moved to the sofa and buried myself into the oversized pillows while Connor turned on the electric fireplace and the rain drop chandelier above the dining table. The previous evening's events rushed back to me when I saw the flowers.

"Connor, should we go next door and check on Mariah?" I asked him after I took a sip of my hot tea.

He was in the kitchen and turned to face me, and even in the soft glow of the suite I could see the discolored mark on his jaw.

"I don't want to see Matt, do you?" He asked me.

"No." I continued to slowly sip my drink, being careful not to scald my tongue. I watched Connor move around the kitchen, preparing a pot on the small glass top stove. He poured dry oatmeal into it and put the lid on. When he joined me on the sofa, he set his own cup of tea down on the coffee table.

"I'm sure she will make her way over here eventually," he said with no attempt to hide his disdain.

"Should we talk about it?" I moved the hot mug around in my hands.

"There isn't much to say. I hit him...he hit me...he's a tool." He paused, before leaning into me and then said, "And you are beautiful." He kissed me gently. The faint taste of honey passed between our lips.

The room had begun to warm from the fireplace and Zoey had stretched out in front of it. When Connor sat next to me she began to thump her tail against the ground. She didn't want to go out in the rain but it was obvious she was done waiting for her potty break.

After Connor returned to the kitchen I went to my room and changed into my jeans. I wasn't ready yet to take off his shirt, so I decided to leave it on, even though it was snug around my chest and the material was thin enough to see my bra. After pulling on some socks and my shoes I searched around for my sweatshirt and carried it out into the sitting room. Connor wasn't in the kitchen anymore. Zoey rushed over to me and whined.

"I'm taking Zoey out, I'll be right back," I said loudly.

"Just a sec, I'll come with you." He hollered from his room. When he joined us at the door he was wearing jeans and a hoodie. He gestured at the V-neck shirt I still had on and said to me with a laugh, "It looks much better on you."

I went up on my tip-toes and planted a kiss on his mouth, "So, you don't mind if I keep it on for the day?" I slipped into my sweatshirt and opened the door. The windows at the ends of the hall did little to help light up the walkway since the clouds outside had swallowed up the sunlight. We walked quickly and quietly past the room next door and pushed the call button when we reached the elevator. I waited nervously for the doors to open. I half-expected Matt to come barreling out of his room wielding an empty whisky bottle above his head as a weapon, but we stepped into the elevator without being seen.

The hotel lobby was freezing, and it was even colder outside. Water was rushing down the street gutters, overflowing the sidewalk in places. I thought to myself we needed the rain, California *always* needed rain, but also considered the fact that not having an infrastructure in place meant no one would be around to help move downed trees and repair flooded roads. I considered this while Zoey ran out to her patch of grass and did her business. She came back to us shaking the rain from her drenched coat.

We took the elevator back upstairs and talked about the weather, and the damage it was most likely creating to the roads we planned on taking into East County. I thought of the resort, and what condition it was in, or if it would even be standing when we found our way to it. Surely if it was built in the mountains it would be designed to withstand rain, wind and even snow. I held onto that hope as we made our way quietly down the hall to our suite.

The rest of the day was spent either on the sofa in each other's arms, or in the kitchen organizing and setting things aside for the journey we agreed to take after the storm subsided. We never heard from Matt or Mariah and by the time the day ended, shrouding the hotel in darkness again, my curiosity got the better of me, and against Connor's wishes I went next door and knocked for almost five minutes. When no one answered, I got down on my knees and peered through the gap below the door. The floor looked empty except for one of Mariah's high heeled shoes, knocked over on its side, near the sofa. I doubted they would have left in the rain and Mariah didn't seem the type to leave without her shoes, so I relaxed a bit and went back to the suite.

We had a simple dinner of rice, black beans and mixed veggies from a can, and afterwards I offered to help Connor pack his things. While we worked, we listened to Connor's MP3 player that was docked into its own speaker system. From his room we began filling a large suitcase with his warmest clothes and an extra pair of shoes. We used his second suitcase for canned goods, packaged foods and bathroom necessities and tucked some candles that Connor had found into the gaps. We set the bulging suitcases on the floor of the sitting room, returned to Connor's room and plopped down on his bed, exhausted. Augustana was playing in the background and as I listened to the lyrics of *Boston* I laughed at the sheer irony of the song's words. No one knew my name anymore. Life was starting over, whether I wanted it to, or not.

The rain was still falling outside but it had softened and lost most of its fury. The wind had also changed, instead of violently slamming into the building with vehemence, it whistled around the window lethargically. The air smelled cleaner and fresher and soon the only light in the room was a soft flicker from a single candle. The Script was playing a mellow beat and the soulful buzz of Danny O'Donoghue's voice echoed around the room.

I rolled onto my side and looked at Connor, who was on his back, his hands linked behind his head, with his eyes closed. At first I thought he was asleep, until he turned and fixed his gaze on me. Shadows danced around his face from the candle flame making it hard to see his features, but I watched as a single tear glimmered down his cheek and disappeared into the curve of his ear.

When he spoke his voice was tight with emotion, "I think my son is dead."

For a moment I thought my blood stilled in my veins. I sat upright and kneeled close to him. "Where is he?" My body was shaking.

"I don't know." He looked away, up at the ceiling. My stomach twisted in knots as I waited for him to elaborate.

Eventually he continued, "He was with his mother, spending the month with her family in London. He's with her a lot because of my work. We never married." He paused to look at me and I nodded for him to go on. "The last time I talked to her, she said all International flights were grounded, hospitals from Britain to China were reporting cases of an illness called the Red Death to the media. The Governments started calling it the Cardinal Plague because of how bloody the death is." He stopped again, his voice wavering and I remembered the reports I had heard myself with the same names. "Her father was sick. It was in their home, Riley; it made its way across the oceans to my son."

I sat perfectly still beside him, stunned, even though I wanted to run into the bathroom and vomit.

The early days of the virus flashed through my mind. When I couldn't get my children into the hospital down the street from my house, I brought them home and put them in bed. I did everything I could to stop the fevers, but nothing worked. I kept the television on to watch the news. Regular programming was suspended and the only channels broadcasting were the major news stations. The images of the sick flooding hospitals and swarming airports was the same all over the country, the written messages appearing at the base of each station kept repeating one statement: *The President has declared a National State Of Emergency. Officials at the CDC have asked all civilians to remain in their homes and to limit all contact with the public. All Military personnel must report to duty. Hospital Staff or those with Medical training are asked to report to their closest Hospital or Clinic.* I knew my own children were dying by then and when the Emergency Broadcast System showed only a bright blue screen on the TV. I turned it off. I left a battery operated radio on in the kitchen but eventually most of the channels became constant static or continuous tones and I shut it off as well. I was numb when my children died. For me it didn't matter if the rest of the World died with them because to me they were my everything.

When Connor described the chaos that fractured Europe and Asia, the severity of it all crashed down on me. I couldn't process it. The whole world - *the entire globe...infected?*

Connor was right, his son probably was dead.

"*I'm so sorry Connor.*" I whispered.

"I should have been there. I should've at least been there, in case...what if he had no one in the end?" He covered his face with his hands and stayed that way for a long time.

I sat next to him, not sure how to comfort him. I decided not to lie. "Being there, as a parent, would have only made it harder for you." My voice wavered.

He sat up and looked at me. His eyes were moist. It made the blue color of his irises brighter, almost turquoise in color. He stared at me intently.

"As a parent...?"

I cleared my throat and braced my arms against my legs. "My daughter's eight...my son is four. Was, *was* eight and four." My body trembled and Connor reached out to me. I couldn't say anymore.

"Oh my god, Riley." He hugged me to him. When I began to softly weep he pulled me under the covers with him and we stayed in bed that way, in our clothes, holding and crying into each other until we ran dry.

Zoey slept fitfully at our feet, lost in her own dark dreams.

***

The next morning we woke at dawn. We left the window curtains wide open the day before and as the sun broke the surface along the eastern side of town it lit up the room with radiant streaks of oranges, ambers, and golden yellows. The room was absolutely ablaze with sunshine. With the light came warmth, and as the shadows were forced under the bed and into the corners, the ability to stay under the covers fully dressed became unbearable and we begrudgingly rolled out of bed.

Connor delegated himself to coffee brewing duty while I sifted through the food on the counter until I found a bag of granola and set out the last of the fresh apples. We hadn't spoken much since rising. We were both mentally and physically drained.

After breakfast we took turns showering and dressed in clean clothes. We threw the little laundry we had into the washer and sat down to write a list for what we wanted to take east. Both of us needed warmer jackets and snow gear. Connor needed boots that were

93

designed with the weather in mind, and his designer footwear, though expensive, wouldn't survive many hikes in the mountains.

We also wanted to find another vehicle, one that would get our gear and us back to my Jeep. This meant a truck and Connor thought he knew just the one to take. In the parking lot there was a brand new F250, and since it was in the lot for the hotel, with only a handful of other cars, it shouldn't be too hard to find the owner. This meant though, that he had to rifle through the dead bodies he had moved into the conference room until he found the right set of keys.

It was just before 7:00 when we planned to head out for the morning, and walk over to the mall where we could get the rest of our supplies. Connor was the first to open the suite door as I searched my room for Zoey's leash.

"Riley, there's a note on the door," Connor said.

I met him at the entrance as he pulled the paper off the door where it had been suspended by a piece of tape. He handed it to me and I read it out loud.

Riley and Connor,
It was early when we left this morning, otherwise we would have said goodbye. Thank you for the room and the company. We are on our way to Las Vegas to hopefully find our family, please wish us luck. I wish, wherever the two of you go, you will find what you are looking for, and I hope to see you again. Who knows, we may end up coming back this way.
Love, Mariah
p.s. Please hug Zoey goodbye for me!

"So...they left," I said quietly to myself. I regretted parting with Mariah this way, although I was happy Matt was gone.

I glanced at Connor and he said, "I hope they make it there." It sounded like he meant it, though I was sure it was only because he hoped they found someone in their family alive, so they would stay in Nevada. I doubted he ever wanted to see Matt's face again either.

***

It took us a few hours and two different stores to find everything on our list. We pushed it all back to the hotel in a drugstore shopping cart. The roads had a different feeling than they did the last time I walked through them. The rain had washed away the dirt and most of the debris, and the dead smell that had been festering from within the buildings was barely noticeable. I still had the feeling I was being watched, though the streets were completely silent, so I continuously scanned the road around us.

We were two blocks from the hotel when Zoey started barking. Connor was pushing the cart and he stopped to glance behind us.

"Riley, look," he said quietly.

I searched the street around us and down the sidewalk, not seeing anything other than parked cars, buildings and a handful of military vehicles. Zoey had stopped barking, and was cowering behind my legs, between me and Connor. I started to turn back towards Connor when I saw her. A girl. She was standing alone, in the middle of the road, a few blocks away. I could see her red overcoat and a red hat sitting atop her long black hair, but she was too far away to make out much more. She was standing in the street, facing our direction, not moving.

"Oh my god," I breathed. I began jogging toward her, straight down the street.

Several seconds later I heard Connor yell, "Wait, Riley, wait!" But I didn't stop. I couldn't. I registered the sound of Connor's feet lightly slapping the ground almost a full block behind me but I didn't turn to look at him.

I pumped my legs harder and when I was close enough to see her clearly I realized she was young...five, maybe six years old. In addition to her coat and hat she was wearing a pair of white tights, with the knees stained a dark color, like she had kneeled in dirt. Blood pounded through my temples and again Connor yelled at me to stop but I couldn't, I was less than a block away from the child.

I ran right up to her and skidded to a stop within arm's reach. My chest was heaving, and I sucked the air in at the same time I reached out and touched her arm. The twill fabric of her coat was rough beneath my fingers. The sunshine broke through the patchy cloud cover and sprayed across her, causing sparkles to bounce through her dark hair.

"Sweetie, are you okay?" The words came out in pants and my breath trailed out before me in puffs. It was cold. I left my hand near her shoulder and shook her gently when she didn't answer me. She was pale, and a familiar red blotchy pattern bloomed out from her nose and mouth. The blood capillaries had burst in different places all around her face and neck like little fireworks had gone off below her skin. Her eyes were so dark I couldn't see the pupils, and her vision was frozen straight ahead, as if she was looking right through me.

"Honey, can you hear me?" I pleaded, but still she didn't answer.

My hand dropped from her shoulder and Connor shouted my name from the curb a hundred feet away. In my peripheral vision I saw movement on my right and left. I looked over my shoulder and dozens of people were walking towards me, their faces all fixed on mine. It was the same from the other side of the street. I jumped to my feet; my breath still ragged from the run, and turned in circles. Men, women and children approached me from all four sides of the street, moving quickly, and filing in next to each other so close that their shoulders bumped together.

Terrified, I yelled for Connor and thought I heard him respond but he sounded muffled and impossibly far away. Every face I saw was either streaked with blood or covered with blotchy skin abrasions like the young girl standing near me. The mass of bodies surrounded us, and the noise from all the cries of anguish and pain was deafening. I squeezed my hands against my ears as I turned around and around, screaming in fear.

The first one to reach me was a man wearing only a sagging pair of pants, with dark, sickly colored blood flowing freely from his nose. His eyes were clouded over with a white mucous substance that oozed down his cheeks and his flesh hung from him like a poorly fitted suit. When he reached for me, grabbing forcefully at my shirt, I shrieked at him in horror. Behind me hands tugged at my hair, pushed against my back, shoved at me, groped me. I tried to smack the hands away but there were too many, hundreds of bodies slammed into me. The smell of death filled my nostrils, and I choked on the rancid odor. An elderly woman clothed in a nightgown snagged my right arm and when I struggled to push her off, some of her long frizzy grey hair tangled in my fingers and came out in fleshy clumps. These people weren't alive, they were rotting. Repulsed, I screeched so high pitched my ears rang.

The mob swayed and pushed and swelled around me until I was sure I would suffocate. Even though my voice was hoarse I screamed over and over for Connor. Someone pulled on my legs and I tumbled to the hot asphalt in a trembling, blubbering mess. I curled into the fetal position as darkness closed in around me. The swarm of dead bodies began to still and move together in a slow sway as a small pair of black dress shoes came to a stop by my head. I looked up and saw the little girl with the red overcoat standing above me, her hand reaching for me. She was looking at me with a pleading expression and when she moved her lips to speak, congealed blood bubbled out of her mouth.

I dropped my head to the street and let the darkness take me.

CHAPTER 9

When Riley saw the little girl, her first instinct was to run to her but Connor froze. He let Riley get more than half a block away before he snapped out of it and pursued her. He noticed the materializing crowd of people before she did and he yelled, screamed at her to stop and come back to him, but before he could reach her, the mob closed tightly around her and he panicked at the sound of Riley's shouts. He ran straight into the legion of crying bodies but only got five feet in before they surrounded him. Arms yanked him back and forth, hands grabbed at his clothing. The smell of rot was so strong he couldn't breathe the air. Even though his eyes saw it happen, his brain refused to believe it. One second the street was empty, and the next the horizon shimmered, as if cooking under a hot desert sun, and they were just…there.

He tried to choke out Riley's name into the pulsating crowd but only heard her screaming in response. A teenage boy reached out at his face and he pushed the arm away, sliding a huge chunk of skin off the young boys arm from the elbow to the wrist. He gagged as the bloody flesh hit the pavement with a wet sound. He kept screaming for Riley, lost in a panic that threatened to drive him mad and until the shoving from the bodies around him halted so suddenly he lost his balance and stumbled to his knees. His hands were covered in dark, lumpy blood and he held them away from him in disgust.

"What the fuck's going on?" He screamed into the sky.

The pack of people began to move backwards, away from him, and gradually dissipated the same way they had appeared until he could only see a few dozen or so bodies moving away from him. He blinked, baffled, as they shimmered, like a mirage…and were gone. They disappeared, right before his eyes.

99

"This isn't happening." He muttered to himself, as movie scenes from every ghost flick he had ever seen flashed through his mind.

The frenzied barking from Zoey in the distance snapped his head back up the street. He struggled to his feet and saw Riley lying motionless in the middle of the intersection, curled into a fetal ball. He ran for her, screaming her name.

"Oh my god! Riley, please be okay!" He slid to a stop beside her.

The clicking of Zoey's nails grew louder as she scurried down the sidewalk behind him. His whole body shook with tremors as he lifted Riley's head off the ground and placed it in his lap. He paused to look at his hands, which were clean, each nail neatly groomed, no traces left of the bloody mess he had just scrambled through and a shiver of anxiety ran through his body. He couldn't have imagined it all, could he?

Riley was unresponsive but breathing. He checked her head for bumps and scrapes and found none. He hoped she simply passed out and that nothing else was wrong with her. Zoey rushed him from behind, whining and nudging Riley's arm as he stood and lifted her carefully into his arms, and began walking the several blocks back to the hotel. His eyes continually scanned the streets, the doorways, the cars, for any sign of movement. He had never been more terrified in his life. There was nothing logical in his mind that could explain what happened, at that moment he didn't want explanations, he wanted Riley safe inside the hotel, away from this street.

He was perspiring heavily by the time they reached the hotel lobby. He grunted as he struggled with the door and cursed when his grip slipped from around Riley's legs, nearly dropping her. When he reached the elevator he pounded the call button but kept his eyes locked on the lobby doors. Zoey brushed against his legs, shaking and whining. When the elevator opened, they rushed inside and he leaned against the wall, holding Riley close to his chest. Even though his arms felt like Jell-O, he refused to set her down, not until he was behind a locked door. His feet stumbled into the twentieth floor hall and he weaved down the walkway to the end and cursed at his keycard after realizing it was in his back pocket. Squatting, he rested Riley's legs against his own and yanked the keycard out, slipping it into the lock. The second he entered the suite he slammed the door shut, engaging the bolt. He laid Riley on the sofa and stumbled into *the kitchen. When he returned, he draped a wet towel across her sweaty forehead and collapsed onto the carpet next to her. No matter how many times he replayed what happened through his mind, it didn't make sense. His temples pounded with a stress headache unlike one he had ever had before, and he thought for sure if his head went on hurting this way it would split in half.*

Riley woke fifteen minutes later, thrashing and screaming. When he tried to hug her she threw his arms off and punched at the air around her. He had to grip her wrists and yell into her face, "Riley! Riley, it's Connor! It's me!" before her eyes focused on him and she sunk into the sofa in sobs. She was trying to talk but the words were swallowed up by convulsive cries. He pulled her heaving body into his and held her while he cried into her neck. He kept telling her it was okay, they were okay, they were safe.

Several minutes passed and gradually her weeping turned to sniveling. Her ragged gulps for air became a steady inhale and exhale and he pushed her away from him just far enough to see her face. Puffy bags protruded from beneath her bloodshot eyes, and she licked at her swollen and chapped lips.

"Can you drink some water?" He asked her, picking up a glass from the coffee table.

She nodded yes, and took a sip before abruptly turning away from him and throwing up onto the carpet.

Once inside his bathroom, he stripped all her clothing off except for her bra and underwear. She let him help her into the massive tub and began filling it with hot water. As the steam curled up around them, fogging up the mirrors and flattening his hair to his head, he used his hand to scoop up the water and pour it over her back. He dribbled the warm water across her neck and shoulders, and watched it trail down her arms in little rivers. She sat in the tub silently with her knees drawn to her chest, and her eyes closed tightly as he washed her, as best he could.

After he drained the tub, she was more alert and aware of his movements. He left her huddled in one of his large bathrobes to retrieve dry clothes from her room, but she called for him to stay with her, so he held a towel out in front of him as she slithered from his robe and out of her wet undergarments, stepping into a pair of his boxers. He stood behind her and pulled one of his shirts over her head and down her bare back while she wiggled her arms into the long sleeves. Wind shook against the side of the building, whistling along the bedroom windows as he guided her to the bed and pulled the covers back for her to climb in. She grabbed onto his arm, and pleaded with him not to leave her.

Zoey had followed them both from the sofa to the bathroom, to the bedroom, and once Riley was in bed, the dog jumped onto the mattress and cuddled up to Riley's back. They were all traumatized, the three of them, clinging to each other.

When he knew that Riley was asleep he whispered over her head at the dog, "Go pee in the bathroom, because I'm not taking you outside." Zoey's dark round eyes darted from him to the door, as if she agreed it was safer where they were.

He told himself they were leaving the next day. He had to get them out of the city. Whatever it was that happened, he sure as hell wasn't going to stick around to see if it would happen again. And that's when he realized the cart they had filled with supplies was still on the sidewalk, at least two blocks from the hotel. The truck, we'll pick it up with the truck...that's if it's still there in the morning, he thought to himself.

He passed out with his arms safely wrapped around Riley and sank into a deep, frightful sleep. He was on an Irish hill, overlooking a valley, holding Roan's hand. When he turned to smile at his son, the boy pulled away from him and the flesh from his hand slid off into his in a bloody and pulpy mess. Terror spread through him as he stared at the chunk of skin smeared between his fingers. When he looked up, Roan was gone, so he ran down the hillside screaming for his son. All he found at the bottom was a puddle of blood surrounded by the grass of the meadow that stretched before him like waves on the sea.

Connor trembled and moaned in his sleep through most of the night, while Riley dreamed of a little girl in a red overcoat. Though they were lost in their own nightmares, neither let go of the other while they slept and both were grateful for dawn, when the sun washed over them, and forced the dreams away.

***

I woke in Connor's arms. He was talking in his sleep, calling out in desperation for someone named 'Roan'. I could tell from the pain in his muffled voice, Roan must have been his son. I shook him gently and eventually he quieted, but the furrow on his brow told me he was still lost in an unfriendly dreamland.

I lifted his arm from my side and carefully rolled away from him, resting on my back in the middle of the bed and stared up at the ceilings antique copper-colored tin tiles that glinted in the early morning sunlight. I traced the Fleur-de-lis style pattern above me in random zigzags until I felt a headache building up behind my eye sockets. My palms felt cool as I pressed them lightly against the swollen heat of my eyes. When I opened my eyes again, an image of the little black-haired girl with blood dripping from her mouth escaped from my memory and I sprang upright...breathing hard and clutching the covers around me.

Jesus, did that really happen?! I thought to myself.

I glanced down at Connor, who was asleep, with a sullen look on his face, and felt compelled to shake him awake and ask him what had really happened on the street. It was obviously morning, and the events from the day before were hazy at best. I remembered running towards the girl, being surrounded by hundreds of dead, rotting people and when the little girl tried to speak to me, foul smelling blood rushed out of her. They touched me, I felt them. I heard their cries. *They seemed so real.*

I had pulled my knees up to my chest and was rocking back and forth on the bed when Zoey came into the room, a guilty look in her eyes. She approached the bed with hesitation until I patted the space next to me. I lowered my knees so she could lay her head in my lap and I murmured soothingly to her.

Connor woke with a gasp, which startled the dog off the bed and scampering to the doorway where she lingered there for a moment before quickly scanning the room and leaving. Her padded feet barely made a sound on the carpet as she walked into the kitchen and seconds later I heard lapping sounds coming from her water bowl.

When I reached out and touched the arm that Connor had draped over his face, he looked at me and smiled faintly but I could see perspiration building up on his forehead.

He swallowed hard before he spoke. "How are you?"

I considered my answer carefully. "I don't know what's real anymore." I paused before asking him, "What happened yesterday?"

"What do you remember?" He sat up and scooted closer, but didn't touch me.

A small trickle of sweat rolled down his temple and I almost reached out to wipe it away. Instead I turned and looked out the window at the bright blue sky.

I closed my eyes and cleared my throat. "Were they real Connor? The girl...the people...were they really there?" I kept my eyes closed, hoping he would ask me - *What people?*

His hand shook slightly as he ran it through his hair and down the back of his neck. "I'm not sure but I think they were real, at least for a little while."

My heart sank into my stomach and I instantly felt nauseous. I whispered, "*That's not possible.*"

He touched me then...his warm hand slid across my back and pulled me to him and I resisted the urge to cry. My throat was dry and hoarse, and sore. I didn't want to cry anymore.

"I think you fainted. You didn't wake up until we got back here. Do you want me to tell you what happened?" His voice wavered slightly.

I turned to look at him and nodded yes.

"After you started running I saw them. It was like they came out of nowhere." He stopped to look around the room. "Riley, they went straight for you - there was nothing I could do. I tried to get to you, I promise. There were just too many of them. I'm so sorry." He looked ashen and paused to take a deep breath before telling me the rest of the story. When he was finished we were both shaking.

"So...they just disappeared?" I asked him.

"I told you, it makes no sense but that's what happened."

"Are you saying we were somehow attacked by a mob of angry ghosts?" I stared at him, wide-eyed.

When he nodded, I let out a humorless laugh that chilled the room.

"Then where do we go now? Somewhere far away, where no one lived, where no one can come back to haunt us?" I spit the words out like they tasted bad.

Connor leaned forward and pushed the hair from my face. "Yes. We go to the mountains, like you said...where less people died."

I pictured the girl, how she seemed oblivious to me on the street until the others came, and I recalled her outstretched hand and the expression on her face.

"Connor, I think she was trying to ask me something." I blurted out.

"Who? You mean...the girl?" He asked, clearly confused.

"She was trying to talk to me. I think she was trying to say something." I looked at him, and he stared blankly back at me. I turned my body towards him and rested my hand on his bent knee.

"I think she wanted...help." I didn't know why, but I felt it was true.

"But..." he stuttered, "She's dead, isn't she? Like the others? How can we possibly help them?"

I thought silently to myself. *I don't know what they want. I don't know what to do, but we should try, we should try to help. The voice inside my head changed, as if my conscience was ripping itself in two. I can't stay here. There's no one to help us. It's hopeless.*

"I don't know what to do Connor, but I can't stay here." I replied painfully.

CHAPTER 10

If the dead were seeking us out by the hundreds, I wanted to be as far away as possible from the miles of metal, concrete and glass that entombed my fallen citizens; it was time to leave the city. Connor had luck finding the keys to the F250 in the employee locker room, which meant neither of us had to search any dead bodies.

By noon we had mostly filled the bed of the truck and I stood before the hotel lobby doors, tightly gripping my black marker. We had both agreed it could be dangerous leaving messages with our exact destinations but I told Connor I wouldn't stop believing someone could be out there, looking for me. Our compromise was leaving the directions to a neutral location where we could set up some sort of two-way communication system that ran on batteries. I had an idea of the place we could use. There was a fire station within a few miles of the lodge. There had to be a radio there but not knowing what sort of communications were in place at the lodge, it made sense to stop somewhere along the way and pick up a set of long range walkie-talkies that we could charge in the cars.

Connor had pulled the truck around to the front of the hotel and the idle of the engine hummed loudly down the empty street. He had already taken the truck down the block to pick up the contents of the shopping cart we had abandoned the day before, so all that was left was for me to leave my last note downtown. I pressed a piece of the hotel letterhead up against the glass and began writing.

1/14

It's time to leave the City. I'm going East with Connor and Zoey...up into the Mountains. I'll leave a message for you at the Mt.

Laguna Fire Station (From the 8, go North on Sunrise Hwy). You'll know how to contact us once you get there. If you're still looking, I hope you find me. – Riley
  p.s. Be careful on the streets. The dead are watching.

***

The sky was bright blue as I navigated our way through the inner and outer streets of downtown, and a sense of relief began to wash over me. I had spent days driving around my part of town knocking on the doors of extended family and friends after my children died. I only went into the city to prove what I already knew was true; that my mother was dead as well. That made it official. I was truly alone. And then Connor found me and that changed things. I had never planned to stay in the city, I didn't want to see what happened there, but Connor was eager and willing to share his resources, and for just a little while, it made sense to stay where other people could find us. But it was obvious to us both, the streets weren't safe.

I worried about what would happen if the wrong people followed us, but I was even more terrified of disappearing without a trace. If anyone I knew came looking for me, I wanted them to be able to find me. So when the skyscrapers and lofts and businesses began to fade behind us into the distance, I was left feeling relief. Relief that we were no longer surrounded by dead bodies or the horror of what happened to them. And relief that I was moving on, that my trail was warm again. I hoped that someone would someday catch up to us.

***

The Jeep was where I had left it and a quick glance inside proved everything was undisturbed and Connor let the truck idle as I transferred my things. The sun was high in the sky - heating the day quickly. As we organized our supplies, and properly packed our items from the previous day's excursion to the mall, we were sweating under our long sleeves and jeans. I stripped down to my tank top before loading Zoey into the Jeep.

Across the street, a large blue Victorian house with ivory shutters stood like a wooden skeleton on the street. Its paint was faded and chipped, and the yellowing grass in the front yard along with the trash that had blown up onto the front steps gave the property a long abandoned look. I sighed, and glanced up and down the street before looking back at Connor.

"There's a sporting goods store a few miles from here. How about we go there first, and find a set of walkie-talkies? We can charge them in the cars as we drive, and also use them to talk." I leaned against the back of the Jeep, wiping sweat off my forehead. My hair was pulled up into a high pony tail but my neck still felt hot.

Connor had also taken off his warmer top and was wearing one of his expensive, tightly fitted white t-shirts that showed the definition of his lean pectoral muscles perfectly. I swallowed hard, and took in the sight of him. He looked rugged and sexy as he leaned onto the truck's dented and scratched front end and crossed his arms loosely at his chest. He had used the truck to push through the blocked intersections, leaving a ragged pathway of broken glass and pieces of plastic behind us on our way to the Jeep.

"Sounds good to me," he replied with a smile.

"You ready?" I asked him, trying not to stare at his chest…with no success.

"Not yet." He shoved himself off the damaged bumper and in two quick steps he was in front of me, blocking out the sun, with his mouth on mine, his hands around my back, and his body pressed against me. He let go as quickly as he had grabbed me and walked back to the truck. My heart thudded wildly against my ribcage at the desire that flooded through me as I watched him hop inside. He winked at me mischievously and in response I sent a casual smirk his way and walked around to the side of the Jeep and climbed in.

While I drove, I listened to the MP3 player I had tucked into my backpack before leaving home by plugging it into the dashboard console. As we traveled the quiet residential streets, I rolled the windows down and let the fresh air envelope us as the music played. The first song we listened to was Kings of Leon's *Radioactive*.

***

After spending almost an hour in the sporting goods store, we walked out with two sets of radios, batteries, cords, and a handful of

109

other things. I led Connor through a maze of side streets, even driving up on curbs when the roads were too packed with parked cars. Out of habit, a few times I heeded traffic signs and each time I stopped or yielded for traffic that wasn't there, Connor's voice would boom through the hand-held radio set and tease me.

When we hit the eastern side of El Cajon, I pulled over and studied my road atlas, marking out the best roads to take into East County. From where we were on the streets, the freeway still appeared congested on both sides, so I decided to take us through Crest, which would eventually spit us out into Alpine. My hope was that anyone that far east of the city would have tried to flee to Arizona, not go west, back *into* the city and I was right. After we passed through Harbison Canyon, we traveled parallel with the freeway going east on Alpine Blvd, driving slowly through the empty mountain town. Zoey sat with her head resting outside the open passenger window, letting the breeze blow her floppy ears around her face.

We turned onto Willows Road and drove over I8 and entered the nearly empty westbound lanes from the exit. Once we were on the freeway the winds picked up speed, and the temperature dropped at least fifteen degrees. Twice we slowed down to a crawl to safely maneuver around crumpled and burnt vehicles that had collided together or struck the median. Every few miles, cars had piled into each other, causing a chain reaction of fender benders. They had gone into the median or over it in places, and smashed into other vehicles on the opposite side of the freeway. With every mile we put between us and the city we saw at least one vehicle pulled over to the shoulder, the dead driver slumped in their seat or across the steering wheel.

I forced a yawn until my ears popped as the elevation steadily rose on our way through the Cleveland National Forest and after we passed the 79 exit I radioed Connor to tell him we would be leaving the freeway soon. I had always been at ease in East County, having spent most of my childhood in the country-side. The shrubby Manzanita of the Cleveland National Forest and the pines that dotted Laguna felt like home. I hoped nature would welcome us more than the city had.

Connor trailed close behind me as we left the freeway and turned north onto Sunrise Highway. At first the road was clear, but after a

110

few turns we slowed to barely a crawl to negotiate around various sized boulders that had fallen down from the hillsides and dried mud. Branches and tumbleweeds littered the asphalt which proved the weather had been unrelenting to the area, but the roads were still passable. I knew the route well and cautiously followed the curves of the road that led to the Mt. Laguna Fire Station. It was late in the afternoon, and the tall pine trees filtered out most of the sunlight which cast long, scraggy shadows across the road.

By dusk we pulled into the large space next to the station and parked. The lot was empty and the building looked dark and still inside. I climbed out of the Jeep and stood next to it while I stretched my back. Zoey ran excitedly through the lot, sniffing everything in sight as Connor climbed out of the heavy duty truck, flexing and stretching his arms.

"That was a long drive." He took in the surroundings.

"Yeah, well normally it doesn't take that long." I smiled at him.

"It's a good thing the truck already had a full tank of gas." He gestured at the Jeep. "What about you?"

"I'm just under half a tank." I looked around at the dark woods. I had pulled my sweatshirt on before stepping out into the cooler mountain air. I was worried we wouldn't have shelter for the night if we didn't hurry at the station.

"So, what are your plans, exactly?" Connor asked me as we stood before the closed station door.

"Let's see what's inside first."

The trees tightened around us as the sun sank closer to the coast. It was hard to make out the shapes inside with night falling, but I could see couches, a table and shelving inside. I turned the knob and the door opened, releasing the trapped stale air from the room. We hollered out a hello or two before entering the building. Connor flipped a switch and an overhead light twinkled above us, which meant the sensor had been tripped when the power went out, turning the generator on. The room consisted of a lounging area, two sets of bunk beds and an open kitchen. A closed door led out into the empty garage, another opened up into a large bathroom. I began setting up one of the walkie-talkies on the kitchen counter while Connor investigated the station radios.

"All I can hear is static," Connor said, as he flipped through channels.

"You know what's interesting? All the trucks are gone, the garage is empty." I said to him.

Connor wandered around the room, and after disappearing into the bathroom I heard a loud flush through the open door.

"Toilet works!" He shouted. A few seconds later I heard a loud squeak and then the sudden rush of water. "Shower works too!"

When he came back out into the main room I was facing one of the walls, looking at the framed photos of a massive fire and other shots of the firefighters in gear, posing in front of their trucks or dragging hoses behind them. Wherever their last call came from, it seemed they hadn't returned and an overwhelming sense of guilt washed over me as I looked from one photo to the next. These people were supposed to be the strongest, the bravest of all, and yet someone like me - a former single mom and 3rd grade teacher, survived. It wasn't fair. I turned away from the wall with an angry expression on my face and Connor stepped away from me.

"What's wrong?" He asked.

"Nothing. It's just upsetting that this place is empty. I was hoping someone would be here," I answered. Wind whirled through the open door, whipping my hair around my face. I smoothed my pony-tail back and squared my shoulders.

"I don't think anyone has been here for weeks." He stepped closer and hugged me to him. "Why don't we stay here tonight?"

"Here?" I asked as I looked into his face.

"Why not? We don't know what we'll find at this lodge of yours. At least here we're inside, there's power and cots. We can leave first thing in the morning if you want." He kept his arms around my back as he waited for my answer.

"You're right. It doesn't make sense to drive over there in the dark." I smiled at him and we both looked outside. The only thing I could make out clearly through the large window was the outline of each of our vehicles. The lot was almost completely shrouded in darkness; even the trees blended into the night.

"You know, a few years ago I got my car stuck in the mud out here with a friend. It took us nearly an hour to walk back to the highway from a little mountain road we were exploring. We were freezing and thought we might have to stand on the side of the road for hours while we waited for a friend to pick us up." Connor leaned gently into me while he listened to my story. "We flagged a car down, since cell phone reception was sketchy, and asked the driver to send the nearest Ranger to wait with us. A fire truck came down the mountain instead. I was mortified, totally embarrassed, but the guys were great. They brought us back here, gave us coffee and made sure we were warm." I swallowed hard and pulled away from Connor's grip so that I could look behind me at the wall of framed faces. "I still remember their names...Ty, Joe and Joel. I wonder where they are now."

It seemed every memory of every person I knew was stained with an overwhelming feeling of guilt that I had survived this global viral killer and they hadn't. I closed my eyes and images of friends, family, coworkers, students, neighbors and even grocery tellers started flashing through my mind like an old-fashioned flip book. I opened my eyes and rubbed the back of my neck before one of those images became my daughter or son. Connor stood awkwardly before me, his hands shoved deeply into his jean pockets, waiting for me to speak.

"Let's bring some things inside before it gets too cold," I suggested. He nodded at me silently.

Later, I offered to make dinner while Connor showered. Zoey was passed out on one of the couches, and by the time Connor re-emerged from the bathroom I had thrown together a modest meal for all three of us. After we ate, Connor turned the big screen T.V. on and put in a DVD and both of us fell asleep on the couch half-way through the movie.

***

At first I thought I was dreaming as the voices of Rob Schneider and Adam Sandler bantered loudly with each other from somewhere nearby, until I felt my shoulders gently shaking and my head lolled to the side. My eyes snapped open and I sat upright so quickly that my forehead struck Connor's chin.

"Ouch!" He leaned away from me, holding his hand to his mouth.

"I'm sorry! Was I asleep?" I rubbed above my eyebrows where my head collided into Connor's.

"I nearly bit a hole through my tongue." He laughed and stood up from the couch, turning off the T.V. "Didn't mean to startle you, I was trying to wake you, thought you might want to sleep on the bed." He stretched backwards slightly, with his hands on his hips and glanced down at me. "I'd offer to help you up, but I'm afraid you might punch me in the nose next." He smiled at me.

I laughed and apologized again while I stood up to copy his stretch. Connor walked around the room, shutting off the few lights we had turned on. By the time he made his way to the beds I had claimed one of the lower bunks, and was already curled up under the covers half-asleep. Zoey cuddled herself up around my feet and sighed deeply.

Beneath the blankets I felt warm and comfortable but outside the breeze whistled through the trees and around the doors, threatening to force the cold air inside. The front window shook in its frame as the wind pulsated against the single paned glass.

"Good night," I murmured.

"G'night," Connor replied softly. I felt the slightest whisper of his lips graze along my cheek before Connor's mattress squeaked beneath him as he settled into his bunk.

I sleepily punched the lumps out of my pillow and opened my eyes just enough to see the edge of the covers so I could tug them up to my neck. Something on the far side of the room caught my eye and I looked up to see the inky shadow of a man standing in the corner facing us. My breath stilled in my chest as I blinked, hoping the figure was a figment of my over-worked mind. But as my eyes adjusted, I could make out the standard issue over-sized fire protective pants with the reflective strip around the ankles, a long sleeved dark top and a dark knit cap on the man's head. I stared at him wide-eyed, and jumped when Zoey let out a long whimper in her sleep. I broke my gaze from the fire fighter and glanced quickly down at the dog but when I looked back up, the room was empty…the corner uninhabited of dark shadowy figures.

There was nowhere for a man to go in merely two seconds time. The only explanation was one I didn't want to consider. What I saw hovering in the corner wasn't a man at all. At least, it wasn't a man *anymore*…but an apparition. I lowered my head onto my pillow and let my breath out nervously. I could hear the change in Connor's

114

breathing, which meant he was asleep, and the dog was snoring softly beside me but I lay rigid...paralyzed in the bed, with only my eyes moving from one object to another, peering into each dark crevice until my head hurt. When I couldn't force my eyelids open any longer, I drifted into a restless sleep.

In the early hours of dawn I woke before Connor, my back cramped from sleeping in a tight ball, my arms numb from spending hours crossed tightly at my chest. I was facing the corner of the room the man had been standing in the night before but with the morning light it simply looked like two white walls meeting together, a normal corner. Nothing more, nothing less, and surely nothing sinister stood before me.

It wasn't until we had packed up our things and began to leave the station later in the morning that I walked by that corner on the way out the front door. Connor led the way, with Zoey rushing outdoors ahead of us. As I walked through the doorway I looked down at the floor, and there in the corner, were two dirty boot impressions facing the sleeping area. I felt the blood drain from my face as I slammed the door shut behind me and I turned around to quickly read the message I had taped to the inside of the glass window.

1/15

We made it in one piece! I left a long range radio on the counter. It should be charged, but if you need more juice the station has a generator. We'll be listening for you every night at sunset on channel 7. Call and you'll find me. – Riley

CHAPTER 11

We left the station the way it was when we arrived. The temperature was slowly rising with the sun but it was still cold enough to stay bundled up in our coats. I turned onto the highway ahead of Connor and watched in the mirror as his truck pulled out behind me. The lodge was less than five miles ahead of us but I kept a slow pace, unsure of when the resort would come into view.

In my mind, I replayed the message we had left at the station. Our goal was to keep the lodge location private, and if, by some slim chance, someone followed my messages, we would be able to choose who to disclose our exact location to. It seemed like a good plan but the further away we got from the station, the more nervous I became.

With just a few more miles to go, I told myself that leaving the city was the right choice. We should be safer in the mountains, away from strangers and the...unknown, and we had enough resources to last a while. Plus, we had the option of going back to Alpine or further north into Julian for more when we ran out. I was anxious and excited when I saw the sign that said *Big Laguna Hideaway Lodge, One Mile* and I tapped my breaks to warn Connor that I was slowing down.

The fresh morning sunlight broke through the tree line as we turned down the gravel road that had the lodge's name printed in bold, white letters on a wooden sign and then we passed through an open metal gate. While we slowly eased the vehicles down the gravel road, a solid shape began to appear through the trees ahead of us.

After passing through a dense grove of tall pines, we followed the driveway around a giant oak tree and our headlights flashed across a modern, cabin-styled structure. The grandiose building that stood before us was flanked by massive pine trees and an uneven row of short Manzanita's that lined the building. The lodge fit so well between the trees that I wondered if it had sprouted from the ground as a seed itself. I parked in front of the entryway steps and jumped out of the Jeep. Connor stood beside me as I took in the rectangular shape of the stylish building with anticipation.

Movement from the second story caught my eye. One of the sheer curtains fluttered slightly behind a closed window and I inched closer to Connor before whispering, "*I don't think we're alone.*"

***

A high-pitched screech reverberated through the tall trees around us, followed by a muffled fluttering sound. I looked into the sky just in time to catch a glimpse of an owl flying overhead. I leaned down and clicked Zoey's leash into her collar without taking my eyes off the dark shadow as it circled us once before it flew into the cover of the forest. I doubted it was considering the dog for dinner, she was more than three times the bird's weight, but owls weren't the only thing to worry about in the country.

I shuffled my feet nervously as Connor gestured at the lodge door. It was a massive, wooden plank framed by two narrow windows. I made no attempt to leave the driveway and go up to it. Connor sensed my hesitation and started up the walkway first, glancing over his shoulder at me as he slowly went up the steps. The sunlight cast a shadow on his face that made his square jaw more angular, and the circles under his eyes more pronounced. But still, Early Morning Connor mixed with Mountain Man Connor took my breath away.

"You coming?" he asked me.

I nodded in affirmation and began following him. Zoey was so close beside me that she rubbed against my legs as we walked. She kept her head low and her tail tucked, ready to bolt at the slightest sound.

Once we reached the door I wasn't sure what to do, so I fidgeted with the end of Zoey's leash while Connor peered through the windows. He tried the doorknob but it was locked. He suggested walking around the building, and maybe finding a way in through a window before he went back to the truck to retrieve a flashlight. When he returned to the building, he leaned against the window pane near the door and pointed the light inside. I watched the fluorescent glow arc around the room, sweeping the floor, the walls, a hallway, and several pieces of empty furniture. It appeared deserted inside.

I sighed deeply, trying to hide the growing uneasiness I felt. "Okay. Let's try the back door."

Our feet made crunching sounds in the gravel as we followed the driveway to the edge of the building. Along the landscaping we found a stone pathway leading to the back and we stopped to look in the windows as we passed them. By the time we made it around to the back door I was sniveling from the cold early morning air.

Behind the main building a pathway trailed around a large open lawn. I gasped as I looked beyond the massive expanse of the lodge and took in the view. A narrow dirt road bordered the sloped lawn and led to an outside pavilion and picnic area. Leading deeper into the trees were a handful of smaller dirt pathways. I saw a solid form in the distance but couldn't make out what it belonged to. The trees moved gently in the breeze, whispering ancient secrets to each other, and I deeply inhaled the fresh and clean air that smelled nothing like the city we just came from.

We stayed along the path that led to the rear porch. It was a wide-open space surrounded by potted bushes and tiny shrubs full of skeletal-like branches. When I leaned down towards one of the rustic ceramic pots, I noticed thorns on some of the bare branches. Spring would turn the naked stumps into colorful rose bushes. Nostalgia and guilt washed over me as I imagined the abandoned rose garden at my house, but I straightened my shoulders and tilted my chin up to the sky, trying not to imagine my garden, because the last time I was there it was to oversee the burning of my dead family.

"Riley...the door is unlocked," Connor said quietly as he rattled the knob around in his hand.

Before he could push the door open, Zoey rushed away from us, her leash trailing behind her in the dirt, and barked once at the building. Both Connor and I jumped, and when we turned back to the door, a man's face was on the other side of the glass, staring suspiciously at us. For a long moment I stood there next to Connor, transfixed on the stranger's shadowy glare. Zoey turned in circles, tangling her leash around her feet and barked repeatedly at the man behind the door. I bent down to free the dog before she panicked and when I turned back to look, he was gone.

"Where'd he go?" I asked Connor. He shrugged at me and ran his hands through his hair nervously.

"What do you want?" a voice from within boomed. The curtain on the door moved and the man's face appeared again. I took a step backwards as he tapped the barrel of a handgun against the glass and then pointed it directly at us.

Connor moved sideways, putting himself between me and the door and used one of his hands to shove me behind him. Annoyed, I pushed him aside and stepped out, in full view of the door, despite Connor's hushed cursing. Shadows from inside cast distorted shapes around the armed man so that I couldn't make out the features of his face. He asked again what we wanted, and I was the first to answer him.

"Hi." I gulped and blinked as plumes of my breath evaporated into the cool air before my face. "We aren't dangerous…" I paused, waiting for the man to react, "…um, we're looking for a place to stay." My knees were shaking and I wasn't exactly sure if it was from the cold temperature of the mountain air or the fact that we might be shot. It was probably both.

The man backed away from the door and cursed loudly. Connor turned to me and suggested we leave.

"Just wait a minute," I said quietly.

"He's got a *gun* Riley." He leaned close to my ear before whispering, "*We can find somewhere else.*"

At that moment the door clicked open, and the tall man inside stepped cautiously backwards. He held his pistol at his side and twitched it as he grumbled, "Hurry up, it's cold out there." Zoey barked several times and I pulled on her leash until she was at my side again. He glared at the dog then up at me. I assured him Zoey was safe on her leash.

We stepped inside and closed the door behind us. Zoey cowered behind my legs as I thrust my hand at the man and said with a smile, "Hi, I'm Riley and this is Connor," I said, gesturing behind me.

He hesitated before reaching out and firmly pumped my hand twice. The skin of his palm felt rough and callused but warm. The cuffs of his checkered flannel shirt were folded up twice, exposing his tanned and thick wrist. After he let go of my hand he offered it to Connor, who shook it just as swiftly.

"Yeah, hi...I'm Fin." He stood awkwardly in front of us and slowly tucked his gun inside the waistband of his jeans. "Well, shit. I guess it was only a matter of time before someone else found this place."

He took a deep breath before he led us through the entryway into a larger room that had a long counter on one side, and several plush arm chairs on the other. Stacks of paperwork were neatly displayed on the nearest side of the counter. A register and a computer took up the far end. The walls were covered with a deep earthy green paint and unfinished oak planks. The lobby was rustic but the designer had obviously taken great measures to give the open space a modern flare as well.

Connor and I stood in the center of the room and looked around while Fin watched us carefully. He was at least one foot taller than Connor and at least five years our senior, with a solid set of shoulders and bulky arms that he held rigidly at his sides. His full head of straw-colored hair was cut short on the sides and combed forward in the front, swirling in small spikes just above his forehead. His unshaven face was peppered with dark stubble; a week's worth of growth, I guessed. And his eyes had a glassy look to them. I doubted he was sober, and that made me nervous.

"So, is anyone else here?" Connor asked Fin.

"No. Why?" Fin made no attempt to hide the distrust from his voice.

Connor raised his hands up in a mocked defensive posture and smiled at Fin casually. "Just checking. We weren't sure if we'd find anyone here, is all." He moved closer to me.

Fin met my eyes when he spoke, "I wasn't exactly expecting you, either." His gaze bore into me so fiercely that I had to look away. "I'm staying down at one of the cabins. I came up here to get something before you showed up. I usually stay away from this building as much as I can." He was still looking at me and folded his arms tightly across his chest. I felt my face warm as Fin's eyes flicked downwards, taking me in from bottom, to top.

"Cabins?" Connor asked him.

"Have you ever been here before?" Fin turned to look at Connor, annoyed.

When we told him no, he shrugged and walked away from us, leaving us alone. He went back the way we had come in, and we heard him call out to follow him. We found him standing at the open door, his hand on the knob, glaring at us.

"Well, there are plenty of rooms upstairs but they ain't exactly empty. And you sure as hell won't be crashing at my place tonight." He glowered at us as he began pulling on a large overcoat that was hanging on the wall. I didn't know what it was he was telling us to do, and my heart sank at the thought that we might have to leave.

I nodded at him and said curtly, "I understand, we'll go."

Fin froze with one arm in his coat, the other hovering in mid-air and then he laughed. I was so startled by the change in his demeanor that I backed into Connor.

"Lady, I'm not kicking you out, but I take it you understand why I don't want a pair of strangers who show up at the butt-crack of dawn wanting to bunk up in the room next to mine?" He smiled at me with a bright-white toothy grin and walked out the door, urging us to hurry out so he could close it behind us. Connor shrugged at me and we moved onto the cold patio area with the dog, not sure where Fin intended on taking us.

We followed him down the dirt pathway that curled around the grounds and listened as he pointed out each building and what its purpose was. The first floor of the main building consisted of the lobby, which we had already seen, the laundry room, main kitchen and pantry, a bathroom, and an over-sized closet that Fin said served as a first aid room, and an office. Upstairs had several cozy rooms.

When Connor asked why Fin wasn't staying in the main building he laughed and said, "You'll see."

After we passed the detached recreation building, the pavilion, and the sauna, Fin led us down a winding pathway surrounded by neatly trimmed foliage and trees. We were nearing the dark shape behind the trees we had seen from the back patio of the main building when the small path split into a fork. To the left was a tall wooden sign posted near the path that said *CABINS 1-7* and to the right was a sign that said *SUITES 8-15.*

When we turned left I asked Fin where he was staying. "I'm at Cabin Three. It's right by the dock." He turned around and casually gestured in my direction. "How long are you planning on staying?"

"Oh. I don't know." I paused to look at Connor who was walking next to me, staring straight ahead of him. He seemed uncomfortable and hadn't said a word since we left the main building. "Is anyone else here?" I asked Fin.

"Nope," he looked around at the trees while he spoke. "You two are the first I've seen since I came up here a few weeks ago."

"Are you from San Diego?" I asked him.

"Yeah. My brother worked up here last year. It's probably one of the few places in the area that has working power, water, and a fully stocked pantry. I thought this would be a good place to hide out for a while."

"We brought our own things, so we should be good for a bit." Connor seemed irritated. I wasn't sure if he would be able to see my dour expression from the corner of his eyesight but I glared at his profile anyway.

Fin shrugged and we kept walking on in silence until the pathway opened up before a curvy row of tall cabins. The structures were identical, each with two stories and a sharply pointed roof, covered in what I first thought were skylights. Fin explained the checkered rectangles of glass were solar panels. The pathway widened and became a wooden walkway that continued down toward a long pier where the unfrozen parts of Laguna Lake glinted in the background.

Fin pointed at the cabin nearest to the dock. "That one's mine." He turned to face us and gestured at the curvy row of cabins behind his. "They all face the lake, which is nice. And they have everything you need...bedrooms, kitchens, bathrooms." He trailed off and looked at us. "Pick whichever one you want, that's what I did." He stuffed his hands in his coat pockets and lifted his shoulders.

"Are they locked?" I asked him.

"No, I walked through all of them when I first got here. Just to make sure no one was inside." He started moving away from us, to his cabin. "I guess I'll let you get settled. You can drive your truck around and park in the dirt lot back there, but you'll still have to carry your stuff down the path."

"Thanks," I said to him.

"Sure." He nodded at Connor, and left us shivering on the open path. I waved at Fin and watched as he went inside his cabin and shut the door. The breeze coming off the lake made my teeth chatter. I tugged my coat collar up close to my ears and tried not to lick my chapped lips. The first thing I intended on unpacking was my Burt's Bees chap-stick.

Connor sighed heavily and pointed at the empty buildings. "Which one do you want?" he grumbled at me, his accent strong.

Without answering him I started down the narrow pathway by myself, pulling Zoey gently on her leash next to me. Sunlight swept across the path in blotchy patches, stretching my shadow out before us and I heard Connor's footsteps fall in behind me.

***

Connor watched Riley's feet pound into the ground, ahead of him. He paced next to the foot impressions she was leaving on the dirt path, careful not to disturb the tread of her tennis shoes, or the small dog prints left behind by Zoey. He was upset with her, that she insisted on staying here before she knew anything about the place or anything about the scruffy looking drunk who called himself Fin. It was barely 8 o'clock in the morning, and judging from the guy's odor, he had vodka for breakfast. Unless he never went to sleep and the vodka was a late, late night-cap. Both scenarios made sense.

He should have tried harder to convince her to stay at the fire house, at least then they wouldn't be shacking up next door to a crazy looking alcoholic mountain man with a very large handgun that he probably slept and showered with. What did he need a gun for anyway, in the middle of the woods, with no people around? As soon as the thought crossed his mind he realized he would feel safer somehow, having a gun of his own. Problem was he didn't know how to handle a real one.

Once he got Riley settled into a cabin, he'd sit her down and talk to her, find out what her plans were, now that they were here...and obviously not alone. What was she planning on doing now? He sure as hell had no idea. The lodge wasn't very secure, and other than the front gate there was no way to lock the whole place down. If they made it here, he imagined others would find their way up the mountain too. Something told him Fin wouldn't be happy sharing the lodge with a large group of people, unless of course there was another woman or two in the group. Fin only seemed to look at Riley when he spoke, and made no effort to hide his interest in her looks. And she seemed too eager to trust Fin, perhaps because he was the first one to the lodge and offered them a place to stay, however begrudgingly, or maybe it was because she didn't want to be alone with Connor indefinitely.

He glared at the dusty footprints as he followed Riley down the pathway to the last cabin. He was starting to wonder why she would choose the building furthest away, but when she walked up onto the cabin's wrap-around deck, he realized the reason. From this cabin they had an unobstructed view of the south side of the lake, and the sloping mountain side beyond it. He turned to look back up the path where they came from, and knew the scene from each cabin was spectacular, but this one on the end definitely had the best view. He watched her blonde braid sway along her back as she peered inside the cabin windows and he realized that if she wanted to stay here forever, he would do it. To wake up every day in this place with her would almost feel like waking up in heaven. He was sure of it.

* * *

The cold breeze pushed against us as we leaned into the wooden deck railing overlooking the half-frozen lake. Zoey was sniffing in the corner, pawing eagerly at the bottom of a flower pot. Eventually a lizard dashed from underneath the container and vanished in between the floorboards. The dog whimpered and scratched frantically at the wood. After circling the area, she plopped down ungraciously and rested her head over the crack, keeping her eyes open and alert.

I chewed on my lower lip to keep from laughing out loud. Even though Connor was standing quietly a few feet away, I didn't want to talk to him just yet…because I wasn't sure what to say to him. After the dog made it clear she wasn't moving from her lizard-watching spot, I pushed myself away from the railing and followed the deck around to the back door. It was locked, so I continued around the deck and circled back to the front entrance and found the front door wide open.

"Connor?" I called from the doorway. I stepped across the threshold and let my eyes adjust to the slightly darker environment indoors. The sitting room was full of plush chairs that sat at both ends of a large, overstuffed couch. Pillows covered the couch, and rested in the center of each chair, dotting the room with sky blues, sea greens and sunny yellows. A sanded and lacquered log with its flat side up served as a coffee table in the center of the room. Similar-styled end tables flanked the couch, each with a lamp made of turquoise-colored glass and dusty brown over-sized shades.

"Not what a little cabin in the woods usually looks like is it?" Connor asked from the far side of the room. He was standing behind a large counter top that separated the sitting room from the kitchen. I slowly crossed the room and leaned onto the counter, looking in at the kitchen. Windows ran the length of the room, which let in a considerable amount of natural light, as well as a magnificent view of the lake. Inside each frosted-glass cabinet were tidy arrangements of brightly colored mugs, plates and bowls. The large drop-in style sink was wide and deep enough to bathe the dog in, not that I considered it…for very long at least.

"It's straight from a magazine, isn't it?" I smiled as I wandered away from the kitchen and located the small bathroom next to an equally small bedroom, and the sunroom where the backdoor was. I unlocked it and peeked outside to see Zoey still guarding the same crack in the deck. She looked at me and swished her tail from side to side but made no move to get up. I left the door open for her and went back inside. I could hear Connor's footsteps going up the stairs and met him on the second floor landing.

"There're two bedrooms up here, another small one downstairs. Plenty of room for you." He stood still for a moment, with his hands resting on his hips, as if he didn't know what else to say.

"Wait, you aren't staying here?" I blinked at him, confused.

"Well, there are enough cabins for both of us, right? I figured you would want your own." He avoided looking straight at me.

"I don't remember saying that." I shoved my hands into my pockets and stared at him. Finally he met my gaze and smiled weakly.

"You didn't have to."

I studied his face. The deep line between his neatly trimmed brows that seemed to have formed overnight and the rigid set of his jaw made him look tired and older.

"Are you upset with me?" I asked him.

"Why would I be upset with you? I just got the feeling you wanted your own space again." He shuffled his feet.

I sighed and stepped close to him and took my hands out of my pockets. When I reached out to him, he took my hands and softly squeezed them.

"Was I wrong?" he said, just above a whisper.

"Yes, you idiot." I raised my mouth to his and gently kissed him.

"How about you stay here 'til we get tired of each other?" I smiled at him. "You can even have your own room."

He laughed at me and pointed to one of the bedrooms, "That one has a better view of the woods," he paused and turned, pointing to the other bedroom before adding, "...and that one there has an excellent view of the lake."

My smile widened. "I'll take that one then."

"Yeah, I figured." He smiled at me, then his expression hardened and he slipped his arms around me tightly, pulling me to him.

He murmured into my neck, "Riley, I don't know what we are, what *this* is...but I want to be with you, wherever you go." He brushed the hair from my skin and kissed the side of my neck.

When he looked at me, his bright blue eyes were glossy. I chewed on my lower lip before telling him, "I'm happy you're here with me, too. And not because you're the first person I met in the city or because you have ridiculously good looks." I laughed at his mocked impression of shock. "Okay, maybe your looks have a little to do with it." I shrugged at him, an innocent expression on my face, and he broke out into a laugh so loud that I heard it echo downstairs.

It felt good to hold him, and have his arms around me. To hear him laugh made something inside me warm up, almost like a flame trying to ignite. When we kissed, that flame sparked between us, pushing away the darkness that threatened to swallow me. It was a feeling I wasn't ready to lose.

CHAPTER 12

After spending nearly an hour retrieving our things and walking them back to the cabin, I was anxious to find Fin again and get more details about the lodge. When we knocked on his door he opened it with a broad smile on his face and a spatula in his hand.

"Figured you'd find your way back here eventually, so I made some breakfast. Hungry?" He turned and casually walked back into his cabin. Connor and I hesitated awkwardly in the doorway before he called out to us, "Come on in. Hope you like pancakes."

I smiled at Connor, and told Zoey to stay on the porch before following Fin into the kitchen, which appeared to be the only clean room on the first floor. His cabin was decorated in a very similar style to ours, but the place had a more masculine feel, especially with his muddy hiking boots inside the front door and coats and clothing draped across the furniture. Several empty beer bottles littered the dusty table tops too, almost like he intended them to be permanent decorative fixtures.

Fin had stacked three plates and a handful of utensils on the bar counter next to a glass pitcher of orange juice. And as if he was expecting us to arrive just in time for breakfast, a heaping stack of large pancakes sat next to the stove. Fin returned to flipping pancakes as I sat down at the counter opposite him. His flannel shirt was rolled up at the sleeves, exposing the dark blonde hairs that covered his impressive forearms.

"Thanks for breakfast. It's very nice of you," I said to him.

He shrugged and wiped one of his hands on the towel he had draped over his shoulder. "No problem. Haven't cooked for anyone in a while," he said, with a shy grin turning a corner of his mouth upwards. "Help yourself to the juice." He gestured at the full pitcher and Connor poured both of us a cup.

"Oh, there's coffee too." He waved the spatula behind him, at the sink, where a large coffee maker sat with a full pot of fresh brew.

"Thank you," Connor said to him. I could tell he was making a genuine effort to be friendly to Fin, despite his rude behavior earlier in the morning. I beamed at him.

We sipped on our orange juice and watched Fin flip two more pancakes out of the pan before I decided to break the silence. "You're very good at that," I told him with a smile.

"Well, I dated a chef ten years ago. I guess you could say I learned a few things." He set the fluffy tower of food before us, next to a small bottle of syrup shaped like a maple leaf and a plate holding a block of butter. "Dig in."

***

After breakfast, we all sat on Fin's back patio in colorfully painted Adirondack chairs sipping hot mugs of coffee while listening to the subtle sounds of bird life in the trees around us. A thin layer of ice had crusted around the edge of the entire lake during the last storm, making it appear smaller than it was. The wind started as a far-away whistle as it came down the mountains before eventually roaring through the trees like a freight train. Every time I heard the rush of air, I froze, thinking it sounded like an approaching truck. Even with the sun beating down directly above us, the air was chilly enough to make my nose run and my fingers stiff.

I sipped my coffee and listened to Fin as he talked about the lodge grounds and his first few days there. Since he had been there before, he knew where everything was, and so far the only problem had been figuring out where to dump the rotten food he found in the main kitchen--he ended up burning it in the fire pit. As he talked about the different buildings, I remembered the split in the pathway on our way to the cabins and asked him what the Suites were.

"Oh, well it's like a little hotel, one long building with a handful of rooms. There's no kitchen but I think there's a small laundry room. You can't see it from here because it's tucked into the trees more than the cabins are."

"This is definitely better than the main building. The view is amazing," I said to no one in particular as I sipped my coffee.

"Yup." Fin winked at me and then glanced at Connor, who was rubbing the top of Zoey's head.

"So, did you two know each other before everything went to shit?" he asked me.

Connor finally looked up from the dog and waited for me to answer. "No, we met downtown," I said.

"Downtown? Damn, how'd that go?" Fin stretched in his chair and watched me. His eyes darted up and down the length of my body as he drank from his mug.

"It was a mess, actually. There were a few...incidents...so we left." I looked at Connor and smiled. "Connor actually saved me from freezing to death in the bay," I said laughing.

"Really?" Fin looked between me and Connor. "You aren't from around here, are you?" Fin asked him.

"No. Dublin, originally." He sipped his coffee.

"Ireland, huh?" Fin's interest was piqued and when Connor nodded yes, he continued pressing for more information. "Connor your first name, or last?"

I watched as Connor stared at Fin suspiciously before asking, "Why?"

Fin shrugged, and sipped from his mug again before glancing at me. I frowned at him and asked with a hint of confusion, "Why would that matter?"

"I guess it don't matter who any of us were before, right?" he replied simply.

"What do you mean?" I asked. I sat up straight in my chair, staring at Connor.

Irritation turned to a sort of panic when Connor blurted out, "Fin, wait..." but Fin was already talking.

"Oh, come on...like you don't know we're sitting next to a rich movie star," he chuckled.

I blinked dumbly at Fin. The color drained from Connor's face as Fin turned to him and asked incredulously, "She doesn't know who you are? Shit, I'm not the biggest movie buff, but even I recognized you the first time I saw you, man."

I stood up and crossed my arms at my chest and the three of us stared at each other in awkward silence until Fin cleared his throat and tugged on the front of his collar, loosening it from his neck. "Uh, sorry, I guess I'll go inside, leave you two to talk." He left me alone with Connor on the deck.

He stood and walked over to me. "Look, Riley..." he started.

I put my hand up and cut him off. "I don't care who you were before, just who you are now. Is your name even Connor?"

"My name is Kevan O'Connor." He stood five feet from me, clearly waiting for my reaction. When I stared blankly at him he sighed heavily and moved closer to me. "It's been awhile since I could just be myself with anyone, and you didn't recognize me...so I thought, 'what the hell, I could just keep it that way.' Until now, that is." He gestured at the closed back door of the cabin.

"You weren't going to tell me? At all?" I was surprised and a little hurt. I brought my hands to my face and rubbed my closed eyes. "Never mind, it doesn't matter. We haven't exactly disclosed our entire lives to each other."

Connor reached out to my arms, and said, "Riley, I'm sorry. It was just easier to start over, you know?"

When I looked at him, his face was worried. "It's fine. Really," I said as he brushed the bangs from my eyes. "So, what should I call you...Kevan or Connor?"

"Oh." He looked over my shoulder, blinking at the lake before he replied, "I think I'm Connor now." He smiled down at me and kissed the top of my nose.

I closed my eyes and chided myself for not listening to my inner voice that kept telling me before that Connor was familiar. As I followed him back into Fin's cabin, I asked myself for the first time if the safe feeling I had with Connor was because I trusted him completely, or if it was because I had seen him somewhere on screen.

My stomach pitched and rolled as another thought came to mind: Connor's job was to act. He was paid to lie for a living. I watched him play with the dog in the kitchen and asked myself...*Is anything between us real?*

***

We spent most of the day allowing Fin to play tour guide around the complex. He seemed overeager to make us comfortable and I had a feeling it was because he felt he owed Connor one for outing his

132

past. Connor stayed close to me, even holding my hand as we walked down some of the many pathways that snaked through the landscaping. I tried hard to relax and tell myself he was the same person I met on the dock, the same person that carried me back to the hotel, the same person who followed me out of the city, but it was true we didn't really know each other. I hadn't shared much of my past either, and reminding myself of this fact kept me from getting too angry with him.

By the time we had made our way back to the main building I couldn't keep from blurting out my thoughts and I surprised even myself by asking, "What were you in?"

Both men stopped to look at me. "Huh?" Fin asked.

I glanced at Connor and felt my cheeks flush with heat. "What were you in?" I asked again.

"Uh." He looked at Fin nervously, who was laughing.

"That's all you brother, don't look at me," Fin said. A gust of wind tousled the already messy blonde hair on top of Fin's head, and the sunshine lit the hazel of his eyes on fire. I imagined his rugged good looks had broken many hearts in his teens and twenties.

Connor cleared his throat before saying, "Well, do you mean *everything...*? Or just recent stuff?"

"There's a lot?" I chewed on my lip, embarrassed to be caught thinking about Fin's eyes.

Connor laughed, and said nonchalantly, "There's a lot of crap, and then there's a few good things, I guess." I smiled at him, glad that he didn't think less of me for obviously being out of touch with the world *before* it ended.

"Okay, I'll start with some older stuff. Let's see...*Day Runner, Collision, Ned...*?" He looked at me with a smile.

I shook my head no, so he continued to list off movie titles, "What about *Shadytown, Full Force, First Bite...*?" I slowly shook my head again.

Fin rose his hands up in the air and with exaggerated enthusiasm said to me, "I've seen all three of those...how could you not see *Shadytown*?!"

"I don't know, maybe I have. What is it about?" I asked Connor, but Fin took over the answer by spending the next five minutes explaining the plot to a movie I not only hadn't seen, but had never heard of.

"I'm sorry; I'm more of a book person." I watched as Zoey sniffed around the base of a nearby pine tree. She started scratching in the dirt with her front paws, and jumped backwards with surprise when she stepped on a small twig. "I do like Indie movies though," I said as an afterthought.

Connor's eyes lit up and he said, "What about *Hello, Margaret Skye*? That one was filmed in Ireland some years back."

"Yes! I remember it. I saw that a few years ago--it was a beautiful story. Oh my god, were you the kid in it?" I asked with excitement. Images of a young Kevan O'Connor began forming in my mind as I remembered the character he played so well.

"Kid? I was twenty when we filmed that," he laughed.

"You were so young! I mean, not that you're old now...you know what I mean." I stopped talking when Fin laughed and I felt the color rise back into my cheeks.

Fin clapped Connor hard on the back before saying to him, "Hey man, at least now she knows who you are."

***

Connor watched her play on the lawn with the dog, chasing the little Black Lab-spaniel mix around with a stick. Yes, now she knows, he thought to himself. He wondered why he assumed someone like Riley would care about his past and his fame...or the money he used to have. She surprised him by asking only a handful of questions before changing the subject. Fin was more eager to talk to him about his career and annoyingly insisted on calling him the Resident Movie Star every chance he got. Every time the phrase came out of the man's mouth, he resisted the urge to punch him in the nose, but Riley just smiled.

She looked up at where he sat underneath a massive pine tree, and waved at him with a happy expression on her face. He thought it was the best thing about her--that smile. It made him feel sappy and almost like a teenager again. He leaned into the rough trunk of the tree and took in the musky scent of the fallen pine needles around him while Zoey chased Riley down the grassy slope, the dog's tail

134

wagging vigorously from side to side, barking in unison with Riley's
laugh. This was the happiest he had seen her since they met. He
hoped the feeling lasted for both of them while he leaned his head
back and closed his eyes, letting the sounds of her laughter lull him to
sleep.

***

"Look at that," Fin said.

I turned to look behind me and saw Connor leaning against a tree with his eyes closed, a peaceful expression on his face. His arms were crossed against his chest, his lean legs straight out in front of him with one ankle over the other. A shift in the breeze swirled his hair around his forehead and ears, and I caught a glimpse of a younger version of him, a carefree boy asleep under a tree. The visual made me smile.

"I think he's asleep." I turned to look at Fin and he nodded.

"Let him sleep, I want to show you something." He started walking up the path to the main building.

I took one more glance at Connor and lightly slapped my thigh, calling Zoey to me before heading up the path behind Fin. When we caught up to him, I asked him where we were going.

"It's a surprise." He turned around and winked at me. "I'm pretty sure you're going to like it though."

We rounded the pathway and took a smaller trail between the recreation area and the back of the main building.

"It's just around the corner, this way," Fin said as he took the lead on the narrow path. From behind, I noticed how tight his coat was around his broad shoulders, how it didn't seem to fit him just right and as I slowly took in the rest of his frame from my vantage point, I concluded his low-hanging jeans fit his curved backside perfectly. His build was totally different from Connor's...tall, muscular, rough around the edges...and I blushed with embarrassment as I let my thoughts wander towards less innocent thoughts.

The lodge was to our right, partially obscured by a row of citrus trees and carefully shaped rosebushes. Even without their blooms, the neat round shrubs looked beautiful alongside the rest of the landscaped plants, and I reached out and touched almost every bush

135

as we passed by them. When the path rounded a corner, Fin stopped and turned to face me.

"Okay, close your eyes," he said with a smile tugging at the corners of his round mouth.

"What? No." I laughed nervously at him and glanced down the empty path.

"Oh, come on, I'm not gonna try anything funny." He reached out to take my hand after I closed my eyes and gently tugged me down the path several more feet. When we stopped he turned me sideways, and said, "Alrighty...open."

I opened my eyes and blinked through the sunshine at a bronzed, aluminum framed, dark-mirrored structure that was attached to the side of the lodge. It ran the width of the building, coming out at least thirty feet, with the pointed roof rising high above the lodge's first floor. I could see our reflections clearly in the tinted glass panels even though we stood more than twenty feet away.

"It's beautiful! What is it?" I asked with excitement.

I jumped when Fin's warm breath hit the side of my neck as he spoke from behind me, "It's a greenhouse. Fully stocked, solar operated, all the bells and whistles. Wanna go inside?"

I nodded yes, and followed him inside the storm doors. The lower half of the glass house was an intricately designed rock wall, with vented windows just above it that ran the length of the building. Inside, there were several rows of plants, mostly vegetables, at different growing stages. Citrus trees filled the corners and ran down the center aisle. Large baskets of colorful perennial flowers hung from the ceiling in no apparent pattern. Low metal benches for sitting and holding gardening tools sat every few feet, surrounded by ceramic and clay pots of all shapes and sizes.

"This is amazing!" I squealed, and turned around to hug Fin. He awkwardly patted my back. When I let go and moved away from him, he stuck his hands into his coat pockets.

"We can grow everything we need here, Fin!" He grinned as I wandered down each isle, reading the plant names off their labels. "Look... there's green beans, eggplant, zucchini squash, carrots, onions, potatoes...how did they do this? There's a little of everything!" I beamed at Fin, excited at the prospect of not having to live off of canned goods and bagged rice indefinitely.

He pointed into the far corner. "Look over there. I call it a salad garden." An enormous round garden pot took up one entire corner of the greenhouse. It was overflowing with red- and green-leaf lettuce, tall shoots of green onions, and several types of tomatoes...cherry, roma and beefsteak, and several different herbs. I plucked a ripe cherry tomato off its vine and popped it into my mouth.

"I think it's the best tomato I've ever had," I said to him.

"Yeah. I haven't done much in here, but obviously some of this has to be harvested and taken care of if we want to keep it going." He walked around to a short avocado tree and pulled a few of the ripe fruits off their branches. "Grab some of those tomatoes and onions and I'll make the best guacamole you've ever had."

"Deal." I grabbed a nearby basket and loaded it with lettuce, tomatoes and onions. I laughed as Fin filled his coat pockets with food, including a wicked-looking Serrano chili pepper, and a handful of cilantro. "There's a lemon tree over there," he pointed down the center aisle, "grab one for me?"

"I could spend all day in here." I smiled at him after meeting him by the doors. Zoey rushed back outside into the cooler air and dashed down the pathway ahead of us, back where we had come from earlier. "Thanks for showing me this place, Fin. It's pretty exciting. How'd you know I'd love it so much?"

We were walking side-by-side along the pathway, our elbows bumping into each other every few feet. I was sure we looked like we had raided a nearby farmer's market--Fin, with his coat pockets brimming with ripe avocados, and me, protectively holding the overflowing woven basket in front of my stomach.

"I saw you checking out the roses," he said quietly, looking straight ahead of him as we walked.

"What do you mean?" I asked him.

"When you first got here, you were checking out the roses on the back porch...like you were admiring them...or something. And you spend more time looking at the landscaping along the trails than you do at the buildings." He looked at me shyly then, and I noticed the sunshine glinted through the stubble on his chin, making the dark hairs look reddish in color.

"You notice quite a lot." I stopped on the trail and we faced each other silently for a moment.

Fin took a step towards me, and pushed his stomach into the basket I held tightly out in front of me. Before I could react, he leaned down and planted a solid, moist kiss on my mouth. The tiny whiskers of his upper lip tickled and teased my skin as I let my own lips part slightly, inviting the silkiness of his tongue in. I almost dropped the basket that was between us, before I realized what I was doing. I pushed gently on his chest with my hand until our mouths parted, but Fin didn't immediately move away He stood before me, with his hands shoved into the back pockets of his jeans, as if he was afraid of what they might do if he released them.

"I'm sorry...I..." I stammered to find words that wouldn't make me feel like more of an idiot.

"Can I ask you something?" His voice was low, husky, and inviting.

"Sure," I said nervously.

"You and Connor...are you a thing?" He asked the question without blinking. The blues, browns and greens of his eyes reminded me of space pictures of the Earth...and I struggled to focus while looking into them.

"A thing?" I finally looked away from his stare to the open trail ahead of us and listened to the creak of the branches in a nearby pine tree before I answered him. "To be honest, I don't know what you'd call it. But, well, we like each other." I looked back at him and he nodded. "Is that a good enough answer?"

"Yeah, that'll do for now," he said and smiled weakly before backing away and continuing down the trail in front of me. "It figures," he said flatly.

"What?" I said from behind him.

"Shit...it figures the only woman alive in what could probably be the whole fucking state is not only beautiful but already taken." He laughed and turned around to look at me. "It's just my luck, you know?"

Not knowing how to respond, I quietly said the first thing that came to mind, "I'm sorry."

He jerked to a stop and whirled around. "Sorry for what? Being beautiful, or being taken?"

"Um, both...I guess." I stared up at him, wide-eyed, waiting for his response.

He laughed out loud and nudged my arm with his elbow. "Shit, Riley...never apologize for being gorgeous. But if you decide Connor ain't doing it for you anymore, well, you know where to find me." He winked and tipped an imaginary hat on his head.

I laughed softly in response and told him, "Great. I'll keep that in mind, Fin."

We both heard Zoey barking from nearby before she burst out of the foliage and ran up the trail to greet me with her tail wagging and her head hung low. I nudged her side with my knee. "Hi girl, where did you run off to?"

"Riley!" I heard Connor's voice somewhere behind the trees, calling out to me.

"Over here!" I responded calmly.

Fin lifted his shoulders in an exaggerated move. "Your boyfriend's looking for ya."

"Very funny." I rolled my eyes at him and hurried down the trail, meeting Connor near the recreation building.

His expression relaxed when he saw me, but hardened slightly at the sight of Fin walking behind me on the trail. "I must have fallen asleep out there...got worried when I didn't find you at the cabin," he said, just barely out of breath.

"I know. I'm sorry. I figured you needed the nap." I thrust the basket at him. "Look! There's an awesome greenhouse here...Fin just showed it to me. He's going to make us some guacamole." I smiled at him while Fin passed us.

"Guacamole?" Connor repeated.

"Yeah, Mr. Movie Star, you know...mashed avocado with some other stuff...you eat it with chips," Fin teased.

"I know what guacamole is." Connor took a deep breath and as Fin walked away, he flipped him off.

I giggled at him and whispered playfully in his ear before sliding my arm around his waist. "Were you worried about me?"

He adjusted the basket so it was tucked underneath one arm and used his free hand to cup my face gently. "Yes." He kissed me on the mouth, then ran his lips along my jaw and whispered into my ear, "Next time, just wake me up...okay?"

"Okay."

I let him take my hand and together we walked back along the path. Twice I almost blurted about the kiss I shared with Fin, but Connor seemed to be waiting for the perfect opportunity to hate the guy. I didn't want to hurt either of them, so I pushed the thought aside. The rules were different. Connor definitely didn't own me, but the guilt grew as I replayed the kiss in my mind, my fingers entwined with Connor's. I promised myself it wouldn't happen again.

When we were halfway to the cabins, small lights flickered on around us, lighting up the walkways, the signs above the buildings and spotlighting some of the trees. We heard Fin holler from some distance ahead of us.

"The lights are on a timer, it'll be dark in less than an hour. Who's cooking dinner?"

* * *

After the meal and a few beers later, we said our good-nights to Fin. We made the short walk to our cabin quickly with Zoey trotting ahead of us, eager to get out of the cold air and onto the couch for a nap. Fin had allowed her inside his place for a bit but wasn't impressed with her cat-like ability to sleep on furniture armrests. After being banished from the couch, she stood around awkwardly most of the evening, watching us with irritated and impatient stares, eager for us to leave.

"Are you okay here Connor?" I asked him, watching Zoey slowly disappear into the darkness ahead of us.

"Yeah, I guess...you?" He put an arm around my shoulders while we walked.

"I love it here, actually. And Fin isn't that bad. You'll see."

Connor said something inaudible under his breath.

"I mean it, he's trying hard. He doesn't want to be completely alone any more than we do," I said to him.

After a brief silence and only the sounds of our feet crunching the occasional leaf underfoot, Connor finally spoke. "You're right, he's not that bad...and this place seems perfect, for now at least." He paused slightly. "How long do you want to stay here?"

"I guess as long as we can, until it doesn't make sense to stay. I don't really have anywhere else to go, you know? But we obviously need to talk with Fin about what to do if others come here."

He nodded but didn't speak. For him it was different, I was sure all he could think about was his family overseas and what happened to them. The not knowing had to be devastating.

Zoey barked from the cabin porch. All we could see of her was an amber reflection in her eyes, making them look like a pair of fireflies dancing in the distance. The air smelled of wet, mossy pine and the subtle undertone of Fin's chimney smoke.

Once inside the cabin, the three of us split off into different directions. Zoey stretched out on top of the sofa and swiftly fell asleep, and I went upstairs to take a bath while Connor began lighting the fireplaces in an effort to warm the chill from the air.

***

I woke up with a start when my lips dipped below the water level and I breathed in a mouthful of tiny, lavender-scented bubbles. I sat up quickly, spitting the soapy residue from my mouth and wiped my face dry with the folded towel that was draped across the edge of the old fashioned claw tub. The bath had chilled to match the temperature of the room--much cooler than the steaming hot water I had slipped into earlier. The bubbles floated thinly in a handful of groups on top of the water, shrunk down to the size of peas.

After smearing on coconut-scented lotion and wrapping the bath towel around my body, I walked lightly into the bedroom, careful not to slip on the hardwood floors. My bags still sat on the bench at the foot of the bed, one of them open, showing my meager wardrobe. I pulled out a softly faded and over-sized cotton scoop-neck shirt with long sleeves the same dark blue color as my eyes, and tugged it on over my wet hair. After I put a thick pair of socks on, I combed the knots out of my hair and twisted it into a messy bun.

Connor must have come into the room while I was in the bath because the fireplace was roaring, warming the room nicely. The wood popped and sizzled as it burned, catching my gaze and holding it there, transfixing me with the mesmerizing flames that leaped upwards. Oranges and yellows and blues burned and twisted into each

141

other, making soft shadows dance around the room bewitchingly. I had to will myself to look away and blinked the flamed-shaped images from my vision.

I found Connor downstairs, asleep on the couch with Zoey draped across his legs. She opened her eyes and looked up at me, slowly thumping her tail onto the sofa cushion a few times while I tip-toed around them and sat on the edge of the massive coffee table. An open book lay face down on Connor's chest. I leaned forward to read the title off the faded cover and smiled...*To Kill A Mockingbird.*

I took the brightly checkered quilt from the back of the sofa and gently draped it across Connor. "Sshh...stay, Zoey," I whispered to the dog when she huffed softly at me. She put her head back down onto her paw, which was resting on one of Connor's ankles and thumped her tail again onto the cushion. I backed away from them quietly, and wandered through the living room checking the locks on the door out of habit more than necessity, and turning off the few lights Connor had switched on. I ended up in the kitchen and pulled one of the colorful, eclectic-styled mugs down from the cabinet and turned the coffee maker on to heat water for tea.

Other than the soft glow that came from the fireplace, I left the downstairs dark and carried my mug of chamomile up to my room. I left the door cracked open, pulled the covers down on the bed, and climbed beneath the sheets where I scrolled through my mp3 player until I found the song that was on my mind...*Hear You Me* by Jimmy Eat World. After sinking into the plethora of cushy pillows that decorated my bed, I closed my eyes and sipped my hot tea every few seconds until half the mug was drained and the weight of it began to fight against my tired grip. I gave in, finally, and set the cup down on the small wooden bedside table and turned off the lamp. Not bothering to shove off any of the pillows, I pushed my ear buds in deeper and buried myself beneath the folds of sheets and blankets...falling asleep somewhere in between the soulful echo of Adele and the guitar thrumming beat and crooning of Cold War Kids.

***

Connor was on top of the hill again. The grass was swishing gently at his feet, the wet wind swirling about him, plastering dark chunks of hair to his face. The roar of water crashed into the bottom of the cliffs beside him, beating into the rugged rocks again and again...relentlessly. He stood still, his naked feet streaked with mud, breathing the crisp air into his lungs in shallow gulps. The clouds blocked out the sun, like they so often did in Ireland, yet he still squinted to see the small dark spot far below him crouching next to a patch of scurvy grass growing around the rocks. He opened his mouth to call out to the young boy picking the white flowers off the plants and tucking them into the curls of his hair but only hot breath escaped past his lips.

The boy turned to him with a smile and Connor's heart swelled. Little Roan stood up, his messy hair full of tiny white flower petals, and ran awkwardly up the hill with his face full of happiness. Connor knelt down and reached out to him, tears spilling onto his cheeks. But when Roan reached the top of the hill, he didn't run into Connor's waiting arms; he ran right through him. He felt all of Roan, the softness and newness of his little boy skin and the silkiness of his hair. He could smell the soap Roan bathed in and the peppermint candy on his breath. And the joy, the total joy only a child can have...he felt it rush around inside him, passing through him briefly, before leaving...leaving him hollow again.

His hands dropped into the grass before him, and he sat down hard, almost crumpling into the earth. He could hear Roan at his back, laughing. When he turned to look over his shoulder, he felt the warmth of his tears run down his neck and dissolve just above his collarbone. The sun broke through the clouds just then and he saw them walk away. Roan, safe between two people...his small hands held by his mother, and a man he thought he knew. He closed his eyes and listened to the family laugh. Roan squealed with delight and he opened his eyes to see the couple lift Roan's arms up, and swing him between them as they walked.

The man and woman looked up from the child and smiled at each other. He saw the man's face for the first time...his own face. He screamed and the air that forced its way from his lungs ran off with the wind. He had no voice to call out to the happy family that never was. He screamed again and again until the little boy turned and looked right at him, a familiar crooked smile on his face. But Connor recoiled in horror as the boys smile began to change into a grimace

143

and his lips dissolved into his chin. His eye sockets stretched out, exposing red muscle and the milky white cartilage of his nose. Roan's flesh split at the top of his head and his hair fell backwards while the skin of his face slid off and landed at his feet in a bloody heap.

Little white flower petals floated in the breeze around the boy's body and drifted towards the cliffs, carried by Connor's silent screams. He didn't stop screaming until he was ripped from his nightmare back into reality, by a long, wet canine tongue licking his face.

CHAPTER 13

For several days, we explored the lodge inside and out, collecting things we wanted or needed from the storage area, stocking up our woodpiles and setting up 'home' as best we could in the cabin. Connor made a genuine attempt to befriend Fin, which eased everyone's anxiety, including Zoey's. Fin returned the favor by giving Connor some gardening lessons. I spent the majority of my time listening to the long-range radio every day at sundown and laughing at Connor's lack of gardening skills. He did little more than poke around in the dirt with a solitary finger, as if he thought the potting soil itself might attack him.

Other than a severe thunderstorm that flooded the trails, downed two trees on the street side of the property and damaged at least one solar panel on the recreation building roof, all was quiet and mellow around our mountain hideaway. In a week's time I saw one rabbit and a set of deer tracks, which meant something other than the birds and the four of us were alive in the woods. I made Fin promise not to hunt the deer, after he saw the prints and remarked that he could track the creature down and shoot it.

"You can't possibly be serious." He stared at me wide-eyed.

"I'm absolutely serious. If you shoot this deer, I'll shoot *you* myself and toss your murdering ass into the lake." I faced him with my hands on my hips.

"Riley, don't be an idiot. That deer's potential food." He stepped forward with a sour look on his face.

I raised a finger and pointed it at him. "Fin, we have the chance to change the things we've done in the past. This deer is a sign of life. Why kill it? We have plenty of food, and we have no idea how important it could be to this ecosystem. What if it's the last one left in these mountains? Did you think about that?" I glared at him.

Fin rocked back on his heels and sighed heavily. "I think you're crazy," he said to me.

"So, maybe I am." I continued to glare at him.

He crossed his arms at his chest and slowly dragged a heel through one of the small deer tracks in the dirt. He looked up at me and laughed before turning to Connor, "She's serious, ain't she?"

Connor shrugged and leaned against a nearby pine tree, picking at the loose bark.

"Shit," Fin grumbled. "You wouldn't really shoot me, would ya?" He smiled. When I didn't smile back, he pulled his lips into a tight line and nodded curtly. "I believe you just might."

I crossed my arms and stood defiantly before him. "Damn straight."

***

Three days later, we saw the deer for the first time. Connor was in the kitchen brewing coffee for breakfast when he called me over to one of the windows. Behind the cabin, a large fawn stood cautiously at the lake's shoreline, lowering her head for a few seconds at a time to lap up water. She was a golden brown color, dotted with a handful of faded cream-colored spots. The white-tailed deer appeared to be alone and monitored the area very well with her dark brown eyes, ears flicking at all angles to the sounds of the forest.

"She's beautiful!" I said with my face nearly pressed against the window glass.

Connor stood behind me with an arm around my shoulders. "Do you think it knows we're here?"

"It must. We haven't made an effort to be quiet really, and it has to be able to smell our food and the fireplaces," I answered him, still watching the deer take turns drinking and surveying.

"Why would it come so close then? If it knows we are here?" He leaned towards the glass, his face just next to mine.

"Maybe it's lonely," I said sadly. I turned away from the window and walked across the kitchen, to the backdoor. "Will you keep Zoey in here for a second?" I asked Connor before quietly slipping outside.

The deer raised its head quickly at the sound of the door and stood still, watching me walk slowly across the deck. She flicked her tail from side to side and stuck her tongue out of her mouth to lick the side of her nose. I leaned onto the deck railing and smiled at her and for several more seconds she simply stared at me. She bent to drink more water but suddenly turned her head to the forest, both ears forward and alert. She glanced at the cabin once more before darting away in long strides and hops along the shoreline and disappearing into the woods, south of us.

Zoey began barking from inside the cabin and Connor tapped on the window, signaling for me to come back inside. Once I joined them, Zoey rushed at me and wiggled between my legs, whimpering.

"Dog...you scared the deer away!" I said to her, as I rubbed the top of her head.

Connor walked past us over to the front door and peered out one of the windows. "Actually, she was barking in this direction, out front."

"Is Fin outside?" I asked him.

"I don't see him." He turned to look at me and shrugged. "Maybe we should go see if he's up?" he asked.

"Okay." I ushered Zoey to the door and then remembered the coffee sitting in mugs on the kitchen counter.

"Oh, wait...let's not forget this. It's cold out there."

I handed a mug to Connor and we left the cabin, taking the trail back up the tree line to Fin's place. He met us out front before we could knock.

"I thought I heard something," he grumbled and nodded vaguely at the dog.

His face was scruffy, his eyes still heavy from sleep, and he was wearing the same shirt from the day before. His hair was pressed comically to one side, the front strands smashed against his forehead like he had passed out face down. He smelled faintly of stale beer. I crinkled my nose at him.

"Sorry if she woke you. We thought she might be barking at you, but looks like this is your first time seeing the sun today." I smirked playfully at him.

"Hey baby-doll, if you don't like my morning look, you can just kiss my-" He was cut off by Connor, who interrupted him with a loud and exaggerated clearing of his throat.

He leaned ungracefully into the door frame with a thump and glowered at Connor. "Oh my god, dude. It's too early in the morning for your chivalry shit."

"Come on now boys. Play nice. It's a beautiful day." I sipped my coffee and listened to Connor and Fin banter back and forth before my attention changed to Zoey. She was emitting a long, low growl from her throat as she faced the trees. I turned behind me and looked into the intricate maze of trunks, branches and treetops, not seeing anything different. The longer I stared the more I realized how quiet the woods were. Too quiet. I sensed more than heard something that was definitely not organic. Something...mechanical.

"Guys..." I urged, "listen."

They continued talking, having moved on from the friendly buddy-bashing banter, to a more adult dialogue of ball busting, before I cut them off with a sharp hiss. "Sshh!" I ran down the porch steps and stood on the path with Zoey whining anxiously at my feet.

"What's got her panties in a twist?" Fin said to Connor and snatched the coffee mug out of his hand and took a long swig.

Connor came down to meet me on the trail and the three of us stood there, staring into the woods. "What is it?" he asked.

"Something in the trees has her spooked. And I think I heard something." I paused and looked behind me at Fin and then to Connor, before saying a bit louder, "I think I heard a car."

**

It took us less than two minutes to arm ourselves with the pistols Fin kept hidden inside one of his cabin closets. Three more minutes and we were halfway up the trail, jogging quietly, shushing the dog and darting behind trees to keep out of sight. We were listening to the woods, for birds, insects, the rustling of leaves, but we heard nothing.

The week before, we sat down one night after dinner and talked about what our options were if anyone showed up at the lodge. Connor and I had been there long enough at that point to know the ins and outs of every trail, every building and every hiding place. Our plan was simple...if anyone arrived, we would remain out of sight if possible, long enough to assess the strangers and get a feel for their intentions. We would make ourselves visible only if necessary. Our biggest fear was if someone showed up at night, or caught us off guard in the front of the property during the day.

We crept through the trees, avoiding the trail so as not to be seen, and circled around the south-east side of the property, staying low to the ground...moving quickly, but carefully. Thankfully, Zoey had rehearsed this enough times with me to know to stay quiet.

When we could see the lodge building in the distance, we stopped and hid behind a pine tree and the dense underbrush, our eyes scanning the back of the property for any signs of movement. Fin was crouched close next to me, so close that I could smell the faint aroma of his deodorant. It was a masculine essence, clean and crisp and surprisingly not unpleasant. I leaned into him slightly, breathing in the scent and when he shifted, my nose bumped into his shoulder. He turned to look down at me.

"*Sorry*," I whispered.

I felt a burst of warmth heat my cheeks and I rubbed the back of my hand across my nose, pretending to wipe away snot that wasn't there. He opened his mouth to speak but snapped it shut when we all heard the unmistakable sound of a car door slamming shut. Zoey huffed and I shushed her, pulling her down to the grassy ground by the collar.

"*Where?*" Connor whispered above my head at Fin, who was peering around the tree trunk.

When he turned back to face us, he slid down the trunk, causing a cascade of broken tree bark to come crashing down around me, and he whispered back, "*I can't see anyone. But that was definitely a car door, right?*"

We nodded yes, and I crawled around Fin's feet, tugging on Zoey's collar as I pushed her over to Connor.

"*What are you doing?*" he hissed.

I was crawling away from him but with his free hand, he grabbed my foot. I shook him off gently.

"*Let go, I'm just going to look through the bushes,*" I whispered at him forcefully.

With my foot free, I crawled on my hands and knees around the tree and through at least ten feet of brush before I was at an angle where I could see a partial view of the front of the property. Four men were crowded around Connor's truck...checking out the front-end damage, kicking the tires and peering inside the windows. One of them, a tall and lanky young guy with thick bottle glasses tried to open the passenger door and looked irritated when he discovered the handle was locked. Connor hadn't left anything valuable inside the truck, but he must have locked it out of habit.

They were talking to each other but I was still too far away to hear them so I dropped down onto my stomach and began pulling myself along the ground slowly and silently. Behind me I could hear both Fin and Connor hissing my name, but I didn't stop. I pulled myself up against a wide pine tree and brushed the twigs and dirt off my thin coat. I didn't dare look back at Connor and Fin, knowing very well they would be furious at how close I had gotten to the strangers. I could hear the flow of their conversation, but not make out the dialogue so I stayed partially hidden behind the tree and did my best to read their faces.

As the men milled around the truck, a very thin woman with long, dark hair and exotic features sauntered around the vehicle and began talking to one of the men. She was wearing a thick, designer winter coat that barely contained her absurdly large breasts and dark skinny jeans with high-heeled boots that went clear up to her knees. She looked completely out of place in the mountains. She also didn't look happy. The man she was talking to pushed past her and disappeared behind the truck while she continued to lash out verbally at whoever stood closest to her. Her high-pitched voice carried into the trees around me, making me feel exposed…though I was sure the group couldn't see me watching from the brush.

A very portly man wearing a bright red bomber hat raised his voice at the saucy woman and she yelled at him in Spanish then spun on her designer heels, kicking up miniature dust clouds as she walked away. I was sure she swung her hips out further than her body was originally designed to accommodate, completely on purpose, so that those watching her walk away would enjoy the show.

I began slowly backing up, having seen enough to know we were outnumbered and most likely in serious trouble, when the long-haired woman's laugh pierced through the silence, causing a bird nearby to startle into flight. When I looked through the brush again to glare at her, a different man was walking next to her along the path that lead around the building. I stared at the tall man with the bushy brown hair and something clicked.

I knew him.

***

I lost every ounce of common sense in that moment. *It's not possible. How could he be here, alive?* I asked myself. Forgetting completely that I was supposed to stay out of sight, that I had two friends also hiding behind me, I sprang to my feet and frantically screamed out his name.

"*Jacks!*"

I burst through the brush, stumbling on the uneven ground and snagging my coat and jeans on every possible branch. It was like the forest itself wouldn't release me without a fight. I was aware that every set of eyes around Connor's truck were on me, and even though I heard the commotion in the brush behind me and a part of my brain registered Zoey's spastic barking somewhere nearby, all I could coherently think and say was his name.

"*Jacks! Jacks!*" Over and over I yelled it, not certain if it was in my head or actually coming out of my mouth. I screamed it every two steps I took, leaping, awkwardly and clumsily out of the trees like big foot on fire until I hit the dirt road that ran around the lodge.

When my feet left the soft and spongy floor of the forest I skidded to a stop and very nearly lost my balance. My arms flailed wildly at my sides, like a baby bird taking its first flying lesson, and I stumbled forward another step. Dust was floating angrily in the air all around me.

Jacks stood near the striking Hispanic woman with his mouth agape and his eyes wide open in stunned disbelief. I heard Fin yelling my name along with the sounds of him and Connor crashing through the trees and that's when Jacks got it. He realized who I was.

An expression somewhere in between panic and bliss came over his face as he rushed at me, grabbing my waist and spinning me in his arms so fast that my knit hat flew off my head and landed in a manzanita tree behind me. Tears began to flow from my eyes and I felt like a dam inside me was finally breaking. Every emotion I had

151

suppressed...all my fears, the loss, the guilt I felt for surviving...it all rushed to the surface and exploded when he touched me.

Jacks stopped twirling in circles long enough for my feet to touch the ground again. He cupped my face in his soft, warm hands before whispering, "*Riley, I found you.*"

We smiled wildly at each other. Me, with fat tears streaking down my dirt-smeared face, and Jacks with his always twinkling green eyes. Just as Fin came crashing out of the trees behind me, Jacks leaned down and kissed me deeply, hungrily...and I kissed him back.

CHAPTER 14

It seemed years had passed in the first few seconds that I held onto Jacks, and for that brief time, it was as if we were lost in a world of our own. The air stilled around me, and the only sound I could hear was my heart thumping madly in my chest as we clung to each other with relief. The early morning sunlight sparkled on the windows of the lodge behind Jacks, almost making him glow.

"What the *hell* is going on, Riley?" Fin's voice, harsh and cold, boomed from behind me.

I jumped as if shocked. I leaned away from Jacks, who moved his hands from my waist to my arms, and slowly down to my wrists. When I turned away from him, he let go of my right hand and squeezed my left tightly. Connor stared at me and Jacks with wide eyes, silent. I couldn't meet his gaze directly, so I spoke to Fin.

"This is Jackson." I paused and looked over my shoulder at him, while he watched me with an expression of awe on his face. "We knew each other years ago." I smiled at him, before looking back at Fin and Connor, who quickly looked away.

"No shit," Fin said. His voice was flat and completely monotone...he wasn't happy.

Without letting go of my hand, Jacks moved around me, taking the few steps towards both the guarded men and stuck his hand out to Fin first.

"Hi, call me Jacks. She always has." His gaze settled on me again and he winked.

Fin hesitated and narrowed his eyes at me before pumping his hand once. Connor folded his arms at his chest and nodded curtly at Jacks who raised his eyebrows but returned the nod. Zoey pulled against Connor and he let her leash slip from his grip and she wriggled around my feet, staring anxiously at the newcomers, not sure

153

who she should look at first. I patted her head and spoke soothingly to her.

Sappy pine needles had stuck to her belly and I bent to tug them off her dark coat as a man spoke from the gawking group by Connor's truck. My skin crawled as I recognized his slow, teasing voice without turning around.

"Well, isn't this a cute family reunion?" the man mocked.

I closed my eyes tightly and unconsciously squeezed Jacks hand so hard, his knuckles ground together. *Matt.*

***

I heard Connor curse under his breath while Zoey barked loudly as Matt walked the short distance from the truck to the woman who had been with Jacks before I came ungraciously thrashing out of the woods. She blinked slowly at Matt when he approached her and loosely draped an arm around her shoulder as if she had never seen him before. Then she shuddered, and by the time she returned her gaze to Jacks, her expression was icy.

"How...where...?" The words stumbled out of my mouth and Matt raised his hand up to cut me off.

"You mean, how did we find you?" he said with a broad smile on his face, but steel in his eyes. "We followed your notes of course."

Jacks moved his fingers in my hand and for the first time I realized how tightly I was holding on to him. I relaxed and straightened my shoulders.

"That's how you got here...you went to my house?" I looked up at Jacks.

"Of course. I would have found you sooner, but I came from Portland." He smiled down at me. His green eyes twinkling like emeralds.

"Portland? Is that where you were living?"

"Yeah, at least for the last two years or so." He swallowed hard and then leaned down by my ear and whispered, "Riley, I'm so sorry. I'm so sorry about the kids..." He stopped talking abruptly, his voice catching with emotion.

I stared at him, unable to process his words. All I could say back was, "Oh."

154

"Right. Okay, this isn't awkward for the rest of us at all," Matt said with a wave behind him at the small crowd of people gathered on the trail.

"Oh," I said again.

Fin cleared his throat. "So, what can we do for you?"

Matt laughed harshly, "Who are you, the guy in charge of this place, or something?"

With no hesitation, Fin replied, "Yep. What do you want?"

Finally snapping out of my haze, I looked at Connor, who had half-turned towards Fin, an angry expression on his face. I didn't hear what the two men said, but when Fin looked back up, he deliberately looked beyond Matt at the rest of the group.

"If anyone is armed, now's a good time to say so." Fin shifted slightly, widening his stance, making his tall frame even bulkier. I remembered the pistol he had tucked in the back of his waistband. I didn't have to reach behind me to know that my own had fallen out somewhere in the trees. I sighed, cursing myself silently.

"Rambo, we're all armed," Matt said dryly.

"Hey, we don't want any trouble." An average-sized man with perfectly trimmed brown hair stepped out hesitantly, raising his hands up in front of him. Though his voice sounded confidant and calm, his hands were shaking slightly. "We met up in the city, three small groups of us, and Matt knew Jacks was looking for you. So, it made sense to come out this way. To try and find you." He smiled, straining to pull his thin lips into a smile. "And we did."

For the first time, Connor spoke. His voice was flat as he aimed his question in Matt's direction. "I thought you and Mariah were on your way to Vegas."

The Hispanic beauty beneath Matt's arm flinched slightly after he jerked his arm back to his side and strode right towards Connor.

"*What did you say?*" he hissed.

I raised my hands up at Matt as he pushed past me. Fin turned sideways, his right arm reaching to his hip and just as his elbow bent behind him where he kept his gun, Jacks lunged forward, grabbing Matt's shoulders and jerking him downward. Matt hit the ground hard on his back, and gulped in a ragged breath.

155

Jacks spun in the dirt to face Matt and dropped a knee into his chest. "Enough! Matt, enough!" he yelled into Matt's reddened face, an arm across his throat, pinning him down.

"*Get off! Get off me!*" Matt growled hoarsely.

"Stop!" Jacks leaned further into Matt's chest, causing him to wheeze. "You fight with everyone, Matt! You have to *stop.*"

"*Get. Off.*" Matt continued to struggle underneath Jacks.

"I'll get off when you calm the hell down. Remember what happened last time, Matt," he said back.

Both men were breathing heavy, and though Matt had a solid college-boy build, he was no match for Jacks' taller and thicker frame. Matt gave one more feeble kick before stilling.

"Okay, okay. When I get up, you're going to walk away. Understand?" Jacks said in a scolding tone.

When Matt didn't answer, Jacks leaned into him again, "*Understand?*"

Matt finally nodded and slowly Jacks released him. He sprang up to his feet facing Connor and Fin.

"You don't say her name, *you got it?*" He pointed at Connor, hissing through his clenched teeth. "And you stay the hell away from me." He ran his dusty hands over the front of his green jacket and glared at me before stomping away from us, and it wasn't until he disappeared around the front corner of the main building that I realized both my hands were clamped over my mouth. Jacks stood up and casually put an arm around my waist before waving the rest of the group over.

He wiped a thin layer of sweat off of his brow and smiled down at me, pulling me into his thick pullover sweater. I breathed in the familiar, musky scent of cedar soap coming from his body. Memories of the two of us spending days between the sheets and taking long walks along the beach flooded through me. We hadn't spoken in over two years, but standing next to him, the time felt erased. As the six newcomers gathered around us, Connor and Fin silently stood their ground.

"Everyone, this is Riley." He stopped and hugged me close to him before adding with a chuckle, "The first and last girl to break my heart."

156

I gulped down the rock that seemed to have found its way into my throat and laughed nervously, thinking about the wild affair Jacks and I had shared in college. I didn't want to look at anyone so I let my gaze wander upward. In the sky, coasting high above the lodge, just inches from the tree tops, an eagle flew in wide circles. I blinked into the brightness of the new day and watched it arc away from us, flying over the woods, and was reminded of a day I picked my daughter up from kindergarten years before.

Mommy, if you could be any animal in the whole world, what would it be?
Any animal? Wow, that's a tough one. I have a lot of favorites.
Would you be a frog?
No! Too slimy!
Would you be an elephant?
No! How would I scratch my nose?
Mommy, elephants don't have noses, they have trunks!
Oh. Hmm. I guess I would want to be a bird.
A bird! Why?
Because, I can't think of anything more exciting than flying.
But, Mommy...wouldn't you be scared?
No way, birds are made to fly. Plus then, I could follow you wherever you go.

***

Connor and Fin stood together in the far corner, watching the group with wary and untrusting eyes. Connor hadn't spoken to me since I ran out of the woods, and even inside the tighter quarters of the lodge lobby, he refused to look at me. He kept his face void of emotion, his eyes transfixed coolly on the bare wall across the room. He tugged at the loose cuff of his shirt so incessantly, I almost begged him to stop before he unraveled the whole sleeve.

Everyone had followed Jacks into the building except for Matt. We didn't see where he went, but he didn't take a vehicle, which meant he was on foot. I doubted he would get far. While the group milled around the room, flipping through the lodge brochures, chatting quietly, I made my way over to Fin and Connor. It was the first time since I had hugged Jacks that his arm was not around me.

"Fin, can we talk?" I said quietly. My hands were jammed tightly into my pockets, much like his.

"What is there to talk about? We had a plan--you didn't follow it," Fin said, with a harsh edge to his voice. He was looking over my shoulder at the people gathered together behind me. Someone laughed and Connor glanced around the room for the first time.

"Look," I started, irritation creeping into my voice. "This wasn't planned. Someone we know showing up. How was I supposed to react?"

Fin shrugged and leaned against the wood paneling on the wall and stretched his neck to the side until it made a popping sound. I grimaced.

"You must have a lot of questions," I said to Connor. He didn't respond.

I waited until the silence between the three of us threatened to choke the oxygen from the entire room before I spoke again. "Okay, fine. If the two of you want to pout, pout. Act like children. I don't care. But I'm going to invite them to stay."

Fin flashed his hazel eyes angrily at me, but said nothing. I didn't even bother to look at Connor before walking away. I was upset at their reaction to Jacks. It was unfair that someone I knew not only survived, but actually *found* me, and I couldn't celebrate it without pangs of guilt rushing through me.

I turned to the group and cleared my throat. "So, there are rooms here in the main building and some more lodging near the lake. If you were planning on staying for a little while, I mean." I watched the small group look around the room at each other.

The man with the neat brown hair and matching oval-shaped eyes spoke up first. "Hi, my name's Winchester. I'm an accountant...was an accountant." He stepped forward and shook my hand firmly. His skin was soft and uncallused and his nails were trimmed just as neatly as his hair. He seemed too delicate and clean to be surrounded by trees and dirt.

"Hi, I'm Riley." I laughed nervously. "But I guess you already figured that out." I smiled at Winchester, who seemed genuinely happy to have found us. He pointed behind him and gestured for some of the others to step forward. The striking Latina was first.

"I'm Ana," she said, with a strong and syrupy accent. She smiled sweetly as she limply shook my hand. When she turned to walk away, she flipped her long dark hair off her shoulders and I caught her rolling her eyes.

A stocky, middle-aged man with a portly stomach and dark features was next to greet me.

"Hey there, Riley. You can call me Skip." He smiled broadly, showing a set of crooked but white teeth. His full head of fluffy salt-and-pepper hair looked as if it spent most of its life underneath a ball cap. He patted me on the shoulder before pumping my hand vigorously. He reminded me of my best friend's father, and I liked him immediately.

Skip moved aside for a tall and overweight man somewhere in his late twenties. His round face was flushed pink--a color I realized later *never* went away. His light blonde hair was short on the sides and buzzed flat on the top, and he was wearing an over-sized pair of stained camouflage hunting pants with a too-tight forest green t-shirt that lifted at the waist-line, exposing his hairy belly when he moved. His hand was rough and clammy and his breath smelled of cheap beer when he introduced himself with a thick southern accent.

"I'm Bobby."

I smiled at him before he turned and shuffled back to the other side of the room, hitching up his loose pants as he walked. I saw enough to know he wasn't wearing anything under them, and I looked away quickly.

A lanky man with stringy, shoulder-length brown hair and a beak-like nose was leaning on the counter, fingering something small when Skip gestured to him with a wave of his hand.

"That there's Alan."

He straightened his glasses with two fingers and nodded curtly before sizing me up. I crossed my arms around my chest when I caught him staring unabashedly at my breasts, but he made no effort to look away.

Skip put one of his heavy hands across a young girl's shoulders. She was wearing a dark hoodie over her head, obscuring most of her features.

She glanced at me cautiously when Skip said, "And this little lady here is Kris."

I smiled at her and she looked down to the floor. I noticed a linear scar on the left side of her face that ran the length of her jaw. It was pink, obviously still healing, which told me it had happened after the city was ravaged with illness. I did my best not to stare at her as I wondered what, or who, had cut her face.

"Well, this is Connor." I turned and gestured to him, without making eye contact and he said a simple hello to the group. "And this is Fin. He was the first here." I smiled weakly and he sighed heavily before grumbling out a hollow hello.

"I guess you already met Matt," Skip said, behind me.

I looked over my shoulder at him and noticed that the group was watching me carefully. Jacks shifted on his feet and sent a glance Connor's way. I noticed Alan pocket the small item he had been holding before he looked around the room.

"Uh. Yes, we met in the City, downtown." I glanced at Connor before aiming my question at Skip. "Where's Mariah?"

He shrugged. "Don't know a Mariah."

"Matt's sister? You haven't seen her?" I looked around the group and Bobby stared at the ground while he shifted his heavy weight around from foot to foot. His red face all but glowed in the dim and natural light of the lobby. If he knew anything, he wasn't going to say so.

"Matt's had some issues with all of us," Jacks said to me. "He hasn't exactly spilled his life story out but he hasn't said anything about a sister."

When I looked away from Jacks, I glanced at Connor, and he met my gaze for the first time during the entire conversation. Part sadness, part confusion, and part mistrust reflected in his eyes. I wasn't sure if the look was meant for me, or for Mariah.

"Hello! I need a place to put my stuff. I don't want to stand around *here* all day," Ana said impatiently.

Jacks sighed and looked at her. "So, go get a room."

She sent a scathing look in his direction before she turned on her heeled boots, clicking and clacking out of the room and cursing under her breath at us in Spanish.

160

"She seems lovely," I said to no one in particular. Jacks and Skip laughed.

Jacks crossed the room and put his arms around my waist. "Hope you have space for me."

I blinked at him, embarrassed, and slightly annoyed. One thing I could count on was that he always spoke what was on his mind.

"Uh, I'm staying by the lake," I answered, fully aware that Connor and Fin were both staring at my back.

"Sounds romantic." Jacks grinned and hugged me.

Skip clapped Jacks on the back and smiled down at me. "I'm really glad we found you, hon. This boy here was pretty worried about you."

I smiled faintly back at him and felt the heat from Jacks body pass through my clothes and warm my skin. Just that morning, Connor's hug was almost identical. I stood still, my feet stuck to the same spot on the floor, with one man holding me, and another man wanting to and I didn't know what to do. For the first time in weeks, I wanted to be alone again.

***

Connor stood outside on the back porch next to Fin, while the group toured the inside of the lodge. He kept wondering when the shock would pass, the shock of seeing Riley flee from the trees and run into the arms of another man. And that kiss...it took his breath away, and not for good reasons. He hadn't said much of anything. He wasn't sure he could speak, even if he wanted to. He knew she wanted to talk to him, but it was obvious that Jacks wasn't going to leave her side any time soon, and what he wanted to talk to her about couldn't be said in front of the other man.

He kicked at the dirt around the path with one foot, while Zoey paced nervously around them. The dog hadn't sat down all morning. She seemed afraid of everything and everyone. He bent down and rubbed her head and tried to soothe her while she waited for Riley to come outside.

"It's okay girl. It's okay," he said to her while stroking her head and back.

Eventually the dog sat down beside his feet with a heavy sigh and he looked up to see Fin watching him with curiosity.

"What?" he asked.

"Nothing. Was just wondering how long it was going to take before you crack, and lose it," Fin replied.

"What, you read minds now?" Connor asked with a sigh.

"Well, it seems like Riley's past has caught up with her. At least for now." Fin shrugged, peering into the windows of the second floor. "He seems to really care about her," he said, almost as an afterthought.

"Jesus, Fin. Is that supposed to make me feel better?" Connor reached his hands behind his neck and looked up at the sky.

"Damn."

"We're all damned, man. You should know that by now." Fin started walking away from the building, across the lawn, in the direction of the cabins.

"No point standing around here." He plodded through the grass, and kicked a twig out in front of him before adding, "I need a damn drink."

Connor watched Fin march down the slope towards the lower pathways until only the top of his blonde head could be seen through the trees. He knew Fin was right. Jacks did care about Riley, it was obvious. And it would be selfish to fight his way in between them. She had a chance to hold onto a piece of her past everyone else had lost. A connection.

"Damn," he said again, into the crisp breeze. "Come on girl, let's go for a walk." He patted at his leg for the dog to follow him in Fin's direction, but she stayed, sitting at the porch door, her ears up and her head cocked to one side as if asking, 'Where ya going?'

He set off through the grass without her, the thickness of it wetting the toes of his shoes from the moisture trapped among the blades from the night before. He had to get back to the cabin and grab his stuff before Riley figured out he was even there. He wasn't going to share the cabin with another man, and she seemed confused enough at Jacks arrival...putting space between them was the right thing to do. It was easier that way. He walked down the winding trail, listening to the insects in the brush, a bird chirping in a tree above him, and the sounds of his own beating heart.

162

When Connor got to the end of the pathway, Fin was sitting on Riley's cabin steps, his arms hung loosely over his knees, a knowing look on his face.

"What?" Connor asked.

"Thought I'd help you pack," Fin said casually.

Connor stared at him, wondering if he had spoken his thoughts out loud on the walk to the cabin.

"I figure, you'll want your own place now, right? I mean, that's what I would do, if my girl was making out with another dude, unless you're into that kind of kinky stuff." Fin winked.

"Nice, very nice, Fin. I love your tact," Connor grumbled at him, but let Fin inside anyway to help him gather up the few things he had in the cabin.

Fin helped him drop off his bags at the cabin next to his, and urged him next door for a beer. He would unpack later. Morning or not, right now all he wanted was to join Fin for a drink...a strong one. As they sat on Fin's messy couch, he drank the steady flow of alcohol that Fin supplied without argument until his body buzzed and the room jumped when he turned his head.

Fin eyed him carefully and then warned him, "Just to be clear, the only room of the house I care about keeping clean is the kitchen. I don't care if your drunk ass crashes here, but I'll toss you out if you take the last cold beer from the fridge and don't replace it. And you better keep your clothes on. I catch you walking around the place naked--I'll shoot you myself."

CHAPTER 15

After coming out of the main building and finding Fin and Connor gone, Jacks pulled me aside and sat me down next to him on a wooden bench. Zoey stretched out along my feet, her eyes flicking quickly back and forth between Jacks and the other strangers who branched out, some to explore the grounds, the others to get their things from the vehicles out front.

"Riley. Tell me everything. What happened?" he asked. He leaned his head into his hands and began absentmindedly twirling his thick hair between his fingers. Some things never change.

I sat quietly for a moment, watching the trees sway gently and listening to the sounds of people around the lodge. People. Talking, laughing, and whispering. Life.

I turned to look at Jacks with his tanned face and bright eyes. While I watched the others, he had pulled a knit hat over his brown hair, which made the ends curl outward from under the woven fabric. He leaned against the bench, watching me. Waiting for the story.

"What is it you want to know, Jacks?" I asked.

He blinked at me, surprised. "Everything. What happened at home? What happened in the city? How you got here." He stared at me, waiting. His arm rested behind my shoulders on the bench, and he reached out to twirl the ends of my hair.

"How'd you find us, Jacks?" I shifted in my seat.

"What do you mean? You told us where you were going. Remember?"

"No. I didn't. I mean I didn't say we were *here*." I looked past him, at the lodge.

"Oh. Well, we drove down every driveway and road near that fire station. Figured you would have to be close. Didn't make sense to sit

165

there and wait for night-fall. Took some time to find you, but it was worth it." He smiled and tugged gently on a section of my hair.

I watched a leaf lift off the ground, and then roll into the grass, pushed by the force of the breeze. I pulled my hair from his grasp, tossing it onto my back, away from his curious finger tips.

I sighed, "Jacks, I haven't seen you in years. I can't just sit here with you and talk about my dead children."

"Right. We used to be able to do this. Talk about anything," he said, after a heavy pause.

"You're kidding, right? You walked out of my life. Then *this* and you show up here." I stood up and raked my hands down my face. "I just can't believe this is happening--any of it."

He pushed off the bench and faced me. "I walked out because you broke my heart." His eyes bore into mine so fiercely I was afraid to blink. "I never stopped loving you, but you didn't choose *me*, remember? You chose that cheating bastard, John, and look how that turned out."

I glared at him and felt my fingers twitch as my brain fought against my will to slap him across the face as hard as I could, even though he was right.

"Marrying John might have been a mistake, but I would never change that. He gave me Shannon and Dean. I'll never feel guilty about marrying him." I stared viciously at Jacks, challenging him to say anything degrading about my dead ex-husband.

He nodded and sighed heavily, studying the tops of his boots. "I'm sorry."

"You should be," I snapped.

After an awkward pause, I was surprised when Jacks leaned forward and hugged me tightly. I tried not to inhale his familiar smell, but I let myself burry my face into his chest for just a moment before he gently pulled away.

"We shouldn't be doing this, Riley. All these people...they lost everything too and now we only have each other." His words stung.

"I know that." I sat down again, exhausted, the fight gone from my entire being.

"How about we start over?" he said, gently as he took the seat next to me again.

"Fine." I took a deep breath. "So...why Portland? Work, fun or a girl?"

"A girl, of course. Some work, maybe a little fun." We laughed together.

"You never could be alone, could you?" I nudged his arm.

"Yep, you know me so well." He grinned.

We sat on the weathered bench together, close and yet far away at the same time. I thought it would feel better finding someone else, someone who knew me. In the first few moments of seeing Jacks I was deliriously happy but after the shock of his arrival wore off, it seemed that even the end of the world couldn't erase our complicated past.

"I was with them when they died. I left, and everywhere, everyone was dead." I started my condensed story. "Connor found us in the city. He helped me and I guess you could say we've been together since." I exhaled sharply.

"Connor. The dark, brooding one." He sat back and folded his arms over his chest. "When you say 'together' what do you mean?"

I didn't answer him, just looked at him and tilted my head to the side.

"Ah. So, *that* kind of 'together'."

"To be honest, it's a bit confusing." I rubbed my hands on my jeans. "And I can't believe I'm talking to *you* about this."

"I'm surprised. He's not really your type." He stretched his legs out straight in front of him, digging his heels into the dirt.

"But the other one, the tall guy...who looks like he was born in a nest at the top of one of these pine trees...Fin, is that his name? He seems your type." Jacks cocked his head to the side and laughed at my shocked expression.

If only he knew about the kiss I shared with Fin. I looked away before he read my mind, something Jacks had always been too good at.

"So, for you and me...does this mean no more kissing?" He playfully kicked one of my feet.

"Jacks don't get me wrong. I'm really happy to see you. But I can't pretend the last several years didn't happen. And I can't pretend the last few months didn't happen with Connor."

"I think I understand," he leaned in close and slowly, softly kissed my cheek, "But *you* understand something. When I found that note on your door, I knew for sure that all the hell I went through to get here became worth it. I couldn't lose you like that. Riley, I'm never leaving you again."

***

I left Jacks with Skip to unload the vehicles after I had given them all a rudimentary tour of the property, but I didn't show anyone the greenhouse. For some reason I wanted to keep that a secret until someone stumbled upon it on their own.

I walked with Zoey down the cabin trail, hoping to find Connor and Fin. The energy was different in the forest. The trees moved and swayed and creaked the same as they did before. I could hear the birds chirping, and a random twig snap in the distance, but the bird calls and shrieks were louder, almost competing with the sounds of the new people. I wanted to apologize to the birds, to tell them it was my fault this new, clamorous group had arrived, but all I did was walk quietly down the trail. Even the dog seemed subdued and a little tired.

I knew as I neared Fin's cabin that both the men were inside, since I could hear their conversation through the open front door. My feet crunched along the dirt and tiny rocks until I stepped onto Fin's wooden deck. Zoey's nails clicked to a stop just before the door, she already knew she wasn't allowed inside Fin's place, so she sat down against the wall and looked up at me curiously before closing her eyes for a nap.

Their voices had stilled when I stepped onto the porch but I announced my arrival anyway. "Hello?" I popped my head into the main room, and waited for my eyes to adjust to the darker space.

"She remembers we exist after all," Fin's animated voice said, from the far corner.

I stepped into the room. They had moved the smaller chairs that had been near the couch to the other side of the cabin, so that they were facing the windows that overlooked the pier. And the trail.

"Ah, so you saw me coming." I smiled at them. Connor lifted his hand up to his face quickly, and then slammed it down hard on his thigh. Something in his grip glinted in the sunlight.

"Are you...drinking?" I asked as I moved closer.

Fin waved a bottle at me, half-full of an amber-colored liquid. "Course we are. What else is there to do?" He chuckled and Connor snorted.

"You're doing shots...before lunch?" I was standing between their chairs when Connor raised his hand out to Fin, who eagerly filled his shot glass, before taking a swig directly from the bottle. Connor laughed and pointed at Fin.

"So, who's going to take care of you boys when you fall on your faces, drunk?" I put my hands on my hips and acted annoyed with them. Truth was, I was happy to see them bonding, even if it was most likely because they were upset with me.

"Oh, no. We've got that covered, baby." Fin winked at me. Connor snorted again.

"Really?" I cocked an eyebrow at him, and crossed my arms at my chest. "Do tell," I said, sweetly.

"We're gonna take care of each other. Cuz Connor's my next-door neighbor now." Fin slapped Connor's arm, and took another long swig from the half-empty bottle.

"Yup," Connor laughed, downing his shot. "Another! Keep them coming, brother."

"What do you mean, neighbor?" I asked, but both men ignored me.

I sighed, no longer pretending to be upset with them. "You know what, fine. Drink yourselves into a coma, I don't care." I stomped out the front door so fast that I startled Zoey awake.

I heard Fin chuckle after Connor said, "Coma sounds nice, don't ya think?"

Not sure where else to go at that moment, I walked back to my cabin and plopped down onto the sofa and leaned into the pillows. I was too edgy to sit still, so I went into the kitchen and began peeling an orange. Halfway through the task, I slammed it down onto the counter, ignoring the gooey puddle that oozed from the smashed fruit. I went up the stairs, taking two at a time. After I looked down the hall, I saw Connor's door standing ajar, and peered in to see the bed neatly made. As I slowly crossed the threshold into the room I realized all of his things were gone. He wasn't joking, he had moved out.

The bed sagged around me as I sat on the edge of the mattress and looked out the window at the pine trees that filled the entire view. While I stared absentmindedly into the forest, a shadow of some kind seemed out of place. I focused on the dark shape standing a few yards inside the tree line. It looked like a person. The hairs on the back of my neck stood on end, and my arms broke out in goose bumps. I blinked slowly, certain that when I opened my eyes, the figure would be gone, but it was still there several seconds later. I moved off the bed and approached the window carefully, not breaking my gaze from the person in the trees. With my nose almost touching the glass, and the lacy curtains tickling my cheeks, the figure took several small steps forward into a patch of sunlight that had filtered through the tree tops.

Matt stood alone in the low brush and looked up at the second floor of the cabin, his hands casually stuffed into his coat pockets, a baseball cap turned backwards on top of his head...and smiled at me.

***

By the time I flung open the front door and sprinted off the porch steps, he was long gone. I walked back inside and closed up the front door, locking it on purpose for the first time since arriving. Zoey sensed my anxiety and ran around me in circles as I rushed back up the stairs to grab my coat, before I bolted out the front door again, jogging up the trail towards the main lodge. There was no point in telling Fin or Connor that Matt was watching me. I doubted they could even walk in a straight line at that point.

I hiked up the trail so fast that a small sheen of sweat had broken out on my forehead. I stripped my coat off, and tossed it over my shoulder as I walked. The forest around me was still and quiet, but I could hear the sounds of people up ahead. Sure enough, when I hit the fork in the trail I stumbled into Skip.

"Hey there, Riley," he said, with a big smile crinkling the deep wrinkles around his eyes into little rainbow shapes.

I panted a hello and moved my coat from one shoulder to the other. "Sorry, but have you seen Matt come through here?" I asked him, slightly out of breath.

"Matt? I haven't seen him since he took off this morning. Why, is everything okay?" He looked at me warily and his smile faded into a frown.

"Oh yes, of course. I just thought I saw him by the cabins. I'm sure I'll find him with the others." I tried to smile up at him.

"Okay." He looked up and down the trail before asking, "How about I come with you?" He smiled at me while we followed the pathway back up to the main building. "I was just checking out the suites. This is a pretty great place."

I nodded in agreement. "It's sort of perfect. I hope we can keep it that way." I looked up at his face, and the wrinkles around his eyes deepened into trenches when he grinned.

"I hope so too," he said.

We talked along the path and Skip told me how he ran into Jacks at a gas station on the outskirts of the northern part of the county. Kris, the young and quiet girl, and Winchester, the neat accountant, were both with him.

"How did you meet up with the others?" I asked.

"Well, we went back and forth in the City for a while, following your messages." He paused to bend over and re-tie his shoe before continuing. "And we stumbled upon Matt and the others at the hotel."

"I'm sorry. For sending you all over like that. It made sense at the time, leaving messages. But I guess it wasn't the best way to go about it." I waited for him to pull his sock up and readjust his pant leg before we started walking again.

"Nonsense. Don't apologize. It's not like any of us had anything better to do. Plus, it had a happy ending, after all, right?" His hiking shoes were worn and dirty, broken in. But his clothing all seemed new which wasn't surprising...most of us had raided a store or two in the last few months.

"So, what did you do before...well, before this?" I asked him, to change the subject.

"Me, I was a coach. High school weight training, and a little football." He stopped abruptly and threw an invisible football through the air, making me laugh. I had almost forgotten why I was walking back to the lodge until I saw the buildings come into view.

"Thanks for walking with us." I gestured down at Zoey, who was wagging her tail at Skip. "She likes you," I said, with a laugh when he patted his chest and Zoey pawed at him with her front feet.

"Ah, I miss my dog," he said sadly. "Roger passed just before my wife and daughter." He paused before looking at me fondly. "She was about your age I'd guess...you know, you remind me of her a bit." A far-away look spread across his face.

"I'm sorry." I hung my head low, suddenly feeling guilty for having Zoey, and finding someone like Connor and then getting Jacks back in my life.

"You're a lucky girl, Riley. Don't forget that." He flashed a genuine smile at me, before patting my shoulder and walking off towards the lodge patio.

I watched Skip's back as he walked away. I sure didn't feel lucky and I was starting to wonder if I was cursed...maybe we all were.

CHAPTER 16

I found Jacks in the hotel lobby speaking with Skip. Kris was sitting in a nearby chair, a small backpack between her feet. She still had the hood of her dark sweatshirt pulled up over her head and she looked tired and a little nervous. Winchester came in the front door, rolling a large black Coach suitcase out behind him. He nodded to me as he passed through the room and took the stairs to the second floor. I could hear each thump of the suitcase as the heavy bag hit step after step.

"Winchester is staying up here?" I asked Jacks.

"Nope. Ana."

I was beyond thrilled when he went on to tell me that Ana had announced the cabins were too far of a walk for her and that she would be taking one of the large hotel-style rooms in the main building. This was great news for me since I was pretty certain we had nothing in common and I didn't relish the idea of having her as a neighbor.

"Bobby said he's staying up here too, and since Alan follows him and Matt everywhere, I'm guessing he'll be somewhere close." Skip said.

"What about you?" I asked him.

"Me, if it's okay with you, I'd love to take a room in one of those cabins."

"Of course! There's plenty of room down there...and each cabin has three bedrooms." I smiled at him, and he seemed to relax a bit.

"Kris," Jacks turned to face the teenager, "Where do you want to stay?"

She shrugged her shoulders just as Ana came in from the front with a set of more Coach travel bags in her arms and pushed past us to

173

the stairway. I doubt she was entirely out of earshot before Kris spoke for the first time.

"Not here." She said sarcastically.

"Hon, you're welcome to bunk with me, but I warn ya, I snore." Skip laughed.

"Yeah, I know." She retorted.

"Which is why I'll stay with Jacks." Winchester said with a soft laugh as he walked into the room.

"Well, Kris, you can stay with me and Zoey if you want. Seems like I have an extra room available now." I grinned at her.

She surprised me by smiling faintly back and saying, "Okay, sure."

"Well, that's settled then. Now everyone has a place." I smiled at the small group. "Who needs help with their stuff?"

Winchester pointed upstairs. "She's the only one that has an actual set of suitcases." We laughed.

"I'll show you the way, if you're ready?" I started walking through the lobby as Jacks snuck up behind me.

He whispered over my shoulder into my ear, "Just remember, I'll be right next door...in case you need me."

I didn't say anything, just nodded and opened the back door. I stood aside while everyone filed out onto the porch. Zoey ran into the grass and rubbed her snout along the ground. Kris laughed and tossed a thick twig across the lawn for the dog to chase. It seemed Kris could smile after-all.

***

I avoided Fin's cabin, even though the front door was still open and the sounds of drunken laughter could be heard from far up the trail. Zoey ran ahead of us down the path, excited to have people around her again. Skip took a cabin right smack in the middle, number four, and we waved at him as he retreated inside to unpack his things. Jacks was true to his word, and claimed cabin number six, right next door to me. Kris and I hovered at the door for a moment while Jacks and Winchester walked through the lower half of the cabin. The interior wasn't exactly the same as ours but the same pieces of furniture were inside, only arranged in a slightly different

174

fashion, opening up the living area more, and filling up the walls with seating and tables. The kitchen had the same glass cabinets but I could see that the colors of the dishes were more muted...full of greys, slate blues and darker greens. For the first time, I realized each cabin had a slightly different color scheme. The sofa pillows were similar to the dishes with the exception of a few bright orange and yellow patterns.

I told the two men that I'd be next door, getting Kris settled in, but that they could come over when they finished exploring their cabin. After Kris quietly followed me next-door, I caught her watching me as I closed the door and peered out the window, and she asked why it had been locked.

"Oh, force of habit, I guess." I smiled at her, not wanting to explain that I had seen Matt watching me from the woods earlier that morning.

She stood awkwardly in the living room, so I walked into the kitchen and pulled out some snacks and glasses for water. After I had neatly displayed everything on the counter in colorful bowls she wandered over and sat on a stool. She seemed tiny, lost in herself, as she picked at the nuts and granola and cut pieces of fruit while she sipped her water slowly.

We ate in silence for a bit, until I told her about the deer. She perked up, and said she might go for a walk later, and try and spot it herself, and I warned her to stay off the lake, since the ice wasn't solid enough to walk across it. Fifteen minutes of small talk later we heard Jacks knock on the front door. Zoey barked at him, but was already wagging her tail before I had a chance to open the door.

Winchester and Skip were standing on the front porch steps, looking at the view, talking about the weather. Jacks smiled and leaned seductively against the door frame, and said in an exaggerated western movie accent, "Howdy, neighbor."

"Howdy." I said back to him, with a chuckle. He always knew how to make others laugh. It was one of the things I used to love about him.

"Come on in. Want a snack?" I asked the men.

They huddled around the kitchen island and I sat on the counter by the sink, my glass in my hand and smiled at the banter back and forth between the men, with the occasional quip from Kris. The group had obviously gotten close over the last several weeks, though it seemed Kris was considerably more guarded than the rest of them.

"Hey kiddo, why don't you take your sweatshirt off, it's not going to rain in the kitchen." Skip said to Kris.

She sighed, and slowly began unzipping her hoodie, and after she pushed it off her head I could see her thick, mousy brown hair, cut just above her shoulders, and another long, pink scar on her neck. I chewed on my lip, trying not to stare at the injuries. She slumped over a bowl of green olives and began slurping the pimentos out, one by one, never looking up at me. I glanced at Jacks, who shrugged his shoulders and tossed a handful of granola into his mouth.

The mood had darkened a bit so I brought up dinner. "What do you say we eat at the Rec building with the group tonight? They have grills, and an entertainment system."

Winchester said, "Sure".

Jacks nodded yes, while still chewing his food.

"I think that sounds like a great idea, Riley." A familiar voice said calmly from the front door.

Zoey barked, jumped off the couch and trotted into the kitchen. She sat down at my feet and did one of her fake sneezes.

I stared at Matt coolly, before forcing a smile. "Hello Matt. Where did you disappear off to?" I asked as casually as I could manage.

Winchester turned on his stool, with a bowl of pretzels in his hand, holding it out to Matt. "Hungry?" He asked him.

I glared at the back of Winchester's head, and made no offer to get Matt a glass of water as he walked to the kitchen.

"A little bit, actually." Matt looked at me while he spoke. "So, dinner in the Rec room tonight, huh?" He smiled broadly but his dark eyes had an icy edge to them.

"It was just an idea. We'll see what the other's say." I looked down at my feet, where Zoey was sitting, her haunches trembling. I scratched her side with my foot and she looked up at me, her brown eyes anxious, but her tail swished gently on the varnished wood floor, letting me know she was okay.

"I think it's a fantastic idea, what do you guys think?" Matt leaned against the kitchen island, next to Kris, causing her to jump a little.

"I think it's up to our hosts to decide." Skip said, taking a sip of his water glass.

"Our *hosts*?" Matt laughed, and again, Kris jumped. I looked between the two of them, and wondered what had happened that made Kris so afraid of him.

I felt the color rise to my cheeks, but I kept my voice calm. "How about we meet at the Rec room around 4:00. That gives you time to gather up the rest of the group, Matt. I'll go let Connor and Fin know."

"Oh, I'm not sure they'll make it. They sound like they're having a great time down there." He looked over his shoulder, in the direction of Fin's cabin. "Maybe I should head over, join the party." He looked at me again with the same piercing stare and fake smile. His short, brown hair had grown out long enough for the edges to brush against his ears.

I swallowed hard and slid off the counter at the same time Jacks stood from his stool. "If you do, let us know how that goes." Jacks said, without looking up at Matt.

He walked around the island and gave me a quick hug before ushering Skip and Winchester out of the kitchen, and nodding at Matt to follow him.

"Come on Matt, let's go find your friends, and get some things together for dinner."

I mouthed a 'thank you' at him while he waited for Matt to stroll onto the front porch ahead of him. He nodded a smile at me and stepped outside, closing the door behind him.

"Matt is such an *asshole*." Kris said flatly.

I blinked at her with surprise - it was the longest sentence she had said to me all day. When she looked up at me, I stared at her with my mouth wide open, and we both burst out laughing.

***

I left Kris in the cabin to shower and change while I trudged over to Fin's place alone. The front door of the cabin was still open but it was eerily quiet inside. I stepped up to the doorway, and slowly leaned my head inside. The smell of alcohol filled the living room and something else...a sugary, burnt smell.

177

I walked inside, stepping over Fin's boots that had been left in front of the couch, and stood in the center of the room, listening to the silence. As I turned towards the staircase to check upstairs, a metallic sound exploded from the kitchen, making me jump.

"Damn it!" Fin's voice boomed.

"Don't move, Fin! Just, stay still!" Connor shouted.

I approached the island barrier of the kitchen carefully and went up on my toes, peering over the unusually messy counter top. Fin was on the ground, on all fours, and Connor was kneeling beside him. They both had their heads tucked inside the cupboard under the sink. Several baking pans were scattered on the ground and two of them appeared to have the remnants of burnt cupcakes inside them still. Flour was everywhere...the counters, the sink, the floor...and all over both men.

Fin slammed the large skillet inside the cupboard again, making me flinch.

"You won't catch it that way, *ye dope!*" Connor yelled again, his Irish accent strong.

I felt a giggle rising up my throat and I clamped a hand over my mouth. Fin wiggled around under the sink some more, and slid the pan over to the wall, banging it up against the wood. Connor jerked his head out and held his left ear.

"Ah, you *bleedin' gimp!*" He hollered. "You trying to make me deaf?!"

I couldn't control my giggles anymore and a choking sound escaped from my lips. I gave up trying to hold it in and leaned onto the counter, laughing out loud while tears began filling my eyes.

Connor tried to turn around and slipped sideways in the flour, spinning on his rear and ending up on his back, one arm holding onto the cupboard door, the other flailing about in the powdery mess on the floor. Fin banged his head on the underside of the sink and came out cursing, and also slid in the flour. Both of them stared at me like I was an alien creature for a minute and I dropped my head down into my arms and howled with laughter.

Half of Fin's face was completely covered with baking flour and Connor's dark hair was white with it. Eventually, Fin cleared his throat and used his long legs to push against the island and leaned against the counters by the open cupboard. "What's so funny?" He said, his voice several octaves higher than usual. When he blinked, white flakes drifted from his eyelashes down his cheeks, like he was crying snow. He wiped at his face casually.

"What, ya never seen a man bake before?" He asked.

The tears from my eyes finally spilled out and ran down my face. "This is baking?" I asked, choking my words out in between bursts of laughter as I waved my hand around the room. "I think the flour has won."

Fin blinked, dusting his cheeks with more of the fine powder. Connor pointed like a little boy at Fin and said, "It's his fault!" I laughed harder.

"You're the one that let it go!" Fin snapped back.

They began to argue back and forth, while I continued to laugh. Connor seemed to be insulting Fin with words I had never heard him use before in a very strong Irish accent. When he called Fin a 'gimp' again Fin's eyes widened and he swung at Connor with a towel.

As Connor struggled to get up from the slick floor, a large brown lizard with dark stripes bolted from the open cupboard and dashed across the room, leaving a zigzag trail in the flour with his feet and tail. I walked around the counter and put my foot down, stopping it from running into the living room. When I bent to look under the lip of the island, the lizard was pressed into the small space between the wood and the floor, having wedged itself into the crack as far as it could.

"Huh. A little alligator lizard caused all this trouble?" I said quietly. The tail was missing - the stump was red and raw. Without moving, I quietly asked Fin for a glass. He crawled across the floor and poked his head out from the other side of the island counter. He pushed a tall glass in my direction.

I smiled, laying the glass near the lizards head, "It's okay little buddy. Let's go outside." I nudged its hind legs in the direction of the glass until it scuttled inside. When I stood up, I topped the container off with my palm and squinted at him. "I think it's alright, but it lost its tail."

"It's lucky that's all it lost." Fin grumbled. "Look what it did to my kitchen!"

"You're the gimp that threw an open bag of flour at it!" Connor said with a chuckle.

I looked at Fin, and bit down on my lower lip to keep from giggling again.

"Damn thing ran across the counter, knocking shit over!" He glared at me, and then Connor before continuing with a slight slur. "I burned the damn cupcakes while we ran all over this kitchen trying to catch it."

"Well, you're safe now, boys." I said, before I walked out the front door. I gently slid the lizard out of the glass into the dirt under the porch. It sat still for a moment, and then ran off when I nudged its back leg again.

I returned the glass to the kitchen. "What a mess."

I smiled at Fin, who was using a rag on the counters. Connor was shaking his hair out over the sink, making white clouds dance around his head in a flurry.

"Exactly how much did you drink before deciding to make cupcakes?"

"Not enough." Fin answered.

"Right." I laughed.

Connor took the broom and started sweeping, stopping every few seconds to pick up a pan or utensil. I sat on a stool and rested my elbows on the counter to watch.

"So, did your friend get boring already?" Fin asked.

"Now that you mention it, I did have a reason for coming over." I paused to push the tipped over mixing bowls across the counter to him.

Connor stopped sweeping and leaned into the sink. "Yeah?" He asked. His eyes were glossed over.

"Um. I helped everyone get settled into rooms. So you'll have new neighbors." I paused to gauge their expressions before Fin cut me off.

"Yeah, we know, it was like rush hour out there." He said sarcastically.

"You have new roommates now?" Connor asked me, as he pulled his flour-dusted t-shirt over his head. The curves of his chest beckoned to me and I found my gaze travelling across his upper body and down his navel, following the thin trail of dark, downy hair that led inside his jeans. Fin walked between us and dumped a handful of dishes into the sink, breaking my gaze.

180

"Yeah, I have a new roommate." I cleared my throat, and tried to clear my mind.

I figured he would find out by the end of the day that Jacks wasn't staying with me, but I wasn't going to stop him from making assumptions since he seemed more willing to do that than have a conversation with me.

"Anyway," I struggled to focus on Connor's face, and not his bare chest. "A few of us thought it would be nice to have dinner together later." I stood up, and brushed flour from my hands. "The rec room, at 4:00...if you're up for it." I smiled and walked away, closing the front door behind me.

Once outside, I let the fake smile plastered to my face fade and shoved my hands into my pockets as I walked back to my cabin. My chest felt heavy, despite the deep mountain air I tried to fill my lungs with. It hurt to see Connor drinking and baking with Fin...without me. I knew he was mad, but deciding to move out without discussing it with me first made me...sad. I walked slowly, and pushed my hair out of my face with irritation as the wind twirled it up and around in the air. I kicked at a stone and watched it bounce down the trail, and forced a smile as Zoey rushed after it with abandon.

If only Connor had waited, and let me explain who Jacks was to me before he took off to get drunk. I wanted to tell him what Jacks had meant to me in the *past*. I hoped that no matter how upset Fin and Connor were, they would go up to the main grounds for dinner later.

I kind of missed them.

CHAPTER 17

It felt good to dress up for dinner. Not that I had any dresses. But I showered, blew my hair almost dry and dabbed on a bit of Kris's mascara. After putting on a cute tank top and clean skinny jeans...well, I felt womanly, more feminine. Definitely more presentable then I was to the group first thing that morning.

There were leaves in my hair when I washed it, which meant I had been walking around all day with foliage on my head. And no one thought it pertinent to tell me. I had also skinned a knee and scraped up my right arm, though I didn't remember exactly how, but I guessed it must have been from crawling and running through the woods.

Kris sat on the edge of my bed while she watched me get ready. I smiled at her in the bedroom vanity mirror and she smiled faintly back.

"Is Kris short for something?" I asked while I twisted large sections of my hair.

"Yeah...Kristina. But no one's called me that in years." She picked at the chipped dark polish on her nails. "Did you have kids?" She asked suddenly.

I looked at her in the mirror. "I did." I turned around to study her face. "I can't imagine going through this, at your age. You're very brave, you know." I paused, and sighed heavily, fighting the urge to tear up. She shrugged, and pulled her knees up to her chest.

I smiled again, and turned back towards the mirror. "So, why did you ask?"

"Cuz you have that way of looking at people like mom's do."

I laughed. "Well, that's better than saying you thought I *looked* like a mom."

She smiled again, and absentmindedly traced the scar on her face with a finger. When she caught me watching, she quickly took her hand away and tucked her chin in between her knees.

I got up and sat down on the bed next to her while she looked at her feet nervously. "Kris, I know you just met me, and this has all been hard. On all of us." I paused, choosing my next words carefully. "But, if you ever want to talk, I'm here. Okay?" I put my hand gently on her shoulder and she looked up at me quickly and nodded. "Are you okay, I mean...is everything okay?" I asked her, while I looked at her scars.

"I'll be fine." She smiled weakly. I nodded and stood up and she said almost under her breath, "But thanks."

Not knowing what else to say, I leaned down and hugged her tight before returning to the vanity. I ran my fingers along the edge of the folded picture of the kids that I had tucked up against the base of the mirror, where only someone looking for it would see it. I didn't want to share it, not yet.

When I was finished getting ready, Kris followed me downstairs and we gathered up our coats. I had slipped a thin sweater over my tank, and ran my fingers through the waves in my hair.

"You ready?" I asked Kris. She nodded that she was, and we let Zoey run out the door first. I had her leash tucked into the pocket of my coat, in case we needed it, and as we walked up the trail I glanced casually at Fin and Connor's cabin, but the door was still closed, and unlike earlier in the day, it was quiet.

As our feet made indents in the dirt and crunched softly on the twigs and leaves, Kris suddenly stopped and grabbed at my arm. Zoey turned to face the woods, her ears forward, and her back rigid.

"Look." Kris said, just barely above a whisper.

I squinted into the tree line and didn't see anything out of the ordinary, until one of the trees appeared to move. As I stared harder, a light brown flick of color moved behind another tree and stopped. We took several steps up the trail until we could see the area from a different angle. Standing not more than thirty feet away was a young deer. It was watching us, her large brown eyes open wide and alert, but she didn't appear to be afraid. She flicked her ears several times, and then bent down to forage from the forest floor. Even though the deer we had seen before had been further away, I was sure the one off the trail was the same one.

I smiled as Kris stared at it with fascination. "She's our resident deer. Young, but obviously healthy. This is the closest I've seen her." I said quietly to Kris.

She whispered back, "I've never seen one up close like this before."

We stood on the trail for almost ten minutes until the sound of music floated through the trees from the lodge. The deer flicked her ears forward, and looked at us before dodging into the dense woods. The graceful spring in her step was delicate and deliberate.

"Come on, let's go." I nudged Kris's arm but she didn't move. She kept her eyes on the trees. "Don't worry, she'll be back." I said with a smile.

I slapped my leg and Zoey rushed up to me, and passed us, where she paused at the fork in the trail and barked impatiently. Kris ran ahead and chased the dog around the bend. I laughed softly at the happy smile that filled her face as the dog dashed playfully away from her and bounced around the awkward teen's feet.

As the lawn area opened up, the steady beat of the music drifted down to me. The sounds of Lenny Kravitz spilled through the grass, circled the trees and danced along the soft breeze. I walked up the graveled part of the trail and followed it along to the Rec room pathway. The large bungalow style building was tucked tightly up against the tree line on its north side, and elevated up high enough to see the mountains behind the lake. It was the perfect viewing spot for sunsets.

I took the six steps up two at a time, and as I reached the landing, *It Ain't Over Till It's Over* faded out and Katy Perry's, *E.T.* boomed through the speakers. The beat thudded in my chest and I all but danced into the pavilion. As I passed through the doorway, an arm grabbed me from behind and spun me in a circle. Jacks grinned as he pulled me into him and danced me around the room. He lifted my arms around his neck and swung his hips in sync with mine and trailed a finger along my collar bone when I leaned my head back and laughed. He spun me away from him, and pulled me back in an exaggerated fashion, mouthing the words to the song. It was obvious he had showered - his thick hair was smoothed down, but was making a valiant effort to curl on the ends regardless of the hair product he had slicked it down with. And he smelled lovely...his familiar Cedar smell was replaced with something fresh...I was sure it was an Ocean smell of some sort. When the song ended, he dipped me over his leg and I heard the sounds of hollering from the far side of the room where Skip and Winchester stood with Alan. I let go of Jacks, my cheeks flushed warm from activity and ran my hands down my jeans nervously. As Train's, *Hey Soul Sister* started, I grabbed Jacks' hand and did my best curtsy at our small but enthusiastic crowd.

We laughed our way across the room, and Winchester turned the music volume down so we didn't have to yell at each other to be heard.

"I plugged my iPod in...hope you don't mind?" Jacks asked, slightly out of breath.

I smiled up at him and laughed. "That explains the playlist."

"It's on shuffle, so don't hold me responsible for what comes on next." He said and casually put an arm around my shoulders, squeezing me gently.

Alan, still in his grungy arrival clothes, and Skip moved around the room, pushing open the large windows and raising the canvas curtains up to let in the late afternoon light and fresh breeze. The fireplace had been started and the sofas were turned sideways, slightly facing each other, so anyone sitting in them could not only enjoy the fire, but also the view of the rest of the room.

Skip came up to me with a basket of canned foods. "So, this is what I scrounged up from the kitchen. We've got peas, green beans and carrots. Rice, pasta, tomato sauce...what sounds good to you?"

I clapped him on the shoulder and said, "Come with me, I've got something better."

He shrugged and followed me back outside and I wound him through the trees until we found the pathway that led to the rear of the main building.

"What's back here?" He said, as he carried the empty basket I had dumped onto one of the tables in the Rec room. I could hear the country twang of a guitar coming from behind us as a Keith Urban song started. I smiled, grateful that Jacks still had a wide range of taste in music.

186

"You'll see." I realized that Fin had taken me back here almost the same way, secretive, hoping to save the surprise for the last minute.

As soon as the greenhouse came into view, Skip knew instantly what it was. "Alright!" He said, and picked up his pace on the trail. I smiled when we stepped inside and Skip's eyes widened with delight.

I wandered down the first aisle, touching each plant gingerly. "How about some fresh green beans, a salad and tomatoes for spaghetti sauce?" I looked at Skip who was still staring at the rows of fresh food in disbelief.

"Wow, sounds great to me!" He said.

We picked several handfuls of beans, what seemed like over a pound of tomatoes and filled the rest of the basket with vegetables for the salad. I laid a handful of herbs on the top and Skip happily carried the basket back to the Rec room. By the time we returned, Aerosmith was playing and the men were huddled by the fire, looking out the windows at the view, each with an open beer in their hand.

"Hey! There you are!" Jacks said, and strolled across the room. He peered down at the basket Skip had set on the table and said, "Holy shit. Where'd this come from?"

"We have our own greenhouse." Skip said happily. "I'll take these to the kitchen and start cleaning them."

"Thanks Skip." I smiled at his back and turned to face Jacks. He was wearing jeans and a dark pullover sweatshirt with frayed edges and every time he raised the beer bottle to his mouth I could see the trim of his green t-shirt underneath.

"So, thanks for taking Kris in at your place." He looked at me from over the lip of the bottle before taking another long swallow. "She needs to be around another woman. And Ana doesn't count."

I nodded. "It's nice having her around actually. Where is Ana by the way?"

He shrugged. "Her and Matt disappeared somewhere a while ago." He winked. I felt like puking.

"I should go help Skip." I smiled and left Jacks to go to the small kitchen in the back of the building. The vegetables had all been rinsed and Skip was cutting the ends off of the green beans. We worked side by side cutting veggies, pureeing the tomatoes, chopping herbs and waiting for the water to boil.

As I lightly sautéed the beans, I looked at the open kitchen door to make sure it was empty.

"Skip, what happened to Kris?" I asked it quietly, not wanting the others to hear from the other room.

"Ahh. You mean the cuts?" He paused and then stirred the sauce before turning to face me. "She hasn't told me the story, but Jacks knows it. He found her hiding out in a gas station somewhere in Los Angeles. All I know is that she ran into the wrong people when everything started falling apart. From the way Jacks said it, she barely got away with her life." He turned to face the simmering sauce again.

I looked at the doorway. "Poor kid." I sighed and slid the beans out of the pan into a large bowl, drizzled them with olive oil and sprinkled some coarse sea salt and cracked pepper all over. "I didn't leave my house for a long time. Not until I needed to get water. By then, well...everyone in my part of town was gone." I twirled the ends of a cheesecloth kitchen towel in between my fingers.

"It still doesn't seem real, does it?" Skip's voice was huskier than usual, emotional.

We stood next to each other, staring down at the rolling pasta as it boiled. Skip put a hand on my shoulder and squeezed gently. I looked up at his round and whiskered face, only a few inches from mine and tried to smile.

"It's going to be okay. You have to believe that, Riley."

I nodded, but I didn't say to him how much I disagreed with his statement at the time.

Kris walked into the kitchen with Zoey at her feet. "Do you need any help?" She asked with a hesitant smile on her face.

"Feel like taking the beans and salad out to one of the tables?" I smiled at her.

"Sure." She picked the two large bowls up off the counter and said over her shoulder on her way into the next room, "Oh, your friends just got here."

***

Dinner was full of amazing conversation and even better food...spreading out over an hour to finish. Three large, rectangular tables were lined up next to each other by the kitchen and with all of us sitting together, we filled two of them. Matt and Ana had showed up just as we all sat down to eat. He seemed to avoid looking in my direction either to please Ana or keep from upsetting Jacks, who had taken one of the seats beside me. Connor and Fin sat across from me, visibly drunk but in good spirits, and Kris sat to my right. Skip was on the far end of our table, and the rest of the group took up the table next to us.

When the food was gone, and the dishes were cleared, we stretched out on the couches, some of us with beers, the rest of us with glasses of wine. Most of the group was gathered around Connor, who seemed more than willing in his drunken state to talk about his movie career. Ana sat perched like a vulture on the armrest of the couch next to him, continuously licking her full lips as if waiting for the right time to pounce on him. Matt sat in a lone chair off in the corner, glaring at the group while he took long sips of a dark liquid he had poured into a small tumbler. His hair was mused, and his clothes seemed thrown on, like he didn't care what he looked like…not at all like the Matt I met downtown, who seemed overly vain.

The room smelled strongly of burning wood, and a whisper of Italian food. I cuddled into the cushions of the couch and stared into the fire, listening to the pop of the engulfed logs. The wine swished in my glass as Fin plopped down heavily beside me.

"Whoa." I said to him as I lifted my glass up and away from him.

"Sorry." He laughed and took a sip of beer before resting one of his hands on my thigh, a goofy grin on his face. We stared at each other for a long moment until someone cleared their throat above me. I looked up and Jacks was leaning on the back of the couch, a twinkle in his eye.

"Can I have this dance?" He said, ignoring Fin, who still had his hand on my leg.

"Uh." I said, not sure how to answer. And then I heard the song playing. *Delicate*, by Damien Rice. I *had* to dance, and Jacks knew it. I stood up and set my wine glass down on an end table and let him lead me to the center of the room. He put his arm around me and pulled me in tight, pressing my chest into his ribs. We swayed and slowly turned in circles and half way through the song I realized the room had gone quiet. Jacks buried his mouth into my neck and murmured the words of the song into my hair and I let myself float away with him.

A flash of Ana's bright red top caught the edge of my vision as she swept past, her arms linked with Connor's while he spun her around us. Connor locked eyes with me as he turned around the room, and I could see the want, the desire in his eyes. And the hurt. Suddenly he dipped Ana and she squealed with delight. The song had ended.

The music changed to the soft piano and swinging beat of Michael Bublé's *Feeling Good*. I stepped back from Jacks and he smiled at me. Kris laughed and I looked over to see Skip dragging her clumsily around the dance floor. Matt cut in on Connor and Ana without saying a word, and she leaned her hips into him, grinding along. He said something into her ear and she threw her head back with delight. Jacks leaned into me again but stopped when a hand tapped him on the shoulder.

Fin grinned as he tipped his head at us and said, "Mind if I step in?"

I smiled shyly, and nodded an okay at Jacks, who stepped back hesitantly.

Fin slid into place, one hand in mine, the other lightly around my waist and I followed his lead away from Jacks. When the drums and cymbals started he pulled me into him, and spun me out, twisting our hands effortlessly. When we came back together we were both smiling and laughing. We danced around the others, his hand on my back, the room whirling around us in a colorful blur, my body feeling light and slightly fuzzy from the wine. Fin had me on my toes as he held me against him, swaying to the close of the song. When he dipped me low at the end, the room clapped around us and Fin held my hand up and bent forward, in a bow. Still laughing, I stood awkwardly next to him as we moved away from the dance area as One Republic came on.

I flopped down onto the couch, and Fin handed me my wine glass. After finishing what was left, I said, "That was fun."

He nodded and took my glass, and walked between Ana and Matt, and Kris who seemed excited to be dancing with Connor. I saw him refill my glass from the far side of the room and weave back through the happy dancers to the couch. He returned my glass and I sipped eagerly, while he set the bottle on the fireplace mantle. When he plopped down next to me again, I sat quietly beside him while we watched the others, trying to ignore the heat radiating between our touching thighs and the curve of his side as it fit into mine.

When *Rock That Body* came on, I squealed at the same time as Kris, and jumped up, swinging my hips as I rushed to the center of the room to join her. We danced next to each other, arms in the air, our shoulders and thighs bumping together, alternating between singing and giggling. Ana slid in next to us and dipped to the beat, her hands roaming her body. Someone lifted my glass from my hand and Kris and I jumped in unison, spinning, and belting the words of the song out. At one point, the three of us were holding hands, moving together fluidly and when Ana slid seductively down my back the men broke out into joyous cries.

For two more dance songs, the three of us frolicked, twisted and swayed around each other. When Florence And The Machines drifted out from the speakers, I was grateful for a break, and the men groaned in protest when Ana, Kris and I broke apart for water and eventually collapsed on the couches. Ana sent a saucy smile my way and I laughed at Kris. *Punching In A Dream* by The Naked And Famous was playing as I rested my head on the cushions. For the first time, I considered Ana might not be so bad after-all.

***

Connor couldn't keep his eyes on her without his vision doubling. He stood off to the side of the room, next to Jacks, with his arms limply at his sides, his thumbs tucked into his pockets, watching Fin's fancy foot work glide Riley around the room. Jacks tapped his upper arm and held out a beer, and he took it with a nod. He knew Jacks was just as irritated to see Riley dancing with another man, but it was obvious neither was going to complain about it to the other. So they watched her twirl around the room and return to the couch with Fin. He couldn't handle seeing him brush the hair back from her face or her playfully smack at his arm when he made a joke, so he asked Kris to dance.

When a club song came on and the girls started dancing together it was hard if not inconceivable for each of the men not to stare. He

191

moved slowly away from the girls and jumped when Fin clapped his shoulder. He refused the urge to shrug him off and watched Ana and Riley instead. Ana was sexy, in a sleazy way. There was something too needy about her that turned him off immediately. Kris was still a kid but it was obvious as he glanced at the others, that some of the men, mainly Matt and his friends, didn't look at her like one. Riley though, she was in a world of her own. It was impossible to not want her.

He watched her blonde, wavy hair dance about her shoulders, her long bangs tumbling into her eyes as her hips swayed seductively from side to side, and felt the desire for her more than ever. He leaned into the couch and loosely crossed his arms and stared, unblinking, at the curve of her breasts. His head spun from drinking all day but he didn't take his eyes off her, couldn't. And once, he was sure she met his gaze, and held it...a flirty smile on her face, a twinkle in her dark blue eyes. And then she turned away, and Ana was behind her, sliding down her backside. Most of the guys hollered but he kept his eyes on Riley. Always on Riley.

***

God, I needed water. I wandered over to the tables, but found none, so I followed the wall with my fingers brushing along the wood paneling, mostly to keep myself from appearing tipsy. And I was. The music drowned all sounds around me and filled my ears like a flood. I found the kitchen doorway and slipped inside, not bothering to turn on the light. I would drink from the tap if I had to.

My hands fumbled through the cupboards until I found a small glass. I gripped it carefully and squinted in the dark at the faucet as I pushed it on. Explosions of laughter erupted from the room next door and I smiled, glad that no one missed me yet.

I was concentrating so hard on filling the glass that I didn't hear the soft footsteps close in behind me. I turned the water off and started raising my arm when a hand slid around my waist. The water sloshed down my wrist and I gasped as I spun around. Even in the dark, I could make out the pale glow of Connor's blue eyes. His face was an inch from mine and his hand went down my side, resting firmly on my hip.

"My god, Connor! You scared me!" I chuckled softly. Water trickled from my wrist, down my arm.

The group laughed loudly again and I looked over Connor's shoulder at the open door. He took the glass from my hand and set it down behind me. I smelled the breezy scent of his cologne, mixed with a subtle undertone of Corona. The metal counter top behind me felt cold, even through my jeans, but my skin flushed and heat radiated through me when Connor's left hand darted under my top and grazed my ribs. His palm slid between my shoulder blades and moved beneath my bra strap, slowly sliding forward, back along my ribs to my breast. A shudder ran up my back when his fingers brushed against my nipple, and he kept his hand there, moving gently inside my bra as the other trailed down my abdomen, inside my jeans. I gasped in surprise as his fingers slid inside my cotton underwear and very slowly began to move up and down.

Connor's mouth started on my collarbone, and his tongue hungrily traced the curves of my throat up to my jaw.

"*Riley.*" He whispered passionately beside my ear before nibbling on it.

I bit down on my lower lip to keep a moan from escaping as his hand firmly cupped my breast. He pressed his hips into me as his mouth found mine, and our tongues twisted together furiously. I felt the bulge of his crotch push against me and I silently cursed the belt he wore, restricting easy access. Time seemed to slow to a crawl as his long and slender fingers rhythmically moved faster and faster between my legs, matching the beat of my racing heart.

I gripped his back and arched against him, feeling the muscles in my stomach tighten and my thighs begin to quiver. With a fistful of his shirt in one hand, and my other holding onto his neck, I let the waves of an intense orgasm completely consume me, shaking my insides to the core. Connor crushed his mouth into mine as I moaned his name loudly.

When his hands slid out from under my clothes, he wrapped his arms around my waist and kissed me until I was breathless and I was certain he could hear the knocking of my heart as it wildly banged against my ribcage. Every sense I had was heightened...the sultry, salty smell of his skin and the lemongrass scented cleaner on the counter behind me made the back of my throat tingle. The multi-tonal laughs coming from the next room and the slow and steady drip of the leaky faucet echoed in my ears. The sweet flavor of Connor's mouth made me hungry to taste all of him, and the softness of his wavy hair tickled my skin when he kissed me. Every nerve ending I had was exposed and throbbing deliciously.

He was nibbling softly on my ear again and tugging on a strand of my hair when the kitchen light flickered on. We both jumped but Connor didn't pull away from me. I peered over his shoulder to see Winchester standing in the doorway.

"There you are." He cleared his throat loudly, and shifted on his feet. From across the room I couldn't be sure, but it looked like he was trying hard not to smile.

Without turning around to face him, Connor said, "We'll be right out. Just getting something to drink." He smiled down at me with a mischievous glint in his eye, and trailed a single finger between my cleavage and my midsection lurched in response.

When he pulled away, I went up on my tip-toes and said softly into his ear, "Finish this later?"

"Hell yes." He said loudly.

He kissed me once more lightly on the lips before winking and walking away. I could hear him talking with Winchester in the other room, so I turned around and gripped the edge of the sink, grinning girlishly from ear to ear. After smoothing my clothes and hair back into place, I gulped the glass of water I had gotten from the tap in one large swallow. I splashed cold water on my cheeks to cool the flush I felt radiating through my skin before I refilled the glass, and took it back with me into the main room.

The group was huddled together, with an end table between the two couches, and Skip was arm wrestling Matt. His hand wavered before slamming Matt's down onto the table and the room erupted in cheers. Connor was standing near Winchester, leaning on the side of the couch. I overheard Winchester say that Skip had won 3-0 against Fin, Bobby and Matt. I laughed and looked around the room, and my eyes met Fin's.

He was watching me with curiosity, and glanced sharply at Connor. When his gaze met mine again a knowing look settled into his expression. He slowly blinked at me and quickly looked away. I was sure he couldn't know exactly what took place between Connor and I in the kitchen, but it was obvious he realized something happened. I brought my palm to my hot cheeks to cool them, and hoped that no one else noticed the flush that I was sure covered my entire body.

Matt stood up and shook his arm with a sullen look on his face and Fin said flatly, "Connor should go next."

Connor glanced at him and then flexed his hands. "Nah, I'm good. Feeling a little tired actually." He avoided looking directly at me but I blushed anyway.

I noticed Kris had tucked herself into the corner of one of the couches. Her head rested on a faded forest-green cushion, a droopy look in her eyes. Kris. I had forgotten that she was sleeping in Connor's old room. A laugh threatened to explode from me as I realized the irony of the situation. There I was, sitting there dreaming about the night I could have with Connor, when a teenager would be sleeping in the next room. I thought to myself…how bad would it be if I left the dog in her room, and snuck Connor into the cabin after she fell asleep?

CHAPTER 18

Something insanely bright was glowing behind my eyelids. I squeezed them shut even tighter, to no avail; the creamy yellowish color penetrated through my closed eyes like radioactive honey. I was face down lying on my left cheek, with an arm tucked under my head, another folded in front of me. I opened one eye gingerly and let the wash of sunlight fill my vision while I blinked, momentarily unaware of what I was looking at. As my vision cleared, I saw the round outline of a man's head and in the background the early morning sun glared through an open window.

Unruly dark curls that flipped up at the base of his neck were glistening in the dawn. I blinked again, and shifted my head so that I could get a level view of the man sleeping on his stomach next to me. The sheets were messily pulled up his back, resting in an uneven bunch just below his shoulder blades. His lean arms were raised above him and tucked under his pillow. I could feel the heat of one of his legs pushed up against my knee. As I blinked at him, flashes of the night before flipped through my memory...and I smiled. I closed my eyes and remembered the feel of his hands and mouth as they explored every inch of my body, slowly, seductively...and the hard feel of him inside me as we pushed against each other; we had fit together perfectly.

With my eyes open again, I raised a hand to his face and carefully pushed back a long strand of wavy hair that was partially obscuring my view of his face. His long, dark lashes fluttered softly against his cheeks, but he didn't wake.

Connor sighed in his sleep. I listened to him inhale and exhale deeply before he was silent again. I was afraid to move for fear I'd wake him, so I stayed on my stomach and watched his back rhythmically rise and fall. I tried to match my breathing to his but couldn't. Just watching him, my heart rate beat faster, my stomach tightened and my own breathing quickened.

The room smelled faintly of sex and the fire we had lit the night before, and something else…coffee. I resisted the urge to bolt from the bed and instead turned my head to the side and checked to make sure my bedroom door was still closed. I wasn't sure why Kris would be awake so early, but if she was making coffee I didn't want her bringing it upstairs to share and finding me naked in bed with Connor.

I slid from underneath the covers and slinked across the room to twist the lock on the knob, then crept back into bed. Before I could roll over back onto my stomach, one of his arms slithered across my waist and pulled me in close to him so that we were lying on our sides, facing each other. He was smiling, a happy and boyish grin. *Damn. Early morning Connor after sex was beautiful.*

"Hi." I said quietly and leaned in for a kiss. His moist lips were warm and inviting.

"Hi." He ran one of his hands down my side to my hip. "Did you sleep okay?" He asked, a sparkle lighting his blue eyes ablaze.

I laughed quietly as his fingers trailed aimlessly along my thigh. "I did, though you didn't leave me much time to sleep."

"*Mmmhmm.*" He purred, and scooted closer to me, so that our bodies touched. I could feel the hardness of him against my pelvic bone and my insides quivered in anticipation. His roaming hand moved from the back to the front of my thigh, and followed my curves until he found my breast. I traced the defined chisels in his chest and abdomen with my own fingers and slid my hand between us, grasping his erection.

The early morning colors of dawn were far gone by the time we left the bed and moved into the shower together. Kris never did knock on my door, but she hollered from the bottom of the stairs sometime around noon to tell me that she was taking Zoey out for a walk. We waited until we heard her go out the front door before we crept downstairs, wrapped only in towels, and fed each other fruit and granola, before making love again on the way up the stairs.

***

198

For several days, Connor felt like a teenager hiding from his parents as they looked for secretive places to make love. Twice he managed to sneak into Riley's bedroom after the lights in Kris's room went dark. The first night they were together, she must have known he was in there because she didn't once knock on Riley's door when she got up in the morning. He understood why Riley wanted to be discreet but after days of dodging behind trees, and sneaking around the lodge, he was exhausted. He knew he wasn't the only one who was interested in her either which made him nervous.

He bit off another chunk of red apple and chewed it as he stepped into his jeans and tugged them over his hips. Riley sat at the foot of the bed, pulling a long sleeved shirt the color of damp moss over her head and he couldn't prevent the swollen reaction of his groin as her blonde hair tumbled loosely out of the shirt and onto her shoulders. He left the button of his fly open and crawled across the bed behind her.

"Do you have any idea what you do to me?" He asked her in a strained voice, as he carefully pushed her silky hair off the back of her neck and she sighed as he kissed her exposed skin. He felt her hands fumbling behind her until she found the front of his jeans and she leaned backwards into his chest.

"I have a pretty good idea." She said, her voice low and sexy.

She turned around to face him, her round eyes fixed on his. She pushed him playfully down onto the comforter and straddled his hips with her naked thighs. Her soft and supple skin trembled as he ran his hands up her inner thighs and gripped her hips firmly. He inhaled deeply, taking in her beachy coconut scent, and groaned with pleasure as she lowered herself onto him and rocked back and forth, slow and teasing at first. But as her breath quickened, she moved faster, eager, hungry for him. They rose and fell together, not at all containing their sighs and moans of pleasure.

He felt the world around him disappear, and all that was left was this woman...this sexy and beautiful woman...making love to him.

When Riley collapsed next to him, he rolled onto his side and buried his face into her hair, kissing the freckles splattered finely across one of her bare shoulders. He didn't realize what he wanted to say, until after the words spilled out of his mouth.

"Riley, I love you."

"It was there, I know it was." Fin's voice rose with anger.

"Man, whatever." Matt said snidely and turned away. Fin grabbed his arm as he tried to walk by.

"Get the fuck off me." Matt gritted through his teeth.

Connor stood next to me in the open doorway of the lodge store room. Winchester was a good ten feet away, clearly not wanting to put himself between Fin and Matt. Jacks practically filled the room with his large frame. His coat hung open, a small revolver tucked into his waistband, which seemed like a foreign accessory for him. He had always been the peacemaker, but it seemed the lodge had turned him into a referee.

"I know you took it, no one else has been in here." Fin growled.

Matt shoved Fin, causing him to slid back a foot but still he kept his grip tightly on Matt's arm.

"Whoa now. What is it you think he took, Fin?" Jacks moved closer to the men, his hands up in a form of surrender.

Fin glared at him. "The Springfield is gone." Matt jerked his arm free, but with no way to edge past Fin and Jacks, he smoothed his clothes out, and leaned against the small gun safe with his arms crossed at his chest. Even though his body language became cool and relaxed, tiny beads of sweat had formed above his brow.

Alan and Bobby materialized behind us. Bobby's red face was stony, while Alan's gaunt face was pinched in irritation. Neither of the men looked happy. For a brief moment I wondered if the group would suddenly be split in two if a fight between Fin and Matt broke out. I glanced at Connor, who stepped closer to me without meeting my gaze. Winchester hovered in the background, clearly nervous, and I was certain in a fight or flight moment, he would absolutely hit the ground...running.

"I have no idea what you're talking about." Matt said calmly.

"You're a damn liar! I saw you in here earlier this morning. And now it's gone." Fin tapped Matt's chest with his finger while he spoke.

Matt stared ahead of him, his expression cool. "Maybe *your* drunk ass took it somewhere."

"What?!" Fin lunged at Matt and again Jacks stepped between the men. He put his palms on their chests and pushed each aside, muttering something under his breath.

"What's going on?" I finally asked.

"The Springfield is gone, and I know he took it." Fin's face was flushed.

"What's that?" I asked him.

"The .30-.06."

"Huh?"

"The damn rifle." He glared at me before turning back to face Jacks.

I felt two things at that moment. My skin went clammy and broke out in goose bumps, and immediately my heart plummeted into my stomach with a hollow thud. Because I knew Fin was probably right. Who else would have gone into the gun safe and taken the hunting rifle? It seemed most if not everyone had pistols of some sort; but a rifle? What would any of us need with a rifle?

"What do you need it for?" I aimed the question at Matt.

"It doesn't matter what he wants it for, the fucker shouldn't have it." Fin spat the words out.

"Okay, so let's assume you're right Fin, that Matt took the rifle." Matt narrowed his eyes at Jacks and even from several feet away I could see the muscles in his jaw twitch. "Why would he do that?" Jacks spoke calmly but kept his stance wide, and never relaxed his hands, as if just waiting for a fight to start.

Fin dragged his hands over his face and cursed loudly. He shoved past Jacks and forced his way between Connor and I. The back door bounced in its framed when he swung it shut behind him.

"I bet the bastard has it tucked under his bed, or propped up in a closet somewhere." Matt said in a mocking voice.

Alan snickered behind me, making the goose bumps return and the hair on the back of my neck stand on end. I glanced at him and he shoved something into his pocket, a guilty look on his face just brief enough for me to notice. I stared at him until he looked away and nervously pushed his thick glasses far up onto his nose.

"I'll go talk to him." I said to the room, and ignored Connor's look of surprise as I left them and stepped outside into the fresh spring air.

I could see Fin taking the lawn in long strides, so I jogged to catch up to him.

"Fin, wait."

"Go away, Riley."

"No." I reached out to his arm and gently grabbed at his elbow but he shook me off. I matched his fast pace on the trail, though I had to skip a bit to keep up. When the cabins came into view, I thought he would turn to the left and take the steps up to his own place, but instead he stayed on the rocky dirt path until it turned into the weathered planks leading onto the pier.

He didn't stop until the toes of his boots literally dangled over the edge of the last wooden board. We hadn't had any snow in weeks, and the ice had long ago melted away from the lake's border, but it was almost April and I was sure the water was still freezing. I stood behind him with my hands shoved into my jeans until he spoke.

"Do you love him?"

I blinked at his shoulder in confusion. "Who?"

He turned to look at me. His normally spiked straw-colored hair had flattened in the last week or so on account of him not having a haircut for the last couple of months. "Connor. Do you love him?"

"Oh." I paused and looked away from his hazel eyes; afraid they would penetrate into my mind and read my thoughts before I could process them. "I do."

"Good." I could feel that he was still staring at me.

"It is good."

"What about Jacks? Connor seems like a good guy. He shouldn't have to compete with Jacks."

I looked at Fin and held his gaze. "I loved Jacks a long time ago. He's a special friend, but we don't really complement each other. It always gets messy between us and I don't want that again...*none* of us need that."

Fin nodded slowly and then shoved his hands in his back pockets, trying to hide his discomfort. "So, someone like me? You would never love someone like me?" His voice was small, almost juvenile.

"What do you mean someone like you?" I laughed softly. "What's wrong with you?"

He chewed on his lower lip and looked out over the lake. When he answered his voice was just above a murmur. "No one like you has ever loved someone like me. That's all."

I stared at him, dumbstruck. "Fin, look at me."

I waited for him to inhale deeply before he brought his eyes to mine. "There's nothing wrong with you. And I'm sorry. I'm so sorry I can't be what you need, because the truth is I think you're great. But me being with Connor has nothing to do with something being wrong with *you*. Okay?" I touched his arm gently and he nodded with a small laugh.

"Right, it's not me...it's you, huh?"

"Exactly."

We both laughed quietly. The pier creaked and moaned slightly and the sound of water gently slapping against the pillars below us was relaxing. I stood next to Fin and stared out at the water of the small lake, watching the treetops on the other side sway.

"You know what's funny? In my life before all...this...I would never have fallen for a guy like Connor. In fact, you're more my type than he is."

Fin turned and looked at me sharply. "Shit, that is not what I need to hear from you."

"Well, it's true. You shouldn't be so hard on yourself."

He looked back over the water and nodded. "Maybe in the next life? You and me?"

I laughed, "Maybe. But for now just friends, okay?" I said it gently, hoping he knew how hard it was for me to have this conversation out loud. Never in my life did I have to make a choice between two totally different men. And part of me thought what Jacks had said was true, there was something about Fin that just seemed to fit with me. I wondered what it would have been like to meet Fin before the virus; what could have happened between us. But the connection I had with Connor wasn't something I could explain in words...he *felt* right. I didn't want to lose that.

Fin looked down at me solemnly before playfully elbowing me in the arm. "Friends." He smiled, and I nodded, hopeful that we could move on without any more hurt exchanging between us. We watched the lake for another few minutes, listening to the water lap below our feet until Fin leaned down against the pier railing and sighed heavily.

"I know he took it, Riley." He sounded tired. "I know Matt took that rifle."

"Okay. I believe you." And I did. "Does it matter so much, though? I mean, we all have some sort of gun now." I kept my voice as gentle as possible, trying not to fuel the fire that burned between Matt and basically everyone else. But the last thing I wanted was for Fin to think I sided with Matt.

He turned around to face me before answering. "Yeah, but does anyone else have a long-range rifle with a scope?"

I felt the blood drain from my face at his implication. He pursed his lips into a crooked smile and laughed hollowly.

"See, now you get it."

***

A shrill scream startled me awake. I sat upright, my heart thudding and my head still heavy with sleep. *Was it Kris?* I listened, waiting for a sound to come from her room at the other end of the hallway. Connor was still asleep next to me. When nothing but the sounds of his relaxed breathing filled the room, I lowered my shoulders and rubbed the back of my neck. *Perhaps I was dreaming?* I slowly leaned back into my pillow and stared up at the ceiling at the lightly stained oak beams that ran lengthwise across the room. It hurt to blink. My dry eyes hurt so I held the heel of my palms to them, hoping to push the brewing headache away.

The scream pierced the night again, from somewhere distant, and Zoey barked from the stair way. I sat up and pulled a shirt over my head and a loose fitting pair of sweats before I pushed my door open and stood quietly in the hallway. The scream couldn't have come from inside the cabin but I checked Kris's room anyway. When I opened her door, she was sitting with her knee's bent up under her chin, the covers pulled up high.

"*Did you hear that too?*" She whispered. Her brown eyes looked like empty caves in the dark.

"*It wasn't you, then?*" I whispered back. She didn't answer, only shook her head vigorously side to side. Zoey barked again, but this time from the lower level of the cabin.

Whoever screamed was outside.

***

Connor was dressing by the time I rushed back into the room. He already had his jeans on and was pulling a sweat-shirt over his head when he saw me.

"Thank God! I thought something happened to you." He rushed forward with his arms still caught in his sleeves, and reached out to touch my face with his fingers.

"Someone's screaming." I said to him, my heart thumping.

"What? You mean that was real?" He stiffened and looked past me, through the doorway.

I shook my head and said, "Kris is fine. It's someone outside."

"Shit." He murmured.

We stumbled around the room, kicking aside pieces of the clothing we wore from the day before and the extra comforter that had slid off the bed sometime during the night, until we found our shoes. Neither of us bothered to put socks on before shoving our feet inside them.

On our way out of the room I saw that Kris was standing in her doorway, a blanket wrapped tightly around her shoulders, her fuzzy hair sticking out like a helmet around her head.

"You aren't both leaving are you?" Her voice was shaky. She didn't seem surprised at all to see Connor coming out of my room in the middle of the night.

"Kris, it's okay. We have to see who that was." I whistled for Zoey and heard her nails clacking rhythmically across the wood floor below us and then padding up the stairs. She greeted all three of us with sniffs.

"Can she stay here?" Kris pleaded.

I looked at Zoey before nodding at Kris. "Okay. Stay inside and lock the door. We'll be right back."

She followed us down the stairs and I heard the click of the lock sliding into place as we ran down the porch steps. The front light flickered on at Skip's place and we met him on the path and stood still for a moment. The screams had stopped but we still weren't sure exactly where they had come from. Jacks stumbled out of his cabin, half-dressed and obviously half-asleep as well. Winchester was the last outside and the sight of him made me want to laugh. His hair was uncombed and tousled wildly on top of his head and his normally baby-smooth face sprouted dark stubble, which surprisingly made him look more attractive than his usual clean and put together countenance.

"It wasn't from down here." I jumped when Fin's husky voice drifted towards us on the cool midnight breeze.

"The lodge." I said, and Skip nodded at me.

"Let's go." Connor said quietly, walking briskly ahead, closing the gap between us and Fin's dark silhouette.

***

We found Ana standing on the back porch in her pajamas, leaning into Alan. She was visibly shaking and choking down sobs. Her black hair was tangled from sleep, her face clean of makeup. I had never seen her not done up.

"I said, *shut up!*" A voice hissed from inside the open doorway. Matt stepped out of the dark into the glow of the porch light. "Get a damn grip, Ana!"

Fin and Connor were ahead of the rest of us by only a handful of paces and approached the trio warily, leaving a wide berth between them and Matt, who was unshaven, and had dark circles under his eyes.

Ana hiccupped and said something in Spanish to Matt. "Speak English, woman." He growled.

Connor and Fin spoke at the same time.

"What's going on?"

"What's wrong?"

Ana seem to finally realize she was in Alan's embrace and pushed him away, rubbing her arms as if she was cold. Alan looked hurt for a second, but ran his hand through his greasy hair and smirked at her.

"Chick is crazy."

She spat out a rapid slur of Spanish words again, while moving further away from him. She had on a short Victoria's Secret number and sandals. She crossed her arms over the sheer top and hugged herself.

Jacks stepped forward and tugged his shirt off. He handed it to Ana, who quickly put it on.

"Gracias." She said quietly.

"What happened, Ana? Are you alright?" I asked her. Rubbing at my eyes where the headache was in full form...throbbing behind the bridge of my nose.

She nodded and began in Spanish before stopping to glare at Matt. When she started talking again, she spoke to us only in English.

"There was a man in the room. I swear it! He grabbed my leg and tried to pull me from the bed."

Matt stood with his arms crossed over his bare chest, a look of either disgust or extreme irritation on his face. His pectoral muscles were shiny with sweat; something I found curious for a guy who supposedly was just woken up.

"The only *man* in our room was me." Everyone stared at him.

"What did you do?" I said just above a whisper.

Ana's eyes got wide as Matt's chest muscles twitched from my implication. "No, no, no...not Matt. Another man. He grabbed me. I swear." She inhaled sharply before continuing, "He was there one minute, then just gone." She gestured to Matt. "He doesn't believe me."

"Of course not! You're saying some damn ghost was in our room. What the hell is wrong with you, bitch?" His words seemed to cut Ana like a knife.

Fin turned his back away from them and looked in my direction. "Now you know why I said those rooms ain't empty." He walked away from the group, toward the cabins without saying anything else.

Ana started arguing with Matt about how she wasn't going back up to their room. He stomped inside and slammed the door shut behind him. Alan stood awkwardly by the door, unsure what to do. He finally followed Matt, closing the door behind him as well.

"I'm not going back in there. And I'm *not* crazy." She sniffled.

"You don't have to." Jacks put his arm around her and gestured toward the cabins. "We've got another room at our place or you can have your own cabin if you want."

"And sleep alone?" She looked at him, her eyes wide, on the brink of panic but then she inhaled deeply and calmly smoothed her hair back from her face. "Maybe just for tonight, I'll stay at your place." She started walking down the trail, with Jacks next to her, but sent a curious look over her shoulder at me. I tried to smile, but the pressure behind my eyes threatened to split my head in half. Something unpleasant twitched inside my stomach as I watched them walk away together, so I turned away from them and rubbed my temples.

"Ghosts, huh?" Skip murmured.

Winchester shifted and looked down at his feet. I didn't have to look at Connor to feel his penetrating stare.

***

"I'm just saying, it's worth discussing...don't' you think?" I looked around the Rec room at the group, hoping they didn't all think I was crazy. Clouds blocked out most of the morning sun which cast a dark glow throughout the room.

Connor cleared his throat and when he spoke, Kris finally looked up. "I think we should at least talk about it. Maybe it would help us understand what's happening." He leaned back into the couch and crossed his arms loosely around his chest.

"I already told you what happened." Ana said. She looked down at her hands, and fiddled with the hem of her denim skirt. She was sitting on the second couch, opposite of Connor and Kris, next to Winchester and Skip.

"That's the only experience you've had?" I asked her, doubt creeping into my voice. She shot me an ugly look but didn't respond.

Skip sighed and patted his thigh a few times, startling Ana. "Well, shoot. I guess I'll go first." He stopped to look around the room, seeming uneasy with the fact that Matt was huddled in the far corner leaning against the wall, sipping from his tumbler. Antisocial and uninterested as usual.

"On one of my solo trips to the grocery store I saw a man in the parking lot, walking by the front of the building. Well, I thought he was a man anyway. But when I got close enough to the poor bastard, I saw he was covered in blood." He paused to glance at Kris, who was watching him intently. "Should I even be saying this in front of the kid?" He smiled awkwardly.

"I'm not a kid." She said defiantly, and tilted her chin up an inch or so. I smiled at her and nodded at Skip to continue.

"Well, it was like he was sick, you know, with the bug. But he came at me, and I sort of freaked out, took off running, and when I looked back, the guy was gone. Just...poof." He sighed heavily.

"That's it?" Connor asked, before glancing at me nervously.

"I guess I've heard things too, voices, stuff like that." Skip looked around the room sharply. "I don't mean in my head or nothing, I mean...you know, like on the wind."

Everyone in the room seemed to be nodding. Winchester leaned forward and hung his head in between his knees and for a second I thought he was getting ready to puke right there, on his feet.

"It's not in your head." He said softly, before lifting his face up at Skip and propping his elbows onto his legs. "There was this girl, I don't know...like fifteen or so, and I saw her twice, wandering around outside my office." He ran his hand across his forehead, wiping at his brow. "She was...naked...and covered with all these bloody spots. I swear, I thought her skin was coming off. I know she wasn't real. But at the time, I don't know, I guess I thought I made the whole thing up."

"Why would you make something like that up, son?" Skip asked him gently.

"Because, it couldn't have been real...I mean, was it?" Winchester stood up and walked past me, closer to the open doorway and gulped in the fresh air.

"Well, I won't stay up here at the lodge because I kept hearing shit. I made it three nights before I thought I might lose my damn mind. And then, in the middle of that last night, I saw something standing in the corner of the room. When I turned the light on, dude was gone. That was it for me. I moved down to the cabins the next day." Fin said.

"So, all y'all had something like that happen?" Bobby spoke for the first time.

He sat on a dining chair pulled close to one of the couches, with his legs opened up in front of him. His belly stuck out above his dirty pants, threatening to pop the top button of his fly off with the slightest change in pressure. With his beady eyes, he scanned the faces in the room quickly.

209

"We did. In the City. Seeing things, hearing shit." Alan said it quietly and shrugged at Bobby's glare.

"They haven't said anything." Ana looked between me and Connor suspiciously.

"Well, we did have a sort of...incident downtown." I said it carefully; unsure of how to tell the story when I still wasn't certain what had happened myself. Connor was watching me thoughtfully.

"Truth is...I don't remember all of it." I shifted on my feet and jammed my hands into my pockets.

"What do you mean?" Winchester asked.

I looked up at Connor for help and exhaled deeply when he gently cleared his throat and began sharing our story of what happened the day before we left the City. I watched as everyone listened, engrossed, as he told about the girl in the street, the mob of dead, and how they all disappeared. Kris seemed visibly upset and held tightly onto Zoey as if the dog was going to dissolve if she took her hand off her.

"That's truly amazing." Skip said quietly.

"Now you understand why I, why we, had to leave the City. Why we wanted to come here." I said.

"If you're talking about ghosts I don't think it matters where we are." Fin said.

"Well, no, but less people lived up here...that also means that less people died up here."

I let my words sink in while the group sent confused and fearful glances at each other as they shifted uncomfortably in their seats.

"Do you think that's why it hasn't happened again?" Kris's voice was tiny, but her eyes were large and clear as she looked between me and Connor.

"You mean the mob?" Connor asked and she nodded.

"The City's full of thousands of people, so it makes sense that up here, that won't happen. When you think about it, millions of people died together...something's keeping them here. We just don't know what it is."

The room was quiet around me. "It's just a theory." I shrugged and looked down at my feet.

"It's a damn good one. Makes sense to me at least." Fin said. I smiled at him, grateful for the support, even if what I suggested sounded wild and unbelievable.

Skip stood and clapped his hands together, startling all of us. "Okay, so until one of us becomes a ghost whisperer...how about we just plan on staying out of the cities for a while?" Soft chuckles and nervous laughs broke out around the room.

"Deal." I said to him.

I let Connor slide his arms around me in a hug as the room gradually emptied, everyone eager to find something else to do, and something else to talk about. Only Matt stayed behind, still standing in his corner with his drink in his hand. Before we passed through the doorway on our way outside, I turned around to glance in his direction and I noticed how the shadows of the room seemed to envelope his space completely. The darkness inside him seemed to be growing, and when he set his icy glare on me, a shiver jolted down the length of my spine.

***

Everyone was on edge around the grounds for days after our group discussion in the Rec room, especially Fin. He skipped whatever group meals we had and spent most of his time in his cabin or the greenhouse. Ana had officially moved into Jacks' cabin, bumping Winchester out of the roomy second bedroom into the small single-bed space off the kitchen. Which made her my neighbor, but fortunately she spent most of her time inside or driving the little golf cart previously reserved for the lodge's gardener between the main buildings and the cabins.

She began spending a considerable amount of time with Jacks and I suspected they had a thing going before showing up at the lodge. I knew the others were aware of the private time Connor and I tried to cut out of the days. Thankfully, no one called us on it and even Jacks didn't mention it. So in a way, I was glad he seemed to be spending time with someone else. I just wished it could have been anyone other than the high-maintenance and whiny Ana.

I sat on Fin's sofa, my elbow propped up on a fuzzy brown pillow. My mind raced, refusing to settle on one thought at a time.

Connor was next door, riffling through his things for a clean change of clothes.

"Is he officially moving back into your place?" I jumped when Fin's voice spoke from behind the sofa.

"Oh, no. He's...just getting something...I think." I stretched and tried to smile at Fin, but he walked past me into the kitchen.

"Was thinking of making vegetable pot-pie for dinner tonight, if you guys want to join me." He moved around the kitchen with ease, pulling pans from cupboards I had yet to explore in my own cabin. He had set a sack on the table and out tumbled several ingredients for his meal onto the counter.

"That would be nice. Thanks Fin." I smiled at him but he didn't look up from his work.

"Gotta eat some of these potatoes; there's a whole bin of them in the greenhouse." He said.

I opened my mouth to comment but what sounded like a single firework blast erupted from the woods and I jumped up and ran to the door, with Fin not far behind me.

"What was that, a back fire?" I asked, my voice shaky.

"No, that was a gunshot." Fin stared at me.

Connor's footsteps pounded down his porch stairs and I matched his worried gaze with my own as he met up with us on Fin's deck. We stood near the railing huddled closely together, craning our necks and straining to hear anything unusual. Silence stilled the forest around us; even the dog was quiet. *Zoey...where was she?* Almost a full minute had passed before we heard Kris's piercing screams echoing off the trees.

CHAPTER 19

I ran into the woods crashing through the waist-high shrubs, oblivious to the branches that snagged my clothes and skin while my eyes darted around wildly, searching for any signs of Kris and the dog. The scream had come from somewhere in the trees. I knew Kris had taken Zoey for a walk, but I didn't ask her where they were going. I cursed myself as I jumped over tree roots and slid on mossy rocks. Connor and Fin were running close behind me, until Fin yelled at me to stop.

"Riley, listen!" He shouted at my back.

I slammed hands first into a large pine tree and leaned against it to catch my breath. In the distance was the distinct sound of a barking dog. My barking dog. *Thank god.* I thought to myself, as I pushed off the tree and cocked my head to the side but I was unable to pinpoint Zoey's location. Her barks were too sporadic, so I whistled sharply and the barking stopped. *Good, at least she knows I'm out here looking for them.* The three of us stood in a semi-circle, waiting anxiously, not sure which direction to go. I whistled again, louder, and Zoey barked in return. All three of us turned to the right and began running south through the trees that bordered the lake. Zoey would bark every time I whistled and she was getting closer to us. When she finally crashed through the bushes and ran up to me, jumping and whining, I realized Kris wasn't behind her.

"Where's Kris, Zoey?" I asked, even though I knew the dog couldn't answer. A succession of sharp gunshots boomed through the trees, much closer than the first one had been.

"*Zoey, go get her, go get Kris!*" I whispered into her ear and off she ran with her bushy black tail straight up in the air, back the way she had come. Fin and Connor followed behind me as we ran through a dense crop of pines. Both men struggled to keep up and I swore to

213

never complain about my short, 5'6" frame again, as Connor and Fin tripped on every root and ran into each low-hanging branch. When the tree line cleared, I could see a small meadow ahead of us, and someone in a dark sweatshirt was sprinting across it. Fin yanked on my shoulder to keep me from running out of the safety of the massive tree trunks.

"Let go, it's Kris!" I hissed.

"I know! Riley, just wait. Something's wrong." He hissed back.

Connor moved around Fin and took my arm. We moved quietly through the woods, circling the meadow hoping to run into Kris who was no longer in sight.

"*There!*" I whispered.

Twenty yards ahead of us was a dark shadow crouching in the bushes at the base of a large tree. When I whistled softly, the bushes shook and Zoey closed the distance between us in a handful of seconds. Kris stood up slowly, peering into the darkness of the woods until her eyes met mine. She looked at me wildly, shook her head and then pointed toward the meadow.

"It's Matt." Fin said through clenched teeth. We dropped to our knees and watched as Matt emerged from the far side of the meadow with the missing rifle held out in front of him. Bobby, his own gun in hand, was directly behind him. Alan took up the rear, also armed.

"What the hell are they doing?" Connor asked quietly.

"*They wouldn't shoot at Kris, would they?*" I whispered, hoping neither of them would answer.

Connor cupped his hand over my mouth to muffle my scream as Matt fired the rifle into the woods. The loudness of the shot rang through my head like a metal pin-ball. From our crouched position I couldn't see Kris anymore. I clamped my hands over Zoey's snout when she let out a low growl.

"*Shush!*" I whispered in the dog's ear.

She quieted but kept her gaze on the three men striding through the tall grass of the meadow. They were arguing and gesturing around them.

"I think they're looking for her." My heart sank. We had to do something before they fired off another random shot from the rifle and actually hit one of us.

"I have my pistol." Fin said quietly. "I could fire in their direction. They won't be expecting her to shoot back, will they?"

"What if you hit one of them?" I asked.

He looked at me flatly before pulling his pistol from the back of his waistband. "I won't. Not unless you want me to."

He leaned against a tree trunk, obscuring most of his tall and wide frame. I slithered up a tree as well, catching loose bark and dead pine needles in my hair, edging around it until I could see Kris. I signaled for her to stay put and pointed at Fin. His hand was steady as he aimed his pistol high above the three men. I didn't think the bullet would make it out of the trees at all. It was only in danger of taking out a branch at best.

When the shot rang out, Matt and Bobby dropped to the ground but Alan stood shocked, before turning and running back into the tree line. Fin fired another bullet into the air and Matt and Bobby scrambled to their feet and took off behind Alan.

I waved Kris over to us and she bolted through the brush, running into my arms. Her freckled nose was scratched and tears had left dirty track marks down her cheeks.

Connor shoved me from behind and we ran back through the woods, not stopping until we reached the cabins. My throat burned and I was sure my heart was going into irregular spasms when I collapsed on my front porch. We took a moment to catch our breath before Fin asked Kris what happened in the woods.

"Let's go inside first." I said between gulps of air, while I scanned the woods nervously.

We huddled around the kitchen-island with tall glasses of water in our hands, waiting for Kris to speak. Fin paced behind the windows, pushing the curtains aside to peer out every few seconds. He tapped his gun against his thigh repeatedly, as if itching to use it.

"I was walking Zoey." She paused to take a sip from her glass. "And she ran away from me, chasing after something in the woods." Another pause for water. "Then there was like, this gunshot and I thought someone shot her. Zoey, I mean." She looked at me before continuing. I nodded for her to keep talking. "Okay, so then I saw her, running through the trees. The deer. You know the one we saw?" Another sip of water. "Matt was shooting at her." She looked down at her hands. "I couldn't let him shoot her. I couldn't." She said quietly.

"Did he know you were out there, Kris?" I leaned against the counter and pinched the bridge of my nose. My headache was back.

"Oh yeah. He knew because I ran through the trees as loud as I could shouting at them. I think the second time he was actually aiming at me. He was really mad." Her eyes darted to the front door. "Will he come here?" Her voice wavered.

"I don't think he will. I mean, right now he thinks you have a gun too." Fin said gently.

Zoey huffed and a knock at the door made us all jump. Connor and Fin approached it cautiously and then relaxed, letting Skip inside.

"What was all the shooting about?" He asked the room, his usually jovial face full of concern.

Kris slipped out of the kitchen quietly and rushed up the stairs and I followed her, trusting the others would be able to fill Skip in without me there. The sounds of the men talking downstairs drifted up the stairway, and even though I couldn't hear exactly what was said, I knew Skip was upset. His voice rose above the others several times.

I sighed and watched her reflection in the bathroom mirror. She looked pale as she rinsed her face with splash after splash of cool water. Her eyes were darker than usual, and her mouth was set into a quivering pout. When she stood, she met my eyes in the mirror for a moment and turned around slowly, leaning her narrow hip against the sink.

With her face buried in a hand towel she mumbled, "So, what do we do now?"

"I don't know. But we have to do something." I squeezed her in a quick hug. "Don't worry. We'll figure it out, okay?" She only nodded.

It didn't take much convincing to get her to lay down on her bed and rest. I pulled a thick cotton blanket over her and tucked her in, much like I did for my own kids. When I patted the mattress, Zoey happily jumped onto the bed and cuddled up against her. I ran my hands over the dog, just to make sure she wasn't injured, before I quietly left the room. I glanced at Kris's small body curled under the white blanket and the black dog that had her head resting on the girl's shoulder. I wondered what would have happened in the woods if Matt had been a better shot. I felt my skin flush with anger at the thought of finding Kris laying in that meadow...bloody...dead.

I crossed the hall and walked into my room and stood in front of my bedside table. Fin's loaded .45 was exactly where I had left it. After I tucked it into the front of my jeans, I pulled my sweater down to hide the bulge. Several hours of target practice with Fin was about to become useful. Matt wouldn't know what hit him.

***

"Where are you going?" Fin's voice rose above the others. My hand was tightly curled around the front doorknob.

"I need some air." I peered at him over my shoulder, trying to act normal. Fin nodded at me from across the room and returned to arguing with Skip and Connor. Winchester had come in at some point while I was upstairs, and he stood quietly in a corner listening to the others. Like the rest of them, he didn't seem concerned when I stepped outside and closed the door behind me.

I held my breath as I walked away from the cabin and didn't release it until I slipped into the driver side of Ana's golf cart, blowing out a gust of air when I saw the key in the ignition. I was sure Connor or Fin would come running after me, as if my thoughts were written across my forehead in permanent marker. But they didn't. The little engine roared to life and I thought then I might get caught. But no one seemed to notice that I had taken the four-seater even as I drove it up the path. Instead of the almost ten minute walk, I made it to the lodge in less than one minute. I parked the cart near the storage building and stepped out onto the gravel, taking in the long expanse of the main building.

The whole area was weirdly quiet, not even birds chirped from the trees. I hoped it would take a while before the others realized I was gone. I slowly approached the door of the back porch, straining to see inside the windows. It wasn't locked. Once inside, I pulled the gun from my waist band, and moved quickly through the rooms on the lower level, holding my arms out in front of me...just like Fin had taught me. The sound of a car door closing led me to the lobby. The open door flooded the entry way with yellow sunlight and I recognized two voices out front...Bobby and Alan.

I slipped unseen around the waist-high counter and moved behind it, hunched forward until I could see out one of the front windows.

The two men were loading a truck with bags and boxes. Bobby's hunting rifle was still slung over his shoulder and his face was such a dark crimson I was sure his blood pressure was going to blow his head clear off his pudgy neck. Alan looked no better; his glasses were missing and his greasy hair was stringy and plastered to his head with sweat. The dirty jeans he wore hung off his bony hips, exposing naked parts of his backside that I cringed upon seeing. Matt wasn't with them.

A string of curse words went through my head while I squatted and leaned against the smooth surface of the check-in counter, letting the coolness of the particle board chill the hot skin of my back. The thumping sounds of Bobby's boots vibrated through the floorboards and I tried to flatten myself against the counter, hoping they didn't have a reason to look behind it.

Alan's raspy voice spoke from just above my head. "He's fucking crazy, man. You know that, right?"

"Shut up." Bobby said tersely.

Something heavy banged onto the counter and I jumped, biting down on the tip of my tongue. A strong odor filled my nostrils, and I clasped a hand over my mouth to keep from gagging. *Gasoline.*

"Just saying. He's fucking lost it, man." Alan squeaked, his voice a manic mixture of terror and excitement.

"Boy, you better shut your mouth. We ain't got time!" Bobby hissed under his breath.

Oh my god, I thought to myself, *what are they planning on doing?* Something metallic banged against one of the nearby walls and I jumped again. My foot slid out from under me and the sole of my shoe made a small squeak against the polished floor. I pressed myself into the flimsy particle board even harder, pain shooting into my shoulder blades. The swish of liquid splashed onto the top of the counter and cascaded over the side. Fat drops of gasoline dripped onto my shoulder and I attempted to lean away from it, horrified.

"That's enough in here; it'll burn." Bobby said, before throwing something against the wall.

A rusty red can rolled along the ground into my view and my stomach lurched. When the sounds of their feet left the room I stood up and turned, ready to bolt out the back door, but stood face to face with Matt instead.

***

He seemed just as surprised to see me as I was to find him standing in the middle of the lobby, his arms holding a large plastic crate full of canned food. Without hesitating, I raised the gun up level to his chest and pulled the trigger. Nothing happened.

"Shit!"

Matt took a step toward me, the sinister look in his eyes betraying the smile that curled his pale lips upward.

"Don't move!" I barked at him. The safety, I had left the damn safety on.

I inched around the counter, trying to fumble the safety switch off while keeping my eyes on Matt. When the hallway was behind me, I turned to run, and made it barely five feet before slipping in a puddle of fuel and landing on my back. The air expelled from my lungs like a popped balloon as dark stars filled my vision.

A dull pain exploded through my right wrist as a tremendous pressure squeezed down on my hand and fingers, grinding them together. I tried to move my arm, but it was pinned to the ground by Matt's boot. I groaned in agony and released my grip on the pistol.

"Good girl." Matt said from above me.

The room spun as he lifted his foot and yanked me up to a standing position. Toxic fumes filled my nose, and something sweet...Matt's breath. I wasn't sure what would make me pass out first: the gasoline that was dumped all over the room or the alcohol vapors escaping from his mouth.

"*Let...go...of me.*" I struggled to talk as he slammed me against the wall, and held me there with his hand around my throat.

"*What were you going to do with your little gun, Riley?*" He hissed in my ear.

"Let *go.*"

No matter how hard I pulled and pushed on his arm, it wouldn't budge. When he started digging his fingers deeper into my throat I began to panic and thrashed against the wall, too aware of how close his face was to mine.

"Stop fighting, you can't get away." He said flatly.

219

No longer able to speak, I lifted a knee upwards as hard as I could, striking his left knee cap. He cursed and reciprocated by punching me in the stomach. My abdomen tightened in knots and the pain brought bile up my throat. I thought I was going to die from choking on my own vomit until Alan's shaky voice came from the front door.

"What the hell?"

"Go away." Matt snapped, without turning to look at Alan.

"What are you *doing*, man?"

"I said go the fuck *away!*"

Matt turned just enough to change the angle of his stance, and I tried again to slam my knee into his groin, but banged into his inner thigh instead. *Not close enough.*

"*Bitch!*"

Spittle flew from his lips as he slammed me against the wall, removing his hand just long enough for me to suck in one ragged breath before he shoved his arm against my chest, once again pinning me to the wooden paneling. A piece of molding broke off the wall behind me and clamored with a crash at my feet.

Able to breathe, I drew air in greedily, my lungs hungry for oxygen. A zipping sound came from below me and I snapped my head up. Matt was tugging at the front of my jeans with his free hand.

"*No.*" I squeaked, my voice barely audible.

"Shut up. You know you want it." I felt the fumble of his hand between us, and he managed to undo the button before shoving the top of my underwear down with his fingertips.

"*No, please stop.*" Tears streamed down my cheeks and left dark spots on his sleeve as I thrashed frantically under his arm.

"Matt!" Bobby's voice boomed from outside. "They're coming man, gotta go!" The sound of a car door slammed shut and an engine roared to life.

Matt leaned against me, cursing. His unshaven face scraped my cheek and I heard the sound of his zipper close. Tears flowed freely from my eyes with relief. *They're coming.* I told myself. *Connor and Fin...Jacks...they'll stop them.* When Matt released me, he gave me a hard shove away from him and even though my body was stiff and sore, I rushed at the doorway and almost made it outside when a sudden heavy weight spread over the back of my head and a sharp pain rang through my ears. The last thing I saw was the light from outside shrinking into a far-away tunnel. And then...only darkness.

**

Connor cursed himself as he sprinted up the path behind Fin. No one knew where Jacks and Ana were...big surprise there. What the hell was Riley thinking? Taking off with the cart. What was she planning on doing to Matt by herself? Fin slid on the trail ahead of him and he almost crashed into the burly man.

"*Damn, Fin!*" *Connor yelled.*

Zoey rushed past them, kicking up dust clouds with her small lab-spaniel feet. Kris and Winchester were somewhere behind them on the trail but he might as well have been in the whole damn woods alone. He had one thought. Where was she? As they rounded the last bend and the lawn opened up in front of them, Fin sprinted the incline easily putting ten, fifteen, twenty feet between them. Zoey yelped and barked at the side of the building, like something spooked her, and she ran in a wide arc away from the shrubbery that lined the wooden structure.

The damn shade tree on the lawn was blocking his view. Fin was already off the grassy area and running after the dog. As Connor passed underneath the giant oak he saw why she feared the building. The entire south side of the lodge was engulfed in a massive wall of flames.

"*Oh fuck!*" *He panted.*

He could hear Kris cry out behind him, but he kept running. The dog and Fin had rounded the front of the lodge and were out of sight. He ran up the drive way, just as they had, putting plenty of room between himself and the fire which had quickly spread to the roof.

"*Riley!*" *He screamed her name at the lodge.*

He heard the screech of tires peeling out away from the lodge, heading towards the long gravel driveway that led to the highway. Zoey was in hot pursuit, barking madly at the truck as it rapidly shrank in size. He jumped when Fin ran at him from his left, from the front of the building.

221

"They torched it!" He exhaled loudly, and waved his arms in the direction of the fleeing truck. "They took her!" Fin bent forward, leaning into his knees and heaved.

"What?" Connor stared at him, not understanding.

"They took her!" Fin stood and pointed down the driveway. The truck seemed to slow before turning to the right and then it was gone. "Did you hear me? That asshole has Riley!" The veins in Fin's forehead popped out and he cursed, kicking up a cloud of dust.

"How do you know?"

"Damn it Connor. I saw Matt carry her, and put her in the back seat!" Fin swore a string of curse words into the sky.

Connor bolted for his truck and slid to a stop half way there. "Oh Jesus." He spun around and collided into Fin's chest. "I don't have the keys. They're at the cabin."

"God damn it!" Fin screamed.

"Fin!" Connor ran over to Riley's Jeep and peered inside, looking for keys. Nothing. "Search the other cars!" He yelled.

Winchester ran up behind them, "Skip's...take Skip's truck!"

Fin ran up to the passenger side and banged his hands down on the roof, "Yes! Keys! Let's go!" Connor pushed him aside and pointed for him to drive. He knew the roads better. Connor whistled out the passenger window when he saw the black dog and the dust that enveloped her like a cloudy aura rushing back to them. Fin slowed to a crawl and after pulling Zoey up into the cab, the tires spun, kicking up dirt and small rocks as Fin floored the old Chevy up the driveway.

In the side mirror, Connor looked at the reflection of the lodge. Fire flicked at the glass from inside the lobby. Dark smoke poured out in coils from under the roof, which meant the fire had spread to the second floor. Before he looked away, he saw Winchester and Skip pulling a garden hose out and aiming it at the front door. It was no use. Connor knew it was hopeless.

CHAPTER 20

Mommy? Mommy, wake up.
Baby, it's too early. Go back to bed.
Mommy? I had a bad dream, can I sleep with you? Please?
Shannon, you slept with Mommy last night...remember?
Mommy...please?
Mommy, wake up. Wake up!

My eyes fluttered open. "*I'm...awake.*" I groaned, bringing my hands to the back of my head. They came back wet with bright red blood. "What?" I blinked, but my eyes wouldn't open all the way.

"Dude, she's awake!"

I bristled, trying to focus on the bright light with flying shadows above my head. "Where...?" I tried to sit up, but a hand pushed me down. And then I remembered. Matt slamming me against the wall. Matt choking me. Something hitting the back of my head. And then what? I couldn't remember how I got wherever I was.

Rubber squealed and I slid into something hard. A door. A car door. I tried to sit up again, this time kicking at the soft person that sat near my feet. I was able to right myself and flattened my back into the small cab window. Not a car, a truck. The shadows outside were trees. And we were shooting past them at speeds I was sure not even the local highway patrol had ever matched on the winding high-elevation road.

Alan sat to my left, smashed up against his own car door, watching me with horror. I wasn't sure if I should kick him or Matt, who was driving. Bobby turned around from the front passenger seat and poked at me with the end of his rifle.

"Don't try anything, sweetheart. Be a good passenger now."

His red face was covered in a layer of sweat and he smelled foul, like he had soiled himself. I brought my knees up to my chest and opened my mouth to speak.

"Stop, stop and let me out. I'll walk back. You can just...leave." Only a whisper of my voice was left.

Bobby looked over at Matt, who was driving so wildly that the tires repeatedly went off the asphalt and tore along the narrow dirt shoulder. A low hanging tree branch hit the passenger side of the truck and I flinched. If he kept driving like this, he was going to kill us all.

"At least slow down, please, Matt." I tried to sound calm, but my mousy voice squeaked like a rusty wheel. I rubbed at my throat and swallowed.

"I don't know why you took her, man. Just open the door and I'll shove her out." Alan was gripping what my Mom used to call the *'Oh Shit'* handle above his head. I glared at him and grabbed my own handle, holding on for dear life as the truck leaned, lurched and skidded along the highway barely making the turns while staying on the road.

"Alan, shut your damn klepto mouth, or I'll throw *you* out of this fucking truck!" Matt's eyes were wild when he looked over his shoulder and both Bobby and I screamed at him to watch the road. The truck slid onto soft ground and gravel spat into the air, pelting the windows like hail.

"Oh my god." I said quietly.

"This is your fault, you know." Matt glanced back at me.

"W-What?" I stared at him incredulous. Another branch slapped the hood of the car and dug a scratch down the side. The shrill sound reminded me of nails on a chalkboard and I shook off a chill.

"All of this." He muttered, his eyes darting across the road, then over his shoulder. "This wouldn't have happened if not for *you.*"

Alan squirmed and took hold of the handle with both hands. I fumbled around my legs for the seat belt and couldn't find it. I dug my fingers into the gaps between the cushions and eventually found the buckle on my left. Matt braked so forcibly that both Alan and I slammed violently into the front seats. As I scrambled backwards a small laugh escaped my lips. I looked at Alan and thought to myself,

So much for the 'Oh Shit' handle. His normally pallid face was an even lighter shade of pale, making him look ghostly.

"Matt, slow down, man!" Bobby hissed. His stench filled the cabin and mixed with the pungent smell of my gasoline soaked clothes to combine a vomit-worthy redolence.

"All your fault...*all your fault.*" Matt muttered over and over to himself.

We hit an open stretch of road and he floored it, hitting almost 100 mph before slamming on the brakes to make a turn.

He laughed bitterly. "You know, Mariah would still be here if it weren't for you and that asshole."

My mouth hung open. "*Mariah?*"

"Don't." Alan warned me, his dark eyes the size of saucers.

Matt looked crazed as he glanced into the rear-view mirror. He snapped, "Alan, why don't you tell the story. You were there after-all, weren't you?"

I gaped at Alan. "What? Where is she?" My voice, though still hoarse, was recovering some of its force. When he didn't answer me, I kicked him.

"Okay!" He shrank back against the door, once again with a death grip on the handle on the roof. "It was all of us...or her." His voice was tiny and weak.

Matt took a turn too fast and I was tossed from my seat into Alan's lap. I pushed myself off him in disgust and began fumbling for my seat belt again.

"I don't understand what you mean." My fingers found the buckle again. I ran my right hand up the side of my seat, digging between the cushion and the door. *Where the hell is the seat belt!?* I screamed in my head.

"Um." He paused to look at Matt and Bobby, who had pressed himself so far away from Matt that even his rolls looked tiny in his seat. "We stumbled upon Matt and Mariah in L.A. These two guys rushed our car at gunpoint at an intersection and forced us all onto the street." He looked down at his knees. They were shaking. "They said...they said they wanted *her*. And they'd let us go." He looked at me sharply and added as an afterthought, "They would have killed all of us if he didn't do it. We owe Matt our lives." He stared back down at his knees.

Terror ran through me as I looked from Alan to Bobby, and focused on the back of Matt's neck. "Oh my god." I clamped a shaky hand over my mouth, imagining what Mariah's abductors would have done to her.

"And you let her go? Your *sister*." I flung the words at Matt like knives.

His head jerked around and he swung his right hand in my direction. A long-barreled revolver shook in his grip. He screamed at me, "*You bitch!* I told her we shouldn't go to Nevada! You and that bastard kicked us out, remember? We had nowhere else to go. We could have stayed there, we could have stayed and *she'd be here!*"

I shook my head at him in terror. "We didn't kick you out Matt, you left." I said quietly.

"Shut up! Shut up! That asshole jumped me; he made it clear we couldn't stay!" The revolver trembled as Matt struggled to keep the truck on the road with one hand on the steering wheel.

"Okay. Okay, I'm sorry. I'm so sorry, Matt." I felt the rough edge of the seat belt with my fingers and yanked at it, but it was wedged too deeply behind the cushion. I would need both hands, which meant I would have to turn my back on Matt's revolver...something I couldn't do. I didn't have to look at Alan to know the sniffling noise I heard was him crying.

"Just put the gun down. You're driving, remember?" I tried to say calmly, but my voice hitched and caught on each syllable.

He shook the revolver in my face and began shouting at me over his shoulder again. This meant he didn't see the next curve and the drop-off alongside it.

"Matt, look out!" I screamed.

I braced my legs against the front seat, grabbed at the handle above me and gripped Bobby's headrest with the other hand. We hit the guardrail head-on and two clouds exploded in the front of the truck. The airbags lost just enough of their cushioning that when Bobby's upper body flew forward as the guardrail broke free and the truck pitched downwards, he slammed face first into the dashboard. Blood flew backwards, running sideways on the passenger window in dozens of tiny rivers before sprinkling my face.

The front tires suspended momentarily in the air before the weight of the truck tilted and we crashed forward, tipping the truck over, front-end first. Cans of green beans and spam tumbled violently from the truck bed onto the roof and rolled down the hood and over the edge as the truck teetered before plummeting. All I could see was bright white, then black, bright white, black, bright white, black as we flipped over and over. Small cubes of glass floated from one side of the cab to the other as the windows imploded, slashing at my face and neck, gouging my arms. A body slammed into me and then disappeared after we hit something large and splinters of wood and pine needles filled the cab. My grip on the 'Oh Shit' handle was ripped free when the truck lurched to the left and began rolling on its side...bright white, black, bright white, black, bright white, black, bright white...black.

***

They had turned south onto the highway, after seeing the back of Matt's truck veer to the right at the end of the lodge driveway. Long and black tread marks tattooed the empty road and Connor's stomach clenched. Fin was driving fast, but clearly not as fast as Matt.

"We've gotta catch up, Fin." He gritted through his teeth, while pulling the harness strap tight around his chest.

"I'm going as fast as I can without flying off the road, okay?" Fin snapped back. For miles they followed the sporadic skid marks that went into the shoulder and across the oncoming lane.

Connor cursed when he saw the missing chunk of guardrail. "There! Stop!"

Fin drove the truck onto the dirt and slammed the brakes so hard Connor's harness locked. He cursed again when he couldn't immediately disengage the latch.

"Christ, get me out of this truck!" He yelled frantically at the empty cab. Fin had already bolted from the driver seat and was peering over the damaged rail. Connor's latch finally released and he threw the door open. Zoey scrambled out of the vehicle behind him, unsure what was going on.

He was three feet away from the drop-off when Fin, his face bloodless, turned and stopped him, grabbing him by the shoulders. "Jesus, Connor, don't look." His voice cracked.

227

He shoved his weight into Fin, gaining a mere foot of ground. "I need to see." He flailed his arms until Fin lost his grip and tried to step away from him. Fin gave him a solid shove to the chest, pushing him back, further away from the railing.

"No. No, no, no. I need to see, Fin!" He screamed in the larger man's face and punched his jaw. Fin barely flinched but stepped aside, raising his hands to the back of his head and dropped down onto his knees.

At least five feet of railing had been ripped out and Connor moved slowly toward the hole. Canned goods were strewn about the dirt along with broken glass, plastic, and pieces of the front end of Matt's truck. The land sloped down steeply, dotted with the occasional tree and boulder. For what looked like several hundred feet, fresh tufts of upturned earth stretched out below him, in a pattern. The bushes and ground glittered with glass and a bag of someone's clothes had ripped apart, sending the contents sprawling over fifty square feet. Connor could see a man's lightweight jacket hanging loosely upside down on a pine tree branch at least two stories high. The thin blue fabric swayed gently against the tree, still caught in the momentum of its flight.

He followed the path of destruction, his insides knotting, his breath stilling, until his eyes settled on the truck. It didn't look like a truck anymore. It looked like a badly crumpled car; the bed was destroyed and bent backwards, away from the cab, and the passenger side door was ripped off. It lay on the driver side, with a steady stream of pale smoke drifting from under what was left of the hood.

He bit down on his hand and screamed. There's no way, no way she could survive this. He dragged his hands down his face and looked around them. Nature was observing in silence. The birds hid in the trees and even the wind had died. All he could hear was the rapid thudding of his heart, the blood pumping behind his ears and his own voice screaming inside his head. He thought he was screaming out loud because the dog started barking at him; the echo vibrating down the highway and below them into the hills.

But the scream wasn't coming from him. He turned in a slow semi-circle and met Fin's eyes, which were moist and bloodshot. Fin wasn't screaming either. Zoey barked at his feet again before rushing down the drop off, skidding through bushes and stumbling over rocks

228

toward the sound of a screaming woman. Riley was somewhere down there, alive, and from the sound of it, in excruciating pain.

Fin and Connor hit the dirt running at the same time. They slid half-way down the hill on their asses, and ran when they could stand upright. Zoey stopped near the bottom and turned around in several tight circles, barking at them as they stumbled their way down the steep embankment. But then she ran off, to the truck, following along the massive gouge marks the vehicle had made on its descent. He saw her pacing around the truck, before gingerly climbing inside the gap where the windshield had been. From his angle, he couldn't see inside the cab.

Riley's screams turned into sobs as they got closer to the wreckage. Zoey barked loudly, as if telling them to hurry and as soon as the land flattened the men bolted. Fin, being half a foot taller, sprinted easily ahead of him.

They almost ran right past the body. Alan's mangled corpse lay in a thick tangle of bushes where the dog had circled before. His bloodied head was unnaturally lumpy and every bone in his body appeared bent at all the wrong angles.

Only pausing for a handful of seconds, they burst into a run again, and reached the truck together. Fin leaned over the hood and peered inside from the gaping hole that used to be the passenger window of the cab. Connor scrambled along the ground, wedging himself partly inside the same way the dog had gone. He found Zoey lying across Riley's midsection.

"Oh god, Riley." He reached in to touch her.

"Connor we have to get her out, can you climb inside?" Fin's tone was commanding and Connor nodded at him without argument.

"Yeah, but I can't get in. The seats are in the way...and...Bobby." The overweight man's face was gone, a bloody mess of crushed bone and brain matter. His right arm had been severed at the shoulder, most likely when the door was ripped off.

Fin tapped on the hood with his hand. "Climb up and drop in."

Riley was crumpled in a ball, her left arm jammed above her head, covered in blood. A long gash ran down her right shin and her ankle was buried beneath the driver seat. Fin lowered him through the side window and he stepped inside the cab, using the front seat as a step ladder.

229

"It's okay, Riley, we're here. Sshh..." He spoke softly. He had to straddle her to get close enough to touch her. When he reached out and put his hand on her awkwardly bent arm, she screamed and then threw up on his foot.

***

For the second time in one afternoon, I woke up disoriented and in pain. But this pain was different. A searing heat erupted from my shoulder and when I tried to move my arm the joint slid loosely, sending waves of intense spasms all through my arm and torso. And I screamed. I screamed until I couldn't handle it anymore, and turned my head to the side and puked. Breathing hurt my shoulder, screaming hurt, but it was all I could do.

When Zoey wriggled into the cab I started sobbing, which shook my arm even more. And eventually, I had to scream again. Everything hurt. Muscles felt ripped, bones felt busted, and blood was everywhere, though I knew it wasn't all mine. Bobby's blood was dripping from his dead body and pooling next to me. I puked again.

Please let them find me before I die, I said in my head.

It seemed like hours before Fin popped his head into the missing passenger window, where I had been sitting when the truck was speeding down the highway. I groaned in agony, unable to talk, not exactly sure what had happened. The cab smelled of blood, bowel and vomit and I was afraid of passing out again from the smell alone.

Connor lowered himself down to me and tried to lift my arm. The pain forced what little was left in my stomach to come out and I choked on the screams.

"Fin, I can't move her without it hurting bad." Connor's voice was terrified.

"*Get me out!*" I wailed.

"You're just going to have to grab her and lift her up; I can pull her through the top." Fin said from above us.

Connor crouched down, and slid his arm underneath me. He lifted my upper body first and I cried in pain as he carefully pulled my left wrist down and into my chest.

"*It's okay baby, almost there. Almost there.*" He whispered against my cheek.

230

He had to kick at the seat to free my foot and strained to pull me upright. I was aware of a throbbing in my shin, but compared to the pain in my head and shoulder, it was easy to dismiss. Connor hoisted me up and Fin tugged on my right arm to pull me through the narrow window. He held me close to him, murmuring softly into my neck while he waited for Connor to climb out and jump to the ground to help Fin lower me off the truck.

Once on the ground, they laid me flat and Zoey resumed her place at my side. Connor tried to shoo her back so he could get a closer look at me but she refused and even growled at his nudges. Fin ran his hands along my left arm and over my shoulder, ignoring my shrieks.

"I think it's dislocated." He said with a deep frown.

"Do you know how to put it back in?" Connor asked.

Fin shrugged. "I've seen it done. It'll hurt."

"*Oh god.*" I moaned.

Fin pushed the bloodied hair off my face that was starting to dry to my forehead. "If we do this right, it shouldn't take long, okay?" I tried to nod and looked away as Fin positioned Connor near my head, to hold my torso still and he straightened my left arm laying it carefully by my side.

"On three." He said to Connor, and then looked down at me, getting close to my face. "This is going to hurt, Riley, but you'll be okay, I promise."

With my wrist in his hand, he bent my elbow and rotated my lower arm into my chest and then out away from my body. He tugged and I thrashed below him, screaming.

"Stop Fin! Stop pulling!" Connor yelled to be heard over my cries.

Again, Fin bent my elbow and rotated my arm in and out. After four tries a loud popping sound came from my shoulder and I felt it slide back into place. The relief was almost immediate and I cried softly into Connor's sleeve as he gently wiped at my face.

"*Thank you. Thank you.*" I said over and over to Fin.

He rubbed my arm and put it back on my chest and tore his flannel shirt open, not bothering to undo the buttons. As they flew off the fabric, I thought they resembled the sound of popping corn. They splayed around us like confetti, and Zoey jumped when one bounced

231

off the top of her head. Fin's thin white t-shirt clung to his sweaty chest, making his muscles more visible. Little tufts of dark hair peeked out of the top of his shirt, decorating his collar bone. I stared at the delicate concave below his throat as he moved above me.

"We can make a sling out of this. But we have to figure out how to get you back up that hill." He nodded up at the road and pulled the shirt around my arm, tying it together behind my neck.

"Do you think you can walk?" Connor asked.

"My leg hurts...but I think so."

Fin lifted the torn fabric of my jeans to peer at my shin. "You'll need stitches for this." He stood up and scanned the area while Connor pulled me into a sitting position. "I'll be right back."

Connor hugged me to him while we waited for Fin to return. He brought a long sleeve thermal shirt and a t-shirt that he found amid the scattered debris. He wrapped the thermal tightly around my leg and folded the shirt in half before wrapping it around my head. Woozy and wobbly, Fin helped me stand with Connor's assistance. I couldn't put weight down on my leg, but with their help I could hop.

"Okay?" Fin asked softly as he slipped his arm around me, like Connor had done from my other side. I nodded, and he leaned down and kissed the side of my head.

Zoey trotted ahead of us but stopped after a few feet and abruptly turned around, her hackles going up along her back, as she let loose a string of vicious barks in our direction.

"What is it, girl?" I asked weakly, too exhausted to lift my head and look around.

A gunshot pierced the silence, its echo ricocheting through the trees. I screamed at the pain in my ears from the deafening noise, while I collapsed to my knees with Connor still holding onto me. Zoey yelped in fear and darted away from us. Fin stumbled and then stood stiffly on my other side before making a soft grunting sound and falling face-first to the ground.

"*Fin!*"

"*Damn.* I was aiming for the *other* asshole. Sorry." Matt's words hung in the air behind us.

Connor scrambled to his feet, splaying his hands out before him, quickly stepping between Matt's revolver and my feet as I crawled frantically to Fin's side. Blood soaked through the back of his shirt from a large, dark hole that was almost perfectly centered between his shoulder blades. I knelt down next to his face and caressed his cheek with my shaky hand. His cloudy gaze settled on mine for a moment, and a soft gust of air passed between his lips. He didn't take another breath.

"Oh no. Please, no." I cried into his shoulder, and shook him gently. "Fin? Please, *no.*" I tried to roll him, but he was too heavy for me to move with one hand.

I wailed at Matt, "*What have you done?*" I tried to stand but collapsed next to Fin's still body. Zoey crawled over to me and rested her shaking head on Fin's arm.

Matt's eyes glowed with wild rage as he looked from me to Connor. One of his arms was obviously broken and he had several gashes on his head and torso. He stood awkwardly, his body trembling with one leg bent to the side unnaturally, causing his whole right side to droop. A stiff breeze would have been enough to bring him crashing down.

"You should watch." He said to me as he raised the revolver and aimed it at Connor's head. I screamed as he pulled the trigger.

***

Matt's mouth opened in a comical 'o' shape as he stared down the barrel of his gun at Connor, who was still standing, his hands held out in front of him in the same defensive position. He pulled the trigger again, with the same result...only a clicking sound. I sucked in a ragged breath and ran my hand across Fin's waist band until my fingers felt the cool steel of his pistol. I tugged on it, pulling it out from under his shirt. I glanced at it once before I aimed it at Matt's chest.

He smiled. His cut and bleeding lips pulled tightly at the corners, showing a large gap where one of his front teeth had been. He pointed his revolver at Connor again. I squeezed the trigger of Fin's gun and felt the recoil jolt through my arm as Matt flew backwards, landing in the dirt with a solid thud.

I crawled past Connor, who was still frozen in shock, until I was lying next to Matt. He tried talking but choked as blood spurted from his mouth instead of words. I held Fin's gun up for him to see, and

233

before he took his last bloody breath, I pressed the barrel against his temple and squeezed the trigger slowly as I whispered into his ear, *"I remembered the safety this time, mother fucker."*

***

Sweat had rinsed some of the blood off my face from the climb up the hillside but it was still nearly impossible to see. At one point, we crawled over the uneven ground on our hands and knees. By the time we made it to the top, we collapsed on the dirt shoulder of the highway, completely spent. My mouth was full of the gritty taste of earth, and the bitter, iron taste of blood.

Connor rolled onto his side and held me until our breathing regulated. The wind had picked up; bringing with it the woody smell of fire and Connor looked up the road with a worried expression. He loaded me quietly into the truck and fastened my seat belt. Zoey climbed onto my lap, despite my hisses of pain.

"We've got to get back." Connor said in a strained voice.

"What's wrong?" I asked, my voice sounding miles away.

He sighed heavily as we pulled back onto the highway. "They set the lodge on fire."

"How bad?" I chewed on the inside of my cheek and warily ran my tongue over a cut on my lower lip.

"I don't know. But the main building is gone...at least."

I looked out the window as Connor turned the truck around and began the climb back up the mountain. Tears flowed freely down my cheeks as I thought of Fin.

"We won't leave him there." Connor said quietly, as if reading my thoughts. "I'll get help, and go back and get him."

I nodded and wiped at my face. My head throbbed steadily and with each wave of pain I struggled to fight back the urge to throw up again.

"Riley, it's a miracle you survived that crash." Connor said weakly as he took the turns slow.

"Well," I said dryly, "I guess you can thank the *'Oh Shit'* handle." I felt him look over at me, but I leaned back into the head rest and watched the scenery in the side mirror shrink as I cried quietly for Fin.

The smell of fire grew stronger as we neared the lodge. I was half expecting to see the trees ablaze when we reached the driveway but they weren't. Nothing was burning actually but the lodge stood an empty, darkened-shell of its former self...smoldering. As we drove closer to the building, we could see right through it to the open lawn and the surrounding buildings...all untouched.

Connor eased the truck slowly down the gravel road and we stared, wide-eyed, like children, at the smoky remains of the main structure. All of the shrubbery around it was gone and the trail that Fin had taken me down as a surprise was scorched. The greenhouse was a melted heap of glass and concrete. I couldn't keep my chin from trembling.

Winchester and Skip jogged toward the truck, both covered in soot and soaking wet. Their happy smiles turned to concern when they got close enough to see the state of me.

"Oh, sweet Jesus." Skip said as he opened my door.

"Where's the cart, Skip?" Connor asked as he hopped out of the truck. "She can't walk very well."

He pointed to the Recreation building, where the cart was parked in front of it. Skip walked with Connor across the lawn while Winchester leaned in to help me stand.

"Did you put this out with just a garden hose?" I had noticed two green hoses curled up in heaps at the front of the building, and another stretched out from the Rec room, pointing at the back of the main house.

His hands were black, the nails gritty and cracked. His hair was messy and ashy. It was the first time I had ever seen Winchester dirty but he beamed with pride.

"Yep." Then his face fell. "We lost the greenhouse though. Skip was able to grab a few things, but most of it is gone." I nodded curtly.

"Is everyone okay?" I looked around for the others, but didn't see them. My damaged voice cracked with emotion.

"Yes. Kris, Ana and Jacks went down to the cabins and started packing up our stuff. For a while there we thought the fire was going to spread out. They just took a bunch of bags back down there, actually."

I looked around at the trees that encroached the entire area. "Yeah, it's amazing it wasn't worse." I paused before asking, "Where was Jacks?"

"What?"

"When the fire started...where was he?" I waited for him to look at me.

"Uh, he was with Ana, on the other side of the lake. They didn't make it back here till after Fin and Connor left." He looked down at his feet and slid his shoe along the ground, making a crescent moon shape in the dirt.

"Oh." I said it with a sigh. So much for Jacks' promise. When we actually needed him, he was off fooling around with Ana. Why didn't that surprise me?

Winchester blinked, and asked, "Speaking of Fin, where is he?"

I looked at him sadly, tears filling my tired eyes. "He didn't...I mean, Matt..." I couldn't finish the sentence and collapsed into his arms, crying into fistfuls of his shirt.

***

The warm wind whipped around my face, tugging strands of hair out of my pony-tail and carrying the dry scent of summer with it. I sat cross-legged in the dirt, twisting a single yellow rose bud in between my fingers. Inhaling deeply, I leaned into the grassy mound with my right hand, and stretched my left arm back and forth. It wasn't completely healed yet, neither was the pain in my shin. Winchester had done a meticulous job of sewing the eight inch long gash up. It had healed nicely on the outside, but the slashed muscle was taking much longer to recover. I worried the limp in my gait would never go away, but considering how badly banged up the accident had left me, it could've been much worse.

The wind changed direction and pushed at my back, causing the pale blue gauzy top I wore to flutter around my waist and a familiar male smell came with it. *Connor.* I smiled over my shoulder at him and he sat down in the grass beside me. His jeans brushed against my thin, cotton shorts and he playfully banged our knees together.

"Hey baby, thought you might be here." He said after tenderly kissing my cheek.

236

"It's a good spot, isn't it?" I rested my head on his shoulder and looked down at the yellow rose. Even though it hadn't fully opened, its fragrant essence fanned out around it, gracing nature with its aroma as only a rose can. Most of the potted roses had burned with the lodge but a few were salvageable. It took several weeks longer than usual for one particular rose bush to bloom and I held the first bud in my hand.

"It's perfect. You know he would love it here, right?" Connor said quietly.

I nodded.

The lake opened up in front of us, contrasting perfectly with the dark pine trees in the background and the tips of the mountains even further away. He put an arm around my shoulder and hugged me tightly. "Kris made an early dinner for everyone but come back whenever you're ready, okay?" I nodded again and smiled at him as he stood and walked away. I watched the breeze push against his shirt, flattening it to his upper body. He had let his hair grow out and the long, wispy dark waves reached just below his ears. At first he complained about the growing length of his hair, but with my assurance that it only made him sexier, he vowed not to cut it. I sighed heavily as he headed back toward the cabins where the others would be waiting. Skip and Winchester. Jacks and Ana...with the small bulge that was showing in her lower abdomen. Kris and Connor. My friends. My family.

A small, fuzzy rabbit hopped out from behind a tree but quickly dashed back under cover when it saw me. I smiled, happy that life had started anew...in the forest, at least. It had taken a while, but even our deer returned to the lake, sometimes coming as close as the cabin steps to say hello. She had filled out, losing her juvenile markings and was spotted most regularly by Kris, who spent at least two hours of each day hiking the trails around the lodge with the dog. In a way, I suppose the deer was a part of the family too.

I carefully dug my painted toes into the soft dirt and wild grass, trying not to badly mess up the pedicure that Kris had given me the day before, while the earth cooled my warm feet and I noticed movement in the sky. A sleek white bird flew in low over the water and dragged an elegant foot along the surface. Zoey raised her head and quietly huffed at the aviary display that rippled the lake water from the center out. Before the water's edge, the bird lifted with the breeze and floated into a nearby tree, timing its landing with rehearsed perfection.

"Fin." I sighed. "We miss you."

I looked at the mound of dirt encircled with dozens of smooth, round stones to my right and laid the flower delicately on top.

"*I hope you find me again in the next life.*" I whispered, as I rested my hand on his grave. "*The first yellow rose is for you.*"

THE END of BOOK ONE

ACKNOWLEDGEMENTS

There are simply too many people to consider in this section, so I will keep my 'thanks' as short and sweet as possible! It took me over thirty-two years to write my first book; which is funny, because the actual 'act' of writing it took less than four months. It's been a dream I've had since I was fifteen years old, so just completing this project is a major accomplishment for me. And it would never have been possible without the ongoing support of my closest family and friends ̀ over the years. You have all been a part of my creative process in some shape or form. I thank each and every one of the people I've encountered over the last three decades or so. Each one of you has touched my life in a way that has made it possible for me to be where I am today. There are a few people I need to mention by name, so let's get that started!

Mom. I love you, and appreciate each sacrifice you have made in your life to ensure I was brought up the best way you could manage as a single parent. I don't say Thank You enough, so now it's in print: Thank You for everything! I love you, like you, and care about you, always.

To my own little family: Shane, not only are you my husband and partner, but you have been a constant support of this writing dream I've had since we've met. I don't think you could ever know how valuable this has been to me. Life has given us challenges, but you chose me and you're still here…for that I thank you and I love you. Rory and Foxx - you two are my rays of sunshine. I love your creative

239

spirit Rory. I hope you reach for the stars and find your dreams up there waiting for you. Foxx, you are my special little man and without you our family would not be complete. Your goofy smiles make everything better. Thanks for being so patient as Mommy works hard during nap times and stays up late at night to write; I'm doing this for you guys. Love you both to the moon and back. And Zoey, you drive me nuts with your neurotic canine behavior but I love you anyway.

Thank you for the push Grandma Dawson. I've appreciated your feedback and interest in my short stories over the years. I love that you have shared my writings with your friends, and that you have encouraged me to actually DO something with it all. Love you lots.

You aren't with us anymore Teresa, but your spirit never leaves me. Even in death you are my personal cheerleader. When I doubt myself, I look at your pictures. It's really that simple, because when I see your smiling face I remember your laugh and know that if you were here you would give me that extra push - no questions asked, no judgments passed. You were like my second mom, I miss you dearly.

Thank you SO MUCH to the amazing ladies and friends that helped Edit this book! You made an exceptional Editing Team: Jennifer Peterson, Kerry Bigelow and Stephanie Perry Aguirre. You are all special friends, and your time and effort to help me make this story the best it can be is invaluable. I thank you all dearly!

To my Beta Readers: You were the first and you loved it! Without your insight, your patience, your questions and suggestions, I would never have made a second draft, a third, or even a fourth. This book is here in large part because YOU loved it. Thank you!

The cover art, one of the most important parts of any book, was done by my good friend Deborah Rogers. Thank you so much for your friendship and for your artistic abilities! I feel blessed to know a woman like you. Thanks for everything, sister!

Gladys Selfridge: You Rock! Thank you for not only being a part of the Beta Reader experience, but for following me on my researching adventures. Thank you for surviving the wilderness with me: muddy bare-feet and all. I appreciate your feedback and help with the eBook conversion too! I know so many keyboard shortcuts now! I have to thank your hubby, Sean Selfridge as well, for driving out into the mountains at night to pick us up from that last researching adventure. I'm glad he thought it was funny.

Hector Aguirre you must remember the total panic on my face when I thought for sure my computer crashed and I lost all of the work that preceded this section of the book. If not for your helpful, calm and always cool demeanor, I would surely have had some sort of massive coronary failure and dropped dead to the floor of my office. But since you fixed my computer, and made it better than it was before, I owe you…well, everything. Thank you, big bro.

Irene Aranda: thanks for being such a dear and long-time friend. I appreciate your patience over the years listening to my crazy dreams and story ideas. Look at what all that talk has amounted to! Thanks for being one of my best friends. Love you.

A very special THANK YOU must go out to the Mt. Laguna Fire Station 49 crew. I have learned that a Ford Focus has absolutely NO business being on a back country dirt road because you never know when a mud puddle is going to try and swallow up your car. Thank you for rescuing me and my friend from the muck and cold weather (Yes, this was a true story). Ty, Joe and Joel - you guys are all awesome, and I'm proud to know you wear the uniform. Can I also thank you…again…for not making me feel like an idiot when you saw exactly what I did to my car. Thank you guys for being amazing, and for laughing *with* me, not *at* me!

To DCBR: you ladies are all amazing and have been nothing but a constant support for me over the last several years. I am proud to call each and every one of you my friend.

Thank you to my fellow Book Club Ladies! I love what we have together as a group. I hope this book makes you proud! Thanks for your love, support and friendship.

To my San Diego Family: I grew up here and have spent the majority of my life in our beautiful City. I did take some liberties with this book however, and feel the need to explain. For starters, Connor's hotel is not real, neither is the Lodge. And anyone that has hiked the Laguna area knows that the lake is not really as big as I make it sound in this book. It's Fiction, after-all. BUT with that said, I hope I did our City proud.

I really don't think I would have gotten far if it weren't for Thesaurus.com. The site is amazing, and helped me tremendously!

Finally...if you've read this book and you are now a fan- thank you! I could have written this story just for myself and kept it hidden away in a folder on my laptop named *ONLY IN MY DREAMS* but when I chose to share it I was happily surprised that people actually wanted to read it! So this is for you! I 'hope' you like it.

ABOUT THE AUTHOR

Trish was born and mostly raised in San Diego, California where she lives now with her family and pets. She's been writing short stories and poetry since high school, and began her first book, 'I Hope You Find Me' in December of 2011. When Trish isn't writing, she's homeschooling her amazing daughter and mildly autistic son, reading whatever she can get her hands on, or enjoying the Southern California sun. As a strict Vegetarian, Trish holds a special place in her heart for animal rights.

You can follow Trish here:

Twitter at https://twitter.com/Trish_Dawson
Facebook at http://www.facebook.com/WriterTrishMarieDawson

29806104R00138

Printed in Great Britain
by Amazon